Standom

Other Bella Books by Maryn Scott

Talented Amateur

About the Author

Maryn Scott lives with her partner in Denver, Colorado. She is the author of *Talented Amateur* and the soon to be published sequel, *Going Under*.

Standom

MARYN SCOTT

BELLA
BOOKS
2022

Bella Books, Inc.
P.O. Box 10543
Tallahassee, FL 32302

Printed in the United States of America on acid-free paper.

First Edition - 2022

Editor: Heather Flournoy
Cover Designer: Sheri Halal

ISBN: 978-1-64247-347-6

PUBLISHER'S NOTE

Acknowledgments

I am so grateful to be a part of the Bella team. Thank you to Jessica Hill for patiently talking me through the steps in this process, to Ann Roberts and Carolyn Elizabeth for their help with social media, and to my fellow authors who have been an inspiration.

I can't say enough about how much I value the support and wisdom of my editor, Heather Flournoy. She's been a master wordsmith, armchair psychologist, and steadfast supporter for both my novels.

For Kathy, one of my oldest friends. I'm so thankful you made it through your own fire. The world is better with you in it.

Thank you to the readers who took a chance on a debut author when they chose to read *Talented Amateur*. I'm grateful for your support.

Dedication

To my parents who created my love of reading.
And always to M.

CHAPTER ONE

"This has been a big year for Sara Silver. In April, her self-titled solo album debuted at number one with the first single, 'Never Alone,' topping the charts for three weeks. The next release, 'Street People,' quickly became this year's song of summer. Now, she's golden again. Her role as Bridget Keogh in the biopic *Enough* has earned her a Golden Globe nomination for Best Supporting Actress." The tiny blonde turned from speaking directly into the camera to face the couch where Sara was sitting. "For those who don't know the story, tell us about the film."

"It's about the seventies band Kindred Strangers and the three months they spent recording their iconic album *Enough*." Sara shifted slightly. "Before the recording sessions began Bridget Keogh, and her bandmate and good friend Rose Nash made a difficult decision. Kindred Strangers was a hugely successful band, but the women were miserable. Rose had been in a relationship with guitarist Keith Dalton for years, but his drug addiction was taking its toll on her.

"Rose's decision to end her relationship encouraged Bridget to make her own changes. Her husband, Peter, who was also in the band, had a series of increasingly public affairs.

"But this isn't a story of women done wrong. Bridget and Rose took control of their futures and decided *Enough* would be the band's last album, and that they would do all they could to create a masterpiece that would carry them forward in their careers."

"An incredible story," the interviewer said. "Things have been pretty incredible for you lately. How does it feel?"

Sara gave the woman a practiced smile. "It's been an amazing time. I can't tell you how much the fan support for the album means to me. It was unnerving branching out on my own." She paused. "But, the opportunity to do *Enough* and play Bridget was a dream come true. She's an incredible talent."

"I've read you had the opportunity to meet Bridget Keogh. What's she like?"

"Very warm and open, which surprised me since she's known for being shy. Fortunately for me, she believed the story of that phenomenal album was worth telling."

The interviewer leaned closer to Sara, her eyes calculating. "Were there any parallels to your own life story?"

A variation of this question had been asked in every interview she'd done for the movie. No one asked her directly about the backstage pictures from her band's last tour or the rumors of her own drug use and rehab. Sara crossed her legs but made sure to keep her upper body relaxed. Rather than move away from the interviewer's intrusion into her space, Sara leaned in. "Deborah, are you asking me if I've been in a relationship with any of the guys in the band?" Deborah's eyes widened and she laughed nervously, and Sara knew she'd once again successfully avoided the question. Just to make sure, she added, "Well, as you know, I exclusively date women, so…" She shrugged.

Deborah shifted in her chair, trying to regroup. Sara wanted to roll her eyes. Straight people were so easy to distract. They were never quite sure what to do if she was the one who brought up being gay. Usually they stumbled over themselves trying to prove they were "okay" with it.

"Let's talk about the album. How hard was it to break away from Range Street?" she asked, referring to Sara's band.

Sara had also been answering this question for months, and the words came out of her mouth without needing thought. "I don't think of it as breaking away. We love each other, but when you've grown up together and made music for as long as we have, at some point you realize your worldview is limited. We decided it was time for us to gain new experiences so we could come back together stronger than ever before. I know it's worked for me. The producers and musicians who worked with me on my solo album taught me so much. I feel very blessed."

"So, what's next? Another Range Street album?" She paused. "Another movie?"

"I've gone nonstop from the end of the Range Street tour to recording my album, to making and promoting *Enough*. I'm looking forward to a little time off. After that?" Sara lifted her palms. "We'll see."

But Deborah wasn't going to let it go that easily. "Will we see you on the big screen again?"

"If the right opportunity comes up, we'll see."

"Sara Silver, Golden Globe nominee and best-selling solo artist, thanks for being here."

Sara leaned forward to clasp the woman's left hand with her right. "You're welcome. Thank you for inviting me."

"And we're out," a disembodied voice announced.

"Thanks, Deborah," Sara said as she stood. "You're always so easy to talk with."

The woman seemed genuinely touched by the compliment. She wrapped one arm around Sara's waist in a side hug. "I think you're going to be getting a lot of calls," she whispered.

Andrew Neiderman, her agent, greeted her with a frown as she walked off set. "Never admit you don't have something lined up."

Sara took her purse from him and pulled out a water bottle. After a long drink, she said, "Andrew, I liked acting. A lot. But I don't know if I want to be an actress. There's nothing wrong with just being a singer."

"You got nominated for a Globe your first time out. There's interest in you. We just need to find the right script." He led her out of the building to the black SUV parked at the curb. Holding the door open, he said, "Get some rest. You want to look good on the red carpet." He started to shut the door, then pulled it back open. "Don't forget the interview with *Rolling Stone* next week. You're the cover. It's a—"

"I know, Andrew. I'll be ready, I promise."

* * *

Mika Williams entered the restaurant and spotted David Stamper right away. "I see my party," she said to the hostess. He was reading something on his phone but looked up when she got close. He stood and kissed her cheek, then waited to sit until she had slid into the opposite side of the horseshoe booth. As she exchanged sunglasses for her signature black-framed glasses, he gave a nod to the waiter, then asked, "Well? What did they say?"

She flashed him a smile and ran a hand over her hair. "As they say, I've got good news and bad news."

David leaned forward. "Tell me the bad news, first."

She ignored him. "The good news is they like the premise. They want a full pitch and a script for the pilot." His eyes lit up, but before he could speak, she held up a hand. "Yes. That's good. The bad news is they expect me to come back with a name. They're right, of course, but there are only so many well-known lesbian actresses."

"So, get a name for the straight part," David said.

"No." Mika looked around. "Has our waiter been by?"

"I've already ordered your martini. I asked him to watch for you." Just as he finished speaking, the waiter appeared at her elbow with a tray of drinks. He placed the martini in front of her and a gin and tonic in front of David.

Mika swirled the skewer of olives in her drink, then lifted it to her mouth. She trapped the first olive between her teeth, then pulled the skewer away, sucking it between red lips. The first bite of salty, gin-dipped fruit always delighted her. She took her time savoring the taste before lifting the glass and taking a delicate sip. "Ooh, that's good. Thank you, David."

"So why not get a name for the daughter?"

"Television being what it is today, we don't have the luxury of building an audience from scratch. We need one before the show premieres. A well-known television actress playing a straight character won't get us that audience. But…" She tapped the rim of her glass. "A well-known lesbian playing a lesbian lead, will."

"Okay," he conceded, "I see that. Who do you have in mind?"

"You haven't asked the worst news yet."

His drink froze in midair. He placed it back on the table. "I thought that was the bad news."

"Oh, no. That's nothing." She looked out the window for a long moment, then reached for her own drink. After a healthy swallow, she said, "The project is contingent on my father acting as creative consultant."

"Shhhit." He pushed the word out through clenched teeth. "How did that happen? He's been out of the business for years."

"I don't know," she said. "It was all very strange. Ostensibly, it's because he has experience with shows like ours. But something doesn't feel right. The development executive was quite smug when they presented the terms."

"I thought you were working with the network head. Who's this guy?"

Mika took another swallow. "I met John Belinski for the initial deal, but each production will have its own network rep. Ours is Larry Rand. Sound familiar?"

"No."

"Not to me, either. He's in his fifties, so I know he's not a contemporary of my father. It's possible he's just a garden-variety misogynist."

"Do you really believe that?"

"That Hollywood is full of arrogant men who believe no woman should ever run a show?"

"Point taken. Forget I asked."

CHAPTER TWO

Nathan Silver ducked his head to peer at the line of limos in front of them. "I think we're getting close. Are you ready?"

"Nooo." Sara drew out the word. "I'm not. Do I look okay?"

"For the hundredth time, you look great. I'm glad you went with this girlie tux thing." He waved his finger up and down to encompass her outfit. "You can't take the Grammys out of the girl."

"I wish this was the Grammys. I know people there. Who am I going to know here?"

"C'mon. You're being a baby. You're going to know the people from your movie. We'll go in, find the table, and people watch. You don't have to mingle."

"Okay, but don't let me drink too much. You know how I get when I get nervous. Nothing until the show starts."

Nathan patted his sister's hand. "You never drink too much." He looked out when he heard the driver's door slam. "Here we go."

Sara stepped onto the plush red carpet and assumed her celebrity persona: shoulders back, head up, eyes and smile bright. When Nathan came around the car, she took his arm and they stepped into the milieu. They hadn't gone more than ten feet when she heard her name called. "Sara, Sara Silver, over here. I want you to meet my friend." And just like that, she was pulled into the crowd of photographers, interviewers, and celebrities. Nathan, as promised, stayed close by, quick to step in when it was time to move. Celebrities were the worst gossips, so any time the conversation turned the slightest bit personal, Nathan stepped in and deftly pulled her away.

After going through the requisite photo stops and interviews, she grabbed his hand and pulled him through the doors of the Beverly Hilton and over to a quiet corner. She wrapped him in a hug. "What would I do without you? You are the best big brother in the world."

"Why hasn't that been a song yet?" He hugged her tightly, then pulled back, holding her hands. "Anything for you. You know that."

"I do, and I appreciate you more than you know," she said. "Now, let's find the bar. I need a drink." She walked away and when she sensed he wasn't behind her, turned back. "You know I didn't mean it when I said we weren't drinking before the show, right?"

Nathan threw his hands in the air. "Who can tell?"

They were at the *Enough* table in the lower tier watching people and laughing with her costars, when she noticed a woman walking toward her. Sara squeezed Nathan's leg under the table. He leaned closer. "Don't be obvious, but there's a woman walking this way, and I can't place her. Black glasses, dark hair. Who is she? I *know* I know her."

He rolled his eyes at his sister. "You don't know anyone. This evening is wasted on you." He scanned the room in the same way they'd been doing all night. He picked up his drink and muttered, "Mika Williams."

Sara was nowhere near as subtle as her brother. She made a face trying to place the name. "Who?"

Rather than answer, Nathan stood. "Hello, Ms. Williams. I love your show. Who knew there were so many ways to…" He hesitated very slightly. "Murder someone?"

"I did." The woman gave him a dismissive look before extending her hand to Sara. "Sara, I'm Mika Williams. Your performance in *Enough* was remarkable. Congratulations on a well-deserved nomination."

Sara had caught Nathan's hint. Mika Williams was the executive producer of the very popular true crime series, *Murder*. She stood and shook the woman's hand. "Thank you. I wanted to do her justice." Sara turned sideways to gesture to Nathan. "Mika, this is my brother, Nathan Silver. I think he watches your show for ideas on how to deal with me." Nathan extended his hand across his sister.

Mika took it, barely giving him a glance. "Nice to meet you, Nathan. It was kind of your sister to bring you along tonight."

Sara didn't like the woman's attitude, and she'd had just enough to drink that she gave voice to her protective instincts. "You've got it backward. I'm fortunate Nathan is willing to put up with all of this superficial Hollywood crap to be here for me."

Their table went silent. The briefest of scowls crossed Mika's face before she threw her head back and laughed. "I don't know when I've been so effectively put in my place," she said. "My apologies, Nathan. I forget there are families who actually love each other."

Nathan, ever the gentleman, smiled and took his seat, turning to the woman next to him to ask a question. Mika Williams gave him a look that bordered on admiration as he easily redirected the attention of the table. "He's very good, isn't he?" she asked Sara.

"He is." Sara's mouth was still set in a thin line. "I'm lucky to have him."

"Yes, you are." Mika put her hand on the back of Sara's chair and moved a little closer to her. "Look, I was hoping to get a chance to talk with you about a project I'm developing. I think you'd be perfect for the lead role. Would you have breakfast with me?"

"Me?" Sara touched her chest with her fingertips. "Do you know anything about me? I'm a musician, not an actress. This"—she gestured to the table—"was a unique opportunity.

I just happen to have the right vocal range and tonality to play Bridget Keogh."

"I disagree. You wouldn't be here if you didn't also have acting talent. Meet me for breakfast and listen to what I have in mind." She touched Sara's forearm. "I think you might like it."

"I don't know," Sara said. "I'm really looking forward to some rest. The last eighteen months have been grueling."

"Yes, it often is in our business. At least hear what I'm offering before you say no."

Sara stared at her for a moment, trying to find a way to politely decline. As much as she enjoyed *Murder*, she was not interested in narrating a television series. A finger dug into her lower back. She flinched and glanced over her shoulder at her brother. He leaned back so she could see Hannah Collins, the actress who had played Rose Nash. Hannah widened her eyes and gave Sara the slightest nod. With her face turned away from Williams, Sara frowned. Hannah widened her eyes even more and tilted her head toward Mika.

With a soft sigh, Sara turned back. "Okay."

"Wonderful. I'll have my assistant contact your agent." Williams smiled and squeezed Sara's arm before leaning over the table. "Nathan, again, apologies for my rudeness." With that, she disappeared into the crowd.

Sara sat down and glared at Nathan and Hannah. "What did you get me into? I don't want to host *Amazing Murder* or *Homicide Survivor* or whatever other hybrid true-crime-reality show they come up with next."

Hannah and Nathan burst out laughing. Hannah slapped at her hand. "She has a scripted show too. It's on cable. The quirky one with the homicide detective who has the hair." Hannah gestured above her head to describe a comb-over.

"Well, that narrows it."

Hannah looked at the rest of the cast around the table and shook her head in a silent, *Can you believe this girl?* She turned back to Sara. "Mika Williams just signed a development deal with that new streaming network, Binge. This is a great opportunity for you, so change your attitude and go with an open mind."

* * *

Sara groaned at the light pouring into the hotel room. It had been a late night. As predicted, Sara didn't win, but she did get to meet the venerable actress who did, making the whole event worthwhile. The *Enough* after-party had gone into the early morning hours, and they'd stayed, drinking and dancing with the cast and crew. At one point, Sara and Hannah draped themselves across the bar and reminisced about the shoot.

"It's never like this," Hannah told her. "Usually someone is a pain in the ass."

"Why did you talk me into meeting with that woman?" Sara whined. "I think she's the pain in the ass."

"You'll be fine. You know she's gay, right?"

"She is?" Sara squinted at Hannah. "How do you know?"

"God, you are the worst power lesbian." Hannah pushed her shoulder, and Sara had to grab the bar to keep from toppling.

"I'm not a power lesbian." Sara righted herself. "Wait. What's a power lesbian?"

Hannah snorted and ticked off on her fingers. "Like you don't know. You're rich, famous, and like girls. Power lesbian."

"Then how come I don't have any power?"

Hannah threw an arm around her shoulder. "You have power, you just don't know how to use it. Now, Mika Williams…" Hannah pointed at Sara. "She knows how to use her power. You should take lessons."

Sara grabbed her phone off the bedside table and flicked through the pictures taken at the party. She smiled as she looked at her drunken colleagues. When she'd first been approached to do *Enough*, she'd been writing and recording her solo album. Acting had never been her dream, but she was captivated by the script. Then the studio arranged for her to meet Bridget Keogh, and that was all it took for her to commit. The surprise had been how much she liked acting. It allowed her to immerse herself in someone else's dreams and struggle through problems that weren't hers to solve.

She put her phone down and stretched. Since she didn't have to meet Nathan until late afternoon, she had most of the day to herself. Last night, she'd been proud of herself for not sneaking into a bathroom stall to Google Mika Williams. Now that she was in the privacy of her hotel room, she let herself go down a rabbit hole and typed "power lesbian" in the search bar. The first thing she saw was a definition in Urban Dictionary: "A lesbian who has lots of money, possessions, and connections. A lesbian elitist. Usually only has lesbian affairs with other power lesbians."

"That doesn't sound very impressive," Sara said aloud. "Well, Mika Williams, if this describes you, I don't think we're going to get along." She typed the producer's name in the search bar. All of the results on the first page were articles detailing the production deal with Binge. "Whoa," Sara murmured when she saw the terms: fifteen million dollars a year to produce an unspecified number of original movies and series. What had made Mika Williams so valuable?

She went on one of her streaming services and pulled up an episode of *Murder*. Mika's distinctive look and low voice added gravitas to the storytelling. It was one of the things that set her show apart from other true-crime offerings. The other was the writing. They didn't rely on a chronological retelling of the crime. Sometimes she started with the guilty verdict, others with discovery of the body. Wherever the story started, *Murder* was much more than a retelling of sensational crimes. Each week was an in-depth study of cause and effect rather than gruesome detail. Mika Williams knew how to tell a story.

The show had been on for eight seasons and in syndication for three years. No one would confirm the syndication money, but an anonymous source hinted the network was getting over a million dollars per episode. With that kind of money, signing Williams made sense. Streaming services were just beginning to sell the syndication rights to their shows to cable networks. They could order as many seasons as they wanted, and since streaming services didn't release viewer numbers, the value of a series in syndication would all be based on word of mouth.

Hannah had said Williams also produced a scripted show. Sara searched for a title and was surprised to find it was one she'd seen. It centered on a homicide detective who was never sure what side of the law he was or should be on. The show dealt in moral ambiguities and played with the audience's loyalty from week to week.

Sara leaned against the pillows. Maybe this meeting was a good idea after all. She was at a crossroads. Range Street had been together for over a dozen years, and it was taking a toll. She loved writing, recording, and even performing. What she didn't love was touring. On the road, she was surrounded by people clamoring for her attention or invading what little privacy she had left. She closed her eyes, thinking of the last tour and all it had taken from her. Afterward, she told the guys she needed a break, but she wasn't sure a break was enough. Maybe a career change was what she needed.

CHAPTER THREE

Sara sipped her latte and checked the time. She expected Mika Williams to arrive late and was prepared to be irritated, but the woman walked in with minutes to spare. She spoke a couple of words to the host, then looked to where Sara was seated. Mika nodded when they made eye contact and walked toward Sara. She was dressed in a black pantsuit tailored to fit her slight frame. Her straight, dark hair was expensively cut in an angular style, and black-framed glasses dominated her face. From her research, Sara knew Williams was forty-six—young for what she'd accomplished.

Mika was halfway to Sara when someone must have called to her. She stopped and turned back to the couple who rose to greet her. Mika extended her hands, air-kissing the couple. Sara groaned. She hated the artificiality of this town. Was this for her benefit? Was Sara supposed to recognize the couple and be impressed? But Williams didn't linger, excusing herself with a casual gesture in Sara's direction.

Sara rose and extended her hand to avoid the Hollywood air-kiss. Mika took it and said, "Sara, I'm so glad you agreed to breakfast. I'm excited to share this project with you."

Sara searched Mika's face but found the greeting sincere. She decided to return it. "I'm looking forward to hearing about it."

"Good." Mika slid in across from her. When they were settled, and the waiter had taken Mika's drink order, she said, "I did my research on you. Sanders Wilson and the studio sang your praises." Mika ticked off on her fingers. "On time, prepared, takes direction, easy to get along with. In other words, the perfect actress." She smiled.

The description meant a lot to Sara. Sanders Wilson directed *Enough*, and Sara had worked hard to meet his exacting standards. She let her guard down at the compliment and asked, "No dirt?" As soon as the words left her mouth, she regretted them. Well, better to get it over with now.

Mika must have read her reaction, because she fixed Sara with a steady gaze. "No. Nothing that a discerning person would believe." After a moment, she said, "Your turn."

"I watched your shows. *Murder* is good. It's compelling, but too heartbreaking for me."

Mika nodded. "Even though that's the point, I often wonder how people can watch every week."

"I couldn't," Sara said. "But, *Malice Aforethought*? Wow. First, how did you ever convince them to go with that title?"

"It was a battle," Mika conceded. "The executives wanted to dumb it down, but I believe in our audience."

"I love the double meaning. You never know if the title refers to the criminal or the detective."

"Thank you," Mika said. "I hope it makes convincing you to work with me a little easier."

"It certainly convinced me to listen to you." Sara was going to say more, but the waiter appeared.

"Do you like eggs Benedict?" Mika asked. "Their hollandaise is wonderful."

"That sounds good."

"I'll have the same," Mika told the waiter. When he left, she adjusted her glasses. With the gesture came a more businesslike tone of voice. "I hope you'll indulge me while I give you a little background. You may know that I'm not the first person in my family to create television shows. My father is Mike Williams."

"I'm sorry, the name is familiar, and I can picture a logo…" Sara trailed off.

"He was known for PI and cop shows in the seventies and eighties. At one time he had six shows on two networks. He was successful, but the shows were moronic. They all had the same tired premise. A world-weary cop or PI fighting a corrupt system out to destroy the little guy. A man's man who looks down on women or anyone who isn't as tough as he is."

Sara thought for a moment. "Did they all have the detective's name in the title?"

"Yes, that's them. He was single-handedly responsible for generations of cop stereotypes."

"What happened to him?"

Mika furrowed her brow. "Happened? Nothing. The genre faded out, but he's still around."

"Oh. Sorry. I thought you were talking about him in the past tense."

"No, not him. Certainly his career. He didn't change with the times, but I guess he didn't need to. He made a fortune in syndication."

Sara was silent, not sure how to respond. Mika reached in her bag for a folder and placed it on the table. "I promise this will all connect, but do you remember the television show *Cagney & Lacey* starring Tyne Daly and Sharon Gless?"

Sara's smile was quick. "Oh, yeah. Not when it was originally out, but I watched it in the afternoons when I got home from school."

"Of course, you did." Mika's smile was indulgent. "Sharon Gless wasn't the original Cagney. An actress by the name of Meg Foster was."

"Oh?" Sara searched her memory. "I don't know her."

"You wouldn't. She was replaced after the first season." Mika flipped through the stapled pages until she came to the section she was looking for. "This is what one of the network execs told *TV Guide* at the time." She picked up the page, adjusted her glasses, and read. "'Too tough, too hard, not feminine. We perceived them as dykes.'"

Sara sat forward. "What? He actually said that in a major publication? He called them dykes and got away with it?"

Mika slid the paper over to Sara. "Oh, yes. They replaced Meg Foster with Sharon Gless because, according to them, she was more feminine."

"That's terrible. What happened to Meg Foster?"

"Meg Foster continued acting, but she was understandably devastated."

Sara read through the highlighted quote again. "I shouldn't be surprised, but I am. He just came out and said it."

"Yes. He did. Because he could." The waiter arrived with their breakfast and the women took several minutes to get settled into their meal. When Mika spoke again, her voice was bitter. "I blame my father. He created this version of the cop genre—this culture."

Sara pointed at the bag where the papers had gone. "The executive quoted—was that your father?"

"No, but I have no doubt he would have said something similar." Anger radiated off Mika.

They made small talk as they ate their breakfast. Mika was interesting and attentive, nothing like the dismissive woman at the Golden Globes. Sara wondered which version was real. Were either? Sara poked at her eggs, lost in thought.

"Sara? Something wrong?" Mika asked.

Sara jumped a little. "No, sorry." She put down her fork and pushed the plate aside. "Yes. I'm trying to figure you out. I have to be honest, the way you treated my brother at the Globes really bothered me."

Mika nodded. "Thank you for saying something." She sighed. "I'm afraid my personal family history colored my introduction to your brother. My father, who was largely absent during my childhood, has recently insinuated himself into my life. When I met Nathan, I allowed my own baggage to surface. As I said that night, I forget that there are families who genuinely love each other and have no hidden agendas."

Sara felt the sincerity in Mika's words. She gave her a warm smile. "Thank you for explaining." The waiter cleared the plates, and after refusing another latte, Sara said, "Tell me about the project."

Mika reached for another folder, this one much thicker. She placed her left hand on it and gave Sara a long look. "You know I'm a lesbian." It wasn't a question.

"I do. Is that important to the conversation?"

"I found that quote when I was doing a research paper in film school. I'd just come out, and even though it happened years before, I took it personally. I've always known that if I had the opportunity, I would make a PI show with a lesbian main character. My version of poetic justice." She paused. "I have that opportunity now." She opened the folder, and Sara could see it was a script. "I'm going to prove that a queer woman will be a compelling lead. And I'm going to show her in a loving, sexual relationship."

Sara looked away from the intensity in Mika's eyes. When she spoke, she chose her words carefully. "That's a lot of pressure to put on your show." She paused. "And your lead."

"Yes. It is. But, I'm up to the challenge, and so is my writing team. As for the lead…" She shrugged, turning her palm up. "It depends on whether I can convince the right actress to come on board." Sara didn't respond to the unspoken question, and Mika let the silence hang for a few moments before saying, "Would you like to see the treatment? Or, I brought the pilot script."

"Tell me about the pilot."

When Mika started to speak, the Hollywood executive faded away and the voice of a storyteller took over. "The pilot opens with new homicide detective Joey Driskell and her older male partner pulling up to an unoccupied house. She doesn't understand why they're there, and he won't tell her. When she starts to unbuckle her seat belt, he tells her to stay in the car. Joey isn't happy about breaking protocol, but he's the senior detective. He's gone for several minutes, and she gets increasingly uneasy. Finally, she gets out of the car, hand on her gun, but still doesn't enter the house. Not until she hears a gunshot." Mika's eyes sparkled behind her glasses.

"The next scene is at the gravesite. Joey is in her dress blues like every other cop, but she stands apart from them. As she walks back to her car alone, a man approaches her and introduces himself. He's Leo Corsetti, and the dead man is his former partner. He invites her to join him for coffee." The waiter appeared with the bill, and Mika pulled it to her, added a tip, and signed. When he left, she gave Sara a teasing smile. "Shall I go on?"

"Definitely."

"Now they're in the coffee shop. They've just settled into a table when two other cops come in, obviously from the funeral. Joey stiffens, anticipating trouble, and she's right. The two walk over to the table and eye her with disdain before telling Corsetti that hanging out with Joey will get him killed. Corsetti tells them to lay off her, she's a good cop. 'Yeah?' they tell him. 'Then you keep her, 'cause no one wants her for a partner.'" Sara held back a chuckle as Mika adopted the voice of a male detective. "What?" she said. "You don't like my accent?"

"It's…well, you're very different when you're telling a story." Sara risked going further. "You come alive."

Mika's blush surprised her. "I do love to create stories." She took a breath and continued, "Fast-forward five years, and Corsetti and Driskell are now partners in a PI firm. Joey lives with her girlfriend, Noelle, and her life is happy." She paused. "As an aside, I like the full circle of it. The queer character is in a stable, loving relationship and the straight woman is dating around."

"Straight woman?"

Mika sighed, looking at her watch. "As much as I'd like to tell you the whole plot, I'd prefer you read the script. But, I will give you a spoiler. About halfway through the pilot, Corsetti is killed in the same manner as Driskell's partner."

Sara frowned. "She has two dead partners? And the murders are linked?"

"Right. The search for the killer or killers will be the serialized component of the story. Every week Joey and her new partner will uncover more of the conspiracy."

"The new partner is the straight woman."

"The new partner is Corsetti's daughter, Bria. She's inherited half of the business and wants to sell, but the will stipulates that the business cannot be sold until all open cases have been closed. And, of course, the biggest unsolved case is her father's murder."

"I like it." Sara nodded slowly. "So, Corsetti and Driskell. Is that what you're calling it?"

"Definitely not." Mika grimaced. "That's too much like my father's shows. No, I'm calling it *Corsetti's Will.*"

"Is it a limited series? One season?"

"Possibly. There is a natural end. The conspiracy has to be unraveled by the end of the first season or we'll have an increasingly improbable arc. That doesn't mean the series has to end. Conceivably, it could go on for multiple seasons with Corsetti and Driskell running the agency," Mika said.

"How will that work with the title? If the murder is solved and the women presumably decide to keep the business, the will is a dead plot point."

"That's if the 'will' in the title is a document."

Sara thought for a moment. "It was Corsetti's wish all along for his daughter to join the agency?"

Mika gave a half-shrug. "Could be, but remember there are two Corsettis—one of whom will be very strong-willed." Sara looked out the window, thinking over what she had just heard. She saw a woman standing on the sidewalk with her phone raised as if she were taking a selfie. Sara had seen the pseudo-selfie move many times and knew the woman was trying to capture a photo of her or Mika. Sara quickly turned her head, not wanting this meeting to be documented. She looked back at Mika, who was smiling. "I'd like you to play Joey Driskell."

"Why?"

If Mika was taken aback by the question, she didn't show it. "Because you're perfect for the part. You showed an emotional range in *Enough* which, I admit, surprised me. You have an innate blend of tough and gentle that I want Joey to embody." Mika picked up her glass and drank from it. "You're openly gay, which I'm sure you understand is a requirement for this role. Fans won't accept a straight actress playing Joey, or Noelle, for that matter."

"Aren't there other lesbian actresses who deserve this opportunity?"

"Certainly. There are many aspiring actresses out there, but if I were to cast one of them as Joey, the show wouldn't last." Once again Mika reached into her leather bag and pulled out yet another folder. She opened it and handed the single page to Sara. "You have over a million followers on Instagram. There are fan accounts for Sara Silver, Range Street, and *Enough*. To put it simply, you come with an audience that I need."

Sara furrowed her brow as she absorbed what Mika had just told her. "You want my fans?"

Mika held up her hand. "No. I want to make a show with a lesbian lead, and I want it to be successful because it's about a lesbian. As I've said, this is personal to me." Mika emphasized the last sentence. "However, my righteous indignation does not sway studios. Numbers do. Binge needs this series to bring in new subscribers. So, yes. I want your fans, but I want to give them something in return." Mika gestured to Sara. "You. Playing a lesbian character in a happy, healthy relationship."

Sara sat back in her chair and blew out a breath. "That's a lot to think about. You weren't expecting an answer today, were you?"

"Of course not, but I do need to know within a week. Once the leads are cast, I'm ready to begin production. The show would film here in LA. We'll let your agent discuss money, but I can promise it will be lucrative up front with potential residual earnings."

"That's fine. The money won't be a deciding factor. Would I have to sign a long-term contract?"

"I would love it if you did, but since we don't know if this will be a limited series, I would say commit to one season, and give me the opportunity to convince you to sign for longer."

Sara's head was spinning, and she wanted to be alone to think. "You've given me a lot to consider." She stood, ready to offer her hand to Mika, but the other woman reached for her bag.

"I'll walk you out."

Once they were outside, Mika placed a thick envelope in Sara's hands. "Here's the full script of the pilot. Read it. Get a sense of Joey." Then she leaned in and air-kissed Sara's cheek. "The car will take you back to your hotel. I'll be in touch." Mika climbed into the back seat of a large black SUV at the curb and was gone. Sara looked after her, then down at the package she was holding. When she looked up, the woman who had absolutely not been taking a selfie in front of the restaurant was hurrying away.

CHAPTER FOUR

Back in the quiet of her hotel, Sara leaned against the pillows and was immediately engrossed in the story. Like Mika's other scripted show, *Corsetti's Will* was well-written with believable characters. When she got to the intimate scene between Joey Driskell and her lover, Noelle Prado, Sara read through it twice before dropping the script in her lap. Although there wasn't much dialogue, and the stage directions were vague, the intent of the scene was clear. She searched for Mika's card.

The call went to voice mail. "Hi, Mika, it's Sara Silver. I'm reading the script, and I've got some concerns. Could you give me a call when you're free? Thanks. Oh, and thanks for breakfast today. No matter what happens with me, I think *Corsetti's Will* is going to be a success."

When Sara finished reading, she dropped the pages on the bed and leaned back on the pillows. It was good. Really good. Unsettled, she reached for her phone. Nathan answered on the third ring. "About time. Tell me everything. Did she ask about me?"

"Funny, you never came up. I can't imagine why," Sara teased.

"You need to meet a producer who's into men. She'd ask about me."

"What if it's a guy?"

"I'm popular with gay guys." He paused. "Tell me about it."

"She wants me to play a lesbian private detective in a series on Binge." Sara waited for his response. When nothing came, she said, "Can't you give me some kind of reaction? What do you think?"

"I think I don't have enough information. Tell me more. Lead or supporting character?"

"Lead. One of two. The other is the PI's eventual partner, well, business partner. She's straight. My character is Joey. She has a girlfriend, and apparently they have a lot of sex."

Nathan laughed. "Wow. You may need acting lessons. How long has it been?"

"Shut up."

"As always, Sar, snappy comeback. So, nudity?" he asked.

"No. Definitely not. I left Mika a message as soon as I read the script. This could be over before it starts if boobs are required."

"Do you have ugly boobs?"

"You and I are not ever going to discuss my boobs."

"I'm just trying to understand why you're against nudity. I don't think it's a big deal anymore." He lowered his voice. "The obvious answer is ugly boobs."

Sara groaned. "Stop it. For the record, my boobs are lovely." She slapped her forehead. "Oh my God, I can't believe I just said that to you."

"If they're lovely, why not show them?"

"Because they're not for public consumption."

"So, you have special reserve boobs? Is that what you're saying? They come out of the vault every few years?"

She knew he could riff for hours once he found a topic, so she cut him off. "Funny guy. I'm not doing nudity, and that's final."

"If nudity wasn't an issue, would you be interested?" he asked.

Sara thought for a moment. "Maybe. I don't know. When I was reading the script, I understood her. Whatever else I think about Mika Williams, she can write. Joey is a complex character."

"How do you feel about acting again? You were happy during *Enough*."

"Yeah, but that was about the people. What are the chances that would happen again?"

"Sara." Nathan's voice was gentle. "The chances are good because you've always been a pleaser. You do whatever it takes to make things around you peaceful. If this is what you want, you'll make it work. It's how you are."

"What if I can't? I couldn't stand Mika at the Globes. What if that's her real personality? I couldn't deal with that every day."

"Was she like that at breakfast?"

"No, and she explained her attitude and apologized again. This morning she was more…" Sara paused, searching for the right word. "Real. There were times she was even cute."

"Cute? As in you found her attractive?"

"No. Cute as in adorably excited about her story."

Nathan wouldn't leave it alone. "Do you find her attractive?"

"Yeah, in a scary *Devil Wears Prada* kinda way, not as someone to date." Sara heard a sound and checked her phone screen. "Hold on a second, will you? I think this is Mika." Before he could answer, Sara switched over. "Hello."

"Sara, Mika Williams. Nudity is not a requirement. I would like to film you topless, but you can wear nipple pads and we'll choreograph the scenes so your modesty is protected."

Sara laughed. "How did you know?"

"As soon as I drove away, I realized we hadn't talked about the sex scenes." Sara could hear papers shuffling. "Do you have concerns other than nudity?"

"No," Sara admitted.

"Are you willing to bare some skin?" Mika pressed.

"I think so. I understand it's important to your vision of the relationship. I know it's cliché, but as long as it's tasteful…" Sara started, then stopped. "Never mind. I don't even know what that means."

"I do," Mika said. "It's about character development. The scene has to reveal character, not just titillate the audience. Did you think the scene as written was tasteful?"

Sara didn't hesitate. "There wasn't a lot written, but what was there was passionate and very loving."

"Excellent. That's exactly how I want the relationship portrayed. Did it resonate? Feel authentic?"

Sara paused to think over what she read. "It did."

She expected Mika to push for more, but all she said was, "Do you have any other questions?"

"No." Then, because she didn't want to hang up without letting Mika know how she felt about the story, she said, "It's good. There's depth to the character. Not just Joey. All the characters have nuance."

There was a smile in Mika's voice. "Thank you. I'm glad you like it. I won't press for more now, but expect my call later in the week."

"I will. Thanks for calling back."

Sara heard Mika's, "Goodbye," as she switched back to her brother.

"Still there?"

"What did she say?"

Sara let out a relieved breath. "It's not required. Topless, yes, but there are nipple pads, and they choreograph the scene to protect modesty."

"Modesty? What are you, a fifties housewife? You can show a little side boob and still maintain an air of mystery."

"I do have good side boob," she mused.

"Am I going to be able to watch this show, or will I get grossed out?"

"Worse. Your girlfriends will want me. Too late, that already happens."

"You're going to do it aren't you?" His teasing tone was gone.

"If I do, will you move here with me? You've always said you can work from anywhere. Just think, no more long Minnesota winters. I'll buy a house with a pool…" She let her voice trail off. Sara hated the thought of living so far from him. He was home to her.

"I could be convinced," he said at last. "I wouldn't mind being farther away from the parents. And I am tired of the cold." He paused. "Okay, I'm in."

"Really?" Sara felt a rush of elation. "Promise?"

"Yes, but, Sara, you should talk to the guys before you make this decision. What if it's a success? What happens to Range Street?"

His question sobered her. "It will have to be part of the contract. I promised the guys I'd always be there when they wanted to record. They know I'm done with big tours, but I said I'd still do a few live shows."

"Then, you better call Jeff before you do anything else."

"I will." Her voice got quieter. "Thanks, Nathan. I don't know what I'd do without you."

"I don't either. Love ya, Sara."

"Love you too." She hung up and jumped off the bed, too excited to laze around the room any longer. The pool beckoned.

CHAPTER FIVE

Several hours later, she'd finished a margarita, nachos, and a third of her book. The afternoon was peaceful. With her long blond hair and blue eyes hidden, she looked like any other tourist enjoying the LA sun. She was pleasantly buzzed by the drink and the thought of living where it was warm. Her phone vibrated beside her. It was Jeff. She needed to talk with him, but not in a public place. She declined the call and texted, *I'm at the pool. Can I call when I get back to my room?*

Have you checked Twitter, today? was his reply.

She frowned and typed, *No.*

Check then call when u can.

"Really?" she said aloud. Jeff and Sara were inseparable growing up on Range Street in their Minnesota town. In the summer, they rode their bikes all through the river valley that separated their working-class neighborhood from the more affluent parts of town. Winters were spent skating, Jeff in black hockey skates and Sara miserable in white figure skates.

Fourth grade was a turning point in their lives. Their teacher, Miss Bailey, ended each day playing her guitar and singing pop songs with the class. Both Jeff and Sara were enamored—Jeff with the guitar, Sara with their teacher. That Christmas they both got cheap acoustic guitars that Miss Bailey taught them to play.

In middle school they started a band with Jeff on lead guitar, Sara on vocals, and Paul, a quiet kid from down the street, playing drums. By the time they got to high school, another neighbor, Greg, quit the school orchestra and taught himself bass guitar. They were surprisingly good, and soon Range Street was popular in the college bars around town.

After graduation, Jeff begged Sara to commit two years full time to the band. Since she wasn't sure what she wanted to study in college, she agreed. The four of them moved to Minneapolis and started including original music in their sets. A year and a half later, as Sara was filling out college applications, the call came. By that summer they'd recorded their first album and were opening for a well-known Minneapolis band. A dozen years later, Range Street had two Grammys, sold-out concert tours, and seven platinum albums.

Sara opened Twitter. What she saw made her heart drop. No wonder Jeff's text was terse. There was picture of her in the restaurant with Mika. Another showed Mika handing Sara the thick envelope containing the script.

She was furious when she saw the tweet: *Is Enough star & Street People singer @real.sarasilver about to ink a deal to play the lesbian lead in @MikaWilliams76 first Binge show? Sources say she's close to signing on. @EnoughMovie @RangeStBand*

Her head spun. How could she explain this to Jeff? She should have listened to Nathan and called right away. While working through what to say, a memory flashed in her mind. The smile. Mika was smiling when Sara noticed the photographer at the restaurant. And her insistence on walking Sara out. It was a setup. Forget calling Jeff. Her first call would be to Mika to vent her rage and turn down the part.

Back in the room, Sara showered, hoping to get her emotions under control before making any calls. She was disappointed and close to tears. Minnesota hadn't felt like home in a long time. Unlike the guys, she didn't have families and a large lake house. She lived in a downtown loft, which was the epitome of cool, but not her.

Dressed in baggy shorts and a college T-shirt, she curled onto the bed and called Jeff. "Hi," she said. "How are you?" No matter what was going on, Minnesota etiquette demanded small talk.

"I'm good. Saw you on the Golden Globes. Looked like fun." Jeff was never a big talker.

"It was fun, but not like the Grammys. I missed having you there." She drew in a shaky breath at the same time Jeff cleared his throat. "Listen, Jeff, I know this is cliché, but it's not what you think. I met Mika Williams at the Golden Globes, and she asked me to have breakfast with her. That was today. So, no, I haven't signed any multiyear deal with her or anyone."

"Huh." Jeff's reply was little more than a grunt. She waited, knowing he was thinking and would talk when he was ready. "Were you going to tell me?"

She quietly exhaled in relief. He was asking as her best friend—the boy who lived next door. "Yeah, but I didn't know what to do, so I decided a margarita and nachos would help me think."

He chuckled. "It usually does."

"She's offering me the lead in a detective series. It might be a limited series—one season—or it might be longer. If I decide to do it, and it's more than one season, I'll have my agent write studio time into the contract. I promise, Range Street will always be my priority."

Jeff grunted another response, and they fell into a comfortable silence. Sara knew his conversational rhythms. He would speak when he had something he wanted her to hear. "Truth is, we all liked the time off. I don't see us keeping the pace we did in our twenties. Greg and Paul want to fish and hunt with their kids. I like producing as much as I like playing, and you know that's a lot." She laughed. "Are you interested in doing this show?"

"I was, Jeff, before this happened. I think Mika Williams staged those pictures, and I'm furious. How can I trust her?"

"Yeah, that could be a problem. Do you think she knew about the backstage photos?"

"Hell, yes, she knew. She kind of alluded to it when we talked. She said a smart person would be able to see through the rumors."

"So, what're you going do?"

"Confront her. Tell her how angry I am."

"About the job."

Sara blew out a long breath, and with it went some of her anger. "I don't know. I liked the idea of living in California. Of having a reason to leave home."

"Shit, Sara, you're thirty-two years old. You don't need a reason to leave home. If you want to live in California, live in California."

"C'mon, Jeff, you know better than that. My whole life is in Minnesota. My parents, Nathan, you guys. We rehearse there. We even record there."

"None of that's a reason to stay. You haven't been happy here for as long as I can remember. But if you need to have a reason to leave, take this one. Don't turn it down just 'cause you're pissed now. If Williams is using you, use her right back. You don't have to be a victim."

They were quiet while Sara absorbed his words. "I didn't think about it like that," she finally said.

"Maybe you should. I'll handle the boys. We should look at putting some time together next spring. Maybe some shows in the summer."

"Okay. No matter what I decide, I'll make sure there's time in my schedule. Yeah?"

"That works."

"Thanks, buddy. I love you."

"Uh-huh," he said and hung up.

Her phone vibrated in her hand. Mika Williams. A surge of anger shot through her. "Mika," she answered. "What the hell was that about?"

To her credit, Mika didn't try to deny responsibility. "That was Dani Copeland, the social media manager for *Corsetti's Will*. The tweet has created quite a bit of buzz."

"I don't appreciate being used to generate"—she paused to emphasize the word—"*buzz* for your show. Don't manipulate me or my fans."

"Sara, maybe I wasn't clear. There's no such thing as unlimited development money. I need an audience, ideally a passionate one, before the show premieres. If I don't bring new subscribers to the network, we won't get past filming the pilot. I never lied to you. I'm interested in your talent and your fans. I also made it clear that social media was key to connecting with the audience and building their passion for our show."

Mika's words deepened her anger. "No, Mika. That's not what we're talking about. You publicized—you sensationalized—what was little more than an exploratory meeting. I've already had to deal with angry colleagues. Mika, you don't know me, but you crossed a line. These are my people you're manipulating. My band, my fans. If you researched me, you know the damage those backstage photos did. I've spent the last couple years fighting rumors that I'm an addict."

Mika's voice was quiet. "Sara, have you read any of the responses on Twitter?"

Was this woman listening? "No."

"You might be surprised by how passionately your fans feel about you. Before you make any decisions, will you at least read what they're saying?"

Sara covered her eyes and breathed. She thought about Jeff's words. When she felt calmer, she said, "I honestly don't know."

"At least promise me you'll sleep on it, and we can talk further tomorrow."

"Fine." To her credit, Mika didn't laugh at Sara's childish response.

"I had another reason for calling." Mika sounded like she was treading cautiously, but Sara suspected it was an act.

"Yes?"

"We've cast the actress who will play Noelle. I thought you'd like to know."

After another quiet exhale, she asked, "Who is it?"

"Christina Landis. She was one of the leads in a popular lesbian film out last year. Maybe you saw it? *Night in Time?*"

"No," Sara said, refusing to engage.

"I've had a copy of the DVD couriered to your hotel. It should arrive within the hour. I hope you'll watch it." She paused. "Thanks for listening, Sara. Good night."

Sara stared at her phone. She wanted to call Nathan or her manager for advice, but she did neither. Instead, she picked up the room service menu and ordered dinner and a bottle of wine. Grabbing the remote, she flicked on the TV. She refused to check Twitter, no matter how intrigued she was by what Mika had said. That lasted as long as it took for her to navigate away from the hotel's promotional screen and search the channel guide. Nothing looked interesting. She turned off the TV, threw the remote onto the nightstand, and picked up her phone.

"Holy shit," she muttered as she scrolled through hundreds of comments. Her fans were thrilled. "Shit," she repeated. The more she read, the calmer she felt. Mika Williams was right; people wanted a mainstream series starring an openly gay actor playing an openly gay character. And her fans wanted it to be her.

She scrolled through Twitter until her meal arrived. As the waitress was setting the table, the courier appeared with the DVD of *Night in Time*. Sara was reading the back of the case when a tentative voice asked, "Will there be anything else, Ms. Silver?"

"I'm sorry, no." She took the folder, added a tip, and scrawled her name. When she handed it back, the woman was staring at the image on the front of the DVD of two women kissing. Sara met her eyes in challenge.

"That's a good movie." The waitress blushed as she spoke. "I've seen it. Twice."

Sara smiled back, ashamed at her assumption. "They just sent it to me. I thought I'd watch during dinner."

"I hope you enjoy it, and your dinner," she added quickly.

"I'm sure I will." The woman was almost at the door when Sara stopped her. "Hey. Um, would you watch a show just because there's a lesbian character?"

She didn't hesitate. "Yes. But if they don't do it right, I'll turn it off. Sometimes shows throw queer characters in to get us to watch, but you can tell if it's just bait."

Sara nodded. She knew several shows that fit that description. "Thanks for sharing," she said.

"You're welcome." Just as the door was about to close, the woman looked back. "I'd watch your show."

Sara set up her laptop and settled in for dinner and a movie. Two hours later, she hadn't moved except to refill her wineglass. When the credits scrolled, she closed her computer and went to wash her face. Her eyes were red from crying, and she felt a little silly. On tour, they watched a lot of movies, and Sara was usually entertained, but *Night in Time* was the first movie in a long time that made her feel an intense connection to the story and its characters.

She looked at herself in the mirror. She was going to do it.

CHAPTER SIX

Sara leaned her forehead against the glass of her loft window. Below her, the frozen Minnesota landscape reflected her mood. After being nominated for a Golden Globe, all of the predictions were that she would get an Oscar nomination. Sara had tried to ignore the talk, to convince herself it wasn't going to happen, but she'd gotten her hopes up. She was disappointed. Her phone rang, and she grimaced when she saw her agent's name. "Hi, Andrew."

His voice was kind. "How're you doing?"

"I'm fine. The Globes were the surprise, not this."

"We need to work on that," he said. "Don't say that to anyone else. What have you put out on social media?"

"I just got up."

"Get something out. The studio will expect you to be supportive of the movie."

"I am supportive of the movie." She picked up her phone. "Okay, how about something like, 'Congratulations to Hannah and the cast and crew of *Enough* on their Oscar nominations.'"

"Needs to be more effusive. Show more excitement. Just make sure you don't say anything like 'well-deserved.'"

"Why not? It is well-deserved."

"No. People are looking for you to be bitter. If you say 'well-deserved' it means you think not everyone deserved to be nominated. You don't want that."

"No, I don't. I'll work on it and make sure it's effusive without judging."

"Good. What time is *Rolling Stone* going to be there?"

"This afternoon."

"Make sure you get all of your crying done before they get there."

Sara was indignant. "I'm not crying."

"You should be. You deserved that fucking nomination."

When they hung up, she grabbed her tablet and considered what to post. After several attempts, she went with her original idea. Screw effusive. *Congrats to everyone who was part of @EnoughMovie, and a special congrats to the talented @hannah_collins11.* She tossed the tablet on the bed and wandered through the loft to the kitchen to make coffee and toast.

More than anything, she wanted to cancel the *Rolling Stone* interview. She hated doing one-on-one interviews. At least the Oscars would move the inevitable questions about rumored drug use to later in the interview. In the meantime, everyone in the room would search for evidence she was using. She'd gotten used to the surreptitious looks while recording her solo album.

Over the next three days, Sara would spend several hours with the *Rolling Stone* photographers and writer in her loft and at various locations around the city. The last day they wanted to see Sara's hometown and visit the small house where she'd grown up. They'd be disappointed. Reporters and tourists always were. After all, Range Street was nothing more than a busy thoroughfare lined with small houses built in the fifties.

* * *

Mika wasn't in the mood to wait, but as with everything that involved her father, what she wanted actually didn't matter. Larry Rand had called to tell her Mike Williams had "notes" on the script for the pilot, and Rand would appreciate it if she met with him. If Rand wondered why her father hadn't called her directly, he didn't ask. Mike must have walked a fine line with the executive. If he hinted there was a problem between them or with her professionalism, he risked tarnishing her reputation. He couldn't do that when he had effectively linked it to his own when he forced his way into the deal.

Mika still didn't know how he'd finagled a role on her production. None of her contacts at Binge had been aware of the caveat to the network's approval of *Corsetti's Will*. Her fear was Mike Williams was planting seeds of doubt with the network executives about her ability to produce a hit. The man had an endless need to prove he was the only talent in the Williams family.

She looked at her watch. He was fifteen minutes late. The first time he'd arranged a command performance like this had been when she was just starting out. She'd been the one to arrive late that time. He punished her by hinting to a tabloid that there was tension between her and the network. When she called him in fury, he laughed and reminded her of the importance of professionalism. Timeliness, for example, he'd said. She got the message, not so much about being on time, but about the power he still wielded.

His entrance didn't have the fanfare it once had, but because this was one of his regular haunts, he still garnered attention. She watched him take his time talking to acquaintances. He wanted her to know how little he cared that she was waiting. Grinding her teeth, she returned to her phone and read reactions to the Oscar nominations.

Unlike others on her team, Mika wasn't surprised when Sara was overlooked by the more conservative Oscar voters. Where the Golden Globes would champion a musician who risked her reputation to portray an icon, the Oscars preferred to acknowledge accomplished actresses. Mika didn't care. Sure, it would have been nice to add "Oscar-nominated" when they announced Sara's signing, but Sara was bringing far more to the project than a nomination.

"You need to learn to put that thing away." While her flinch made him smile, she knew it also irked him that she hadn't watched his tour through the restaurant.

"Father," she said, using the formal term he hated. When she refused to call him "Dad" all those years ago, he tried to get her to use his first name. She'd laughed and told him the name suggested a familiarity they would never have.

"Mika," he said, a broad smile playing to any audience that might still be watching. She wanted to tell him not to bother, no one was paying attention, but she knew it wasn't worth the tiny moment of triumphant. "I hope you haven't been waiting long."

"How very passive-aggressive of you." She barely looked up from her phone. The waiter arrived and he ordered a double scotch. "The water's fine," she said.

"For God's sake, Mika." He looked at the waiter. "Bring her a martini. Gin."

She slid her phone into the inside pocket of her purse, then clasped her hands on the table. She felt like a Catholic schoolteacher waiting for the class to come to order.

"How's your mother?" he asked.

"Let's not do this. I'll have a drink with you and take your notes on the script. There's no need for small talk."

He glared. She watched him search for a scathing reply. Finding none, he said, "That show, what're you calling it? Serpico's Will? It won't last. You're going to blow any credibility you had. Stupid move." Mika didn't bother correcting him on the title or replying. "You need a man in one of the lead roles. No one will ever believe two women without experience can be PIs."

Mika gave him a slow blink. "Yes, you're certainly the expert on believability. Wasn't one of your detectives a mayor? Of New York City? Yet, he had time to sneak off to crime scenes and interrogate witnesses. How believable."

His face reddened, but the drinks arrived, saving him from coming up with a reply. He took two large swallows while she stirred her drink. By the time she'd eaten her olives, he was waving to the waiter to bring him a refill. Another small victory that gained her nothing. The drink bolstered his bravado. "And, this lesbian thing. The guys tell me you're convinced you can draw an audience. We both know that's bullshit. I haven't told them what I think. Not yet. I hope you'll make the right decision before I have to."

This should be good, she thought. "Oh? And what is the right decision according to Mike Williams?"

"There's too much queer sex. Sure, guys might like it the first couple of shows, but that's not going to last. You need a man in the lead. I understand you want a lesbian in your show. Fine, but make it a small part. Maybe the cop who gets killed."

She shouldn't take the bait, but he was the one person who could always break her iron control. "What was your last show again? *Barnaby Jones?*" Her reference to the 1970s show about an elderly detective hit its mark. It was a casual reminder of his own age and of a successful show he didn't produce. His face reddened again, and he opened his mouth to speak, but she'd had enough. "Be very careful, Father. You're dangerously close to overplaying your hand. What will happen when you do? When you've whispered to Rand that my show is going to fail, but it succeeds wildly?" She let that hang for a beat. "I'll tell you what. They're going to realize you're a pathetic has-been trying to ride his daughter's coattails. You better pray for a soft landing when they do. If it were up to me, it wouldn't be."

She stood, gathered her purse, and pushed her martini in front of him. "Why don't you finish this? I don't need alcohol to get through the day."

* * *

After more than a decade of doing press, Sara had come to recognize "the shift." It was the subtle words or movement an interviewer used to show the softball questions were over. The reporter in front of her probably wouldn't even try to hide his shift. She guessed he was somewhere in his forties. He'd layered his flannel shirt over a thermal, the front of which he'd tucked into his jeans, revealing a wooden belt buckle in a honeycomb pattern. The French tuck, the buckle, and the Timberland boots told Sara all she needed to know about the man: he tried too hard to be younger and hipper than he was.

He'd been leaning back, his right ankle resting on his left knee, showing only a casual interest in her answers. She watched him look down at his pad of questions. Here it comes, she thought. He'll drop the foot. Then he'll lean forward, probably rest his forearms on his thighs.

"Sara." He dropped the foot to the floor. "How did you feel when you found out you'd been overlooked for an Oscar nod?" He leaned forward, legs spread wide.

She couldn't help a small smile as she took in the new posture. He was leaning on one thigh, his notebook resting on the other. "I don't look at it as being overlooked," she said.

"So, you don't think your performance deserved a nomination?"

"What I'm saying is the women who were nominated had outstanding performances." She reached for her tablet and pulled up the list of nominees. "Who in this group doesn't deserve to be recognized?" She read the names aloud, then looked up. "Who would you exclude?" She'd been happy when she came up with the idea to turn the nomination question back on the interviewer. It should end the conversation, and, if reported accurately, show she admired the women who were honored.

"At the end of the last Range Street tour, photographs of you looking exhausted and emaciated were taken backstage. Shortly after, the band announced a three-year hiatus. Some suggest you have a drug problem and your bandmates demanded you seek help."

"That was the speculation," Sara said.

"Is it true?"

"No."

"Which part isn't true?"

She kept her gaze fixed on him, knowing any flicker of her eyes would be interpreted as a lie. "It's easier to tell you what is true. The pictures were taken of me during a backstage wardrobe change. The band is on hiatus."

"You don't have a drug problem?"

"No. I don't use drugs."

"Is that because you went to rehab? Were you using during the tour?"

"No. I've never used drugs."

"What about alcohol?"

"I drink socially, but I don't have a problem with alcohol."

"You haven't sought professional help?"

"I want to be careful, here. I don't use drugs and I don't abuse alcohol, so I haven't needed professional help to overcome an addiction."

He jumped on her response. "Have you sought professional help for an eating disorder?"

She tried not to roll her eyes. "I don't have an eating disorder, nor am I suffering from a debilitating illness." She'd considered reminding him that the pictures were taken the last night of a three-month tour. She'd been overwhelmed with fatigue and trapped by her commitment to Range Street. She didn't say any of that. "Those photos were a gross violation of my privacy. The fact they were shared on social media was bad enough, but when mainstream media, like *Rolling Stone* report rumors, well, let's just say I expected more from your publication."

"Whose idea was it for the Range Street to take three years off?"

Sara thought before answering, trying to predict any possible traps in the question. "It was a mutual decision."

"Jeff Peterson didn't demand you seek help?"

Sara breathed in, fighting to maintain her cool. "Jeff has been my dearest friend for years. If I had a health problem of any kind, he would have moved mountains to get me help. He didn't, because it wasn't necessary."

"How do you explain the pictures?"

"I won't comment on the pictures."

He raised his eyebrows. "Why is that?" Sara looked at him, careful not to show how irritated she was. When he finally realized she would outwait him, he went in a different direction. "Your solo album is already platinum. Why didn't you tour last summer?"

She tried for a lighthearted answer. "Tour without my three best friends? What would be the fun in that?"

"Do you feel you can't do it without Jeff, Greg, and Paul?"

Okay, that was it. Sara made a show of reaching for her phone. "That's all the time I have for now." She stood.

"I have several more questions," he said, crossing his legs.

"You can ask them tomorrow. Or when we do the cover shoot."

He slowly closed his notebook and took his time turning off the recording. She'd shut him down, so he was going to make her wait while he organized his canvas messenger bag. She bit her lip, trying not to laugh at his tiny tantrum.

When he finally left, Sara closed the door and let her shoulders relax. After that last tour, her bandmates and family had wanted her to take time off to rest, but she knew what she needed. She spent the next month doing what she loved: writing and recording. Being away from the crowds and doing work that was meaningful to her was energizing. When the opportunity to do *Enough* had come, she felt ready for a challenge. The surprise was how much she like her time on set.

And so she'd agreed to take the part on *Corsetti's Will* despite her lingering concerns about Mika Williams. She hadn't lied to the reporter. She needed to pack her loft and arrange for it to be sold. She had several days with the *Rolling Stone* team, and then she'd be in LA for preproduction publicity.

She went back to the window and watched the snow blow along the bank of the river. She couldn't wait for this view to be a distant memory.

CHAPTER SEVEN

Mika gambled when she cast Sara and Christina without testing their chemistry, but the timeline was tight, and she worried Sara wouldn't commit. If she hadn't, casting Christina to play Noelle, Joey Driskell's lover, was essential to building their queer audience. Today they were bringing the actresses in for a publicity shoot.

"How sexy do you want this to be?" Dani Copeland asked.

"I want it clear that they have a sexual relationship, but I'm not looking for skin. That's why we're on this set and not the apartment." As she spoke, Mika walked around the desks in Corsetti's office, considering options.

Christina stepped on set dressed in a tank top and long flowing skirt. Layered necklaces fell between her breasts. Her long hair was pulled up into a messy bun, revealing her flawless skin.

"You look perfect," Mika said. Wardrobe had captured the bohemian-artist vibe she wanted Noelle to embody. She stepped closer to look over the work of the makeup team. The outline around Christina's large dark eyes brought out gold flecks Mika hadn't noticed before. Mika turned to her assistant. "Get some shots of this. Her makeup is exactly what I want for the pilot. In fact, this whole look is what I want. Let everyone know."

Christina stood still while Renee took pictures with her phone. Mika went back to Dani. "I like the bare feet. Find a way to get that into the shot."

Dani nodded. "Maybe something on the desk? We can hike the skirt and put Sara between her legs."

Mika pursed her lips. "No, that's not what I want. I don't want it to look like she's being taken on the desk. Put Sara on the desk. She's wearing jeans, so it won't be as sexual."

Dani nodded, and they all turned when Sara stepped out of the shadows. Her hair was styled in loose waves accenting the blue of her eyes. Mika looked between the two actresses. Normally she would have preferred more contrast in their hair color, but Christina refused to go darker than her natural dirty blond, and Mika decided to see how they looked on-screen before insisting. Changing Sara's Scandinavian blond was out of the question. Not when the combination of her light hair and bright blue eyes had been driving women crazy for years.

Mika looked Sara's wardrobe over, deciding whether it worked for the character. She was in boyfriend jeans and a blazer pulled up at the sleeves. A chunky chain rested in the vee of her white T-shirt. Mika wanted Joey to have a unique style ranging from androgynous to femme. For scenes where she was working, she'd wear a variation on this look, but Mika wanted the audience comfortable when they played up her femininity.

Dani joined the group. She, too, was blond, only hers was a platinum pixie cut that highlighted her fine features and dark eyes. She was dressed in high-waisted plaid pants and a simple silk shell. "This is Dani Copeland, social media manager for the show and an accomplished photographer," Mika said.

A flicker of recognition crossed Sara's face, and she frowned slightly before stepping forward with a smile. "Hi, Dani, I'm Sara." They shook hands. Good, Mika thought. She expected professionalism on her sets, and Sara Silver had just passed the first test.

Dani turned back to Mika. "What about a few black-and-white shots? If I light behind them, we'll get a soft silhouette."

"Good idea." Mika looked at the two women standing next to each other, not talking. Sara met her eyes and smiled. Christina stared at her phone instead of engaging with the group. "Christina, Renee will hold your phone during the shoot." Renee stepped forward, plucked the phone from Christina's fingers, and made sure it was silenced.

Dani adjusted the lighting. "Sara, let's put you on the desk with Christina between your legs."

Sara lifted herself onto the desk and smiled at Christina. "Come here, baby," she teased. Christina didn't return the smile. She took her position, arms stiff at her sides. Sara's smile faltered.

Dani stepped forward. "Okay, take her hands, Sara. Yes. Like that. Smile at each other. Christina, relax your forearms." Dani looked up from her camera, frowning slightly. "Let's try lifting your hands up and touching palms. Yes. Now clasp your fingers. Gentle smiles. Lean toward each other. Little more. Christina, step forward."

Mika knew what Dani was seeing through the camera. Christina was stiff, her movements toward Sara awkward. She waved at Dani and stepped close to her actresses. "Christina, hug Sara." Sara opened her arms and Christina stepped into them. She bent forward to hug Sara, their shoulders the only point of contact. "Scoot forward on the desk," Mika told Sara. "Let your feet drop so just your toes touch the floor." With Sara positioned, she said, "Okay, now hug Christina." Sara pulled the other woman into her arms, and they all saw Christina stiffen. Sara dropped her arms immediately.

"I'm sorry," she said. "Did I hurt you?"

"No," Christina said. "No, I just wasn't expecting you to pull so hard. Let's try again."

"Ready?" Mika asked. At Christina's nod, she stepped back and said, "Sara, pull Christina to you." This time Christina stepped into her arms, and they embraced. The room was silent except for the sound of camera clicks.

Mika looked to Dani, who gave her a nod to continue. "Okay, Christina, half a step back. Good. Now, Sara, reach with your left hand and tuck a strand of hair behind her ear." Sara looked at Christina, a question in her eyes. Mika heard Dani capture the look. That might be the best one, she thought. Then Sara reached out and with gentle fingertips, tucked the long strand of hair. "Good. Lean your head into the hand. No, too far, come back a little. Good. Close your eyes, Christina. Open your lips slightly. Hold." Mika let Dani move around the couple, getting several shots. "Sara, move forward like you're going to kiss her. Look down at her lips but keep your eyes open. Lips parted both of you." Again, Mika let Dani get the shot before stepping forward. "Are you ready for your first kiss?" she asked the pair.

They both straightened and looked at her. "Sure," Sara answered. She reached down for Christina's hand and squeezed it. "Are you ready?"

"Yes," Christina answered in a whisper. She didn't make eye contact.

Sara looked from Christina to Mika. "Do you think we could have a couple of minutes?"

Mika paused, then decided to trust her. "Okay, everyone, take five." Dani, Renee, and Mika moved off the set and gathered around the camera. Mika touched Dani when she started to speak and shook her head. She wanted to hear what was going on.

"I've never done this before," Sara said. Christina gave her a look, and Sara laughed. "On-screen, I mean. I haven't had an on-screen kiss." She gave Christina a helpless shrug. "I'm really nervous."

Mika couldn't hear Christina's response, but she saw the younger woman relax. The low hum told her they were both talking. She turned to the other two women and whispered, "Do we have anything?"

"I think we can use these," Dani showed Mika a few of the near-kiss photos, then went back to the early shot where Sara looked at Christina for permission to touch her. The look read differently on camera, like Sara was silently asking for something more intimate. "This would make a good first post," Dani said. "Whet the appetite."

Mika laughed. "Nice word choice. Okay, let's get a couple of them kissing. Maybe just barely. Then I have an idea for what I want to release last." They stepped back onto the set where Sara and Christina were still talking. "Ready?" Mika called out.

Christina looked to Sara. Sara smiled, and Christina answered, "We're ready."

"I want the relationship between these two women to be one of equals. For this shot, I need Noelle to be in command of the kiss. Let's talk about how to stage it. Thoughts?"

Christina looked at her without blinking. After a few moments of silence, she said, "Against the wall."

Mika and Sara both looked over to the brick-paneled side wall. "Let's do it," Mika said, and the group moved behind the desk. The image flashed in Mika's mind, and she set the women up before she lost it. "Sara, lean against the wall. Now arms down, palms flat, and put your left foot against the wall. A little higher. Good. Christina, one hand on her thigh. Yes, like that, and the other just below her neck. Slide your fingers inside her shirt. Perfect. Now, press your body into her and touch her lips with yours. Open mouth. Christina, your bottom lip in between Sara's. Hold." Mika didn't look away from the two. "Now, kiss her, Christina."

Christina's movements were still tentative, but she was better than she had been earlier in the shoot. Sara tried to make up for it by leaning her head forward to reach for Christina's lips. It made her look like she was chasing the kiss, like Noelle was teasing Joey, keeping just out of reach. "It's perfect," Mika whispered.

After a couple more minutes, Mika gave the actresses a break. "I think we have plenty," she said as Dani scrolled through the shots. "Get those to me as soon as you can. Do you have everything ready for tomorrow?" she asked.

"Yes. Do you want me to talk to them before the table read?"

"I think that would be best. You can take a few pictures during the read, and we'll see if we want to use them. They need to get used to you being around with your camera."

Mika looked up at the actresses who still stood at the wall. "That's all we need. Thank you for coming in today." She gave them a broad smile. "Get some rest tonight. Tomorrow is a big day."

CHAPTER EIGHT

Abby Farina craved a large latte. She held her hand out, hoping her nerves had improved enough to risk the caffeine. When she saw the tremor, she dropped her hand in disgust. If she was this nervous without caffeine, her voice would quake with it. Not a good impression on her first day. "I don't have to decide now," she said aloud. "They'll have coffee there. Probably really good coffee. By the time I get there, I'll be calm." She hoped her nerves were listening.

They weren't. At the craft services table, Abby poked through the pods of coffee, her hand still noticeably shaking as she reached for the breakfast blend. She put it back and was reaching for decaf when a familiar voice said, "Hey, are you Abby? I'm Sara." Abby jumped but managed to keep the container of pods from toppling. "I'm sorry, I thought you heard me walk up."

Abby turned and caught herself before she did that up-and-down thing women do to each other. But she really wanted to take in all of Sara Silver. Despite being casually dressed in jeans and a hoodie, she looked like a Nordic ski champion.

Abby expected the hair and bright blue eyes, but her skin? It was porcelain and dewy and perfect. Then there was the smile. Her mouth was a little too wide for her face, but all that did was make her smile more pronounced. Abby wanted to touch her to see if she was real.

Sara looked down at her clothes, touching the front of her hoodie. "I get cold in air-conditioning," she explained. "I do have a nicer shirt on under this."

Abby flushed. "Sorry, I was a little starstruck." She looked at her own sleeveless dress. "I didn't know what to wear, so I threw on this old thing," she said.

"Really?" Sara asked. "How many?"

Abby furrowed her brow, trying to figure out the question. What had she missed while she'd been staring? Was Sara asking how much coffee she'd had this morning? Did she notice Abby's hands shaking? She clenched her fists, trying to force the extra energy out.

Sara crossed her arms and gave Abby that big smile, obviously pleased with herself. "How many outfits? I know that's not the first one you put on."

Abby unclenched her fists. "Oh, I see how this is going to be," she said. "I'll have you know this is the first outfit I put on today."

"Picked out your clothes last night?" Sara teased.

"No. I didn't say it was the only outfit I put on, just that it was the first. There were many others before I came back to it."

"You look nice. For the record, I chose my clothes last night, but since I live in jeans, it was a matter of which pair." She pointed to the coffee maker. "Are you planning to actually use that?"

Abby couldn't help smiling. "I can tell you're going to be a problem." She extended her palm toward the coffee. "After you."

"I wouldn't think of going first. It just wasn't clear if you were actually a coffee drinker." Sara emphasized the word *drinker*.

"As opposed to what?" Abby crossed her arms over her chest and leaned against the table.

"I don't know," Sara said. "You spent a lot of time staring at the pods. I think there might have been a little caressing too."

"You're strange."

"I am. In my defense, I've spent far too much time on a tour bus with three smelly men."

Abby laughed out loud, the conversation easing her nerves. "That should be a song. Have you considered it?"

"Already written and recorded. They weren't amused." Sara took the pod Abby was holding and popped it into the machine. "What size?" she asked.

"Eight." Abby tucked a large container under the spout. "I need a lot of milk too," she explained.

"Is this your first show? I'm sorry if it's not, and I don't recognize you."

"It's my first." Abby lowered her voice. "That's why I was hesitating about the coffee. I'm nervous, and I don't want my voice to shake during the reading."

"You'll be fine," Sara assured her. "You don't have any lines until the second part of the show."

"You've seen the script?"

Sara looked guilty. "Yes?"

Abby frowned. "It's not a question. Have you read it? How does it look?"

"Mika let me read it before I took the role." She paused. "I thought it was good. You haven't seen it?"

"Just the part I read at the audition."

"If it helps, your character is pretty feisty," Sara told her.

"I got that from the audition. I read the scene where Joey and Bria argue about selling the business." She pulled her coffee out and stepped back. "It's all yours. I'd better go find my place."

"You're next to me. Over there." Sara pointed to a rectangular table across the room.

"Why are there so many tables?" Abby asked. "There aren't that many characters in the pilot, are there?"

"No, but if it's like the other set I was on…"

Abby raised her eyebrows and a hand. "Excuse me? You mean the role for which you were nominated for a Golden Globe and robbed of an Oscar nomination? That set?"

Sara blushed and turned away to check her coffee. "Well, on that set," she continued as if Abby hadn't spoken. "Everybody was at the table read. Director, producers, all the department heads. Everybody."

"Were you nervous?" Abby asked, then held up her hand to stop Sara from answering. "Sorry. Dumb question. You're used to performing in front of huge crowds."

"Did you get your milk?" Sara looked at Abby's coffee. "I think it's over there." She pointed down the table.

Abby looked in her own cup. "God, I'm out of it today." She followed Sara over to the other table, and they both added milk to their cups. "I hope I get it together."

"Don't worry. You will." Sara touched her arm. "I was terrified. I didn't know whether we were reading or if we were acting. And, if we were acting, I didn't know what to do."

Abby looked up for a moment, deep in thought. "Didn't the movie open with you singing?"

Sara smiled. "Wow. Good memory. Yes. 'Why Try?'"

"It was the perfect opening. It was like Bridget Keogh knew someday, someone would make a movie about that album."

"Yeah, it was good. I can admit it now. At the time, I thought it was a terrible idea."

"Really? Why?"

"They made me sing it at the table read." Sara rolled her eyes. "Cold. Thank God, I'd been working with my vocal coach, or I might have walked out. No." She lifted a finger. "They would have fired me."

Mika called to the group, and Sara led Abby to their seats. Christina, who was on the other side of Sara, looked up when they sat. "Christina, this is Abby Farina. She plays Bria Corsetti." Sara looked at Abby. "Christina plays Noelle Prado."

The women waved to each other, and the three settled into their chairs. Abby tried to pay attention as Mika introduced the people around the table but lost track of names after the third person. Next to her, Sara scrawled notes. When the introductions moved to the other side of the room, Abby surreptitiously looked at her notepad. Sara was writing down the names and positions of each person introduced. She caught her looking, and mouthed, "Focus." Abby raised an eyebrow and tilted her head at the paper. Sara winked.

When the last person had been introduced, Mika straightened. "Welcome to the first day of production for *Corsetti's Will*. I'm thrilled to be here with all of you. Each of you and the teams you've put together bring something unique to the production. Among you are fresh perspectives, underrepresented experiences, and broad knowledge. It will take all of us working together to make a quality show that audiences will believe in.

"I hired each of you, and when I did, I told you this show is special to me. It's personal. From you, I ask two things. Help me make my vision a reality." She paused. "And ensure that my vision doesn't blind me. Let's create something memorable."

"Wow." Abby whispered as the room applauded.

"Right? I could run a marathon after that."

Abby snorted. "I don't think that's what she's looking for from you."

The room settled when Mika spoke again. "Before we get started with the script, Dani Copeland is going to go over social media marketing. Dani?"

All heads turned to a woman who looked to Abby to be in her late twenties. From her platinum pixie cut to her platform espadrilles, Dani Copeland was a uniquely stylish woman. "As Mika said, I'm in charge of our social media feeds which for us will primarily be Twitter and Instagram. We have a Facebook page, but most of our audience gears to the other two platforms. I know Mika has explained the importance of creating an audience for *Corsetti's Will* before the premiere. Our primary venue for that will be social media. We'll do some traditional press, but with the number of shows on the air, it's difficult to get a mainstream mag to pay attention.

"Since the casting announcements, there's been a jump in Binge subscriptions. That's good for us, particularly when we can tie it directly to the show. The numbers have plateaued lately, but that's because there hasn't been any new content. That'll change starting today. We have some photos of Sara and

Christina that will post over the course of the next couple of weeks. I'll also be on set getting more pictures, and little teasers to keep our fans interested."

Dani looked at the three actresses. "Sara, Christina, and Abby, you'll have to be active on Twitter and Instagram. I'll meet with each of you in the next couple of days to direct your posts." Abby stiffened at that statement. Direct her posts? As if reading her mind, Dani continued, "Each of you has a different demographic to appeal to. We need to make sure you're giving your audience the kind of content that will keep them engaged." Dani looked to Mika. "Anything else?"

"I think that covers it for now." She looked at the people assembled around the table. "We're going to make a quality show, but if we want our quality show to air, we have to connect with an audience." She pointed to Dani. "That's how we do it."

CHAPTER NINE

The first assistant director read the stage directions for the first scene. The actor who played Joey Driskell's detective partner oozed disdain at being saddled with a woman. It's a shame he'll only be here for one scene, Abby thought. She was happy to see Sara hold her own with the actor. When her character Joey argued about waiting in the car, Sara revealed a hint of her strength, but also how easily the experienced detective cowed her. In her line following what would be the sound of gunshots, Sara captured the breathless panic of the character calling for help. Abby flipped the page with the rest of the room, already engrossed in the story.

Exterior. A hundred police officers stand at attention around a flag-draped casket. A bell tolls in the background. Joey Driskell stands apart from the other officers, hidden in the trees. She salutes with a white-gloved hand. Tears stream down her face. She slowly lowers the salute. Leo Corsetti approaches, and she turns to get away.

The actor next to Abby played Leo Corsetti, the retired partner of the dead detective and father of Abby's character, Bria Corsetti.

L. Corsetti: *You Joey Driskell?*
Driskell: *Yes.*
L. Corsetti: *Leo Corsetti. I was his partner before you.*
Driskell: *I…I'm sorry. I shouldn't have let him go in alone.*
L. Corsetti: *Bullshit, those other assholes may not want to admit it, but he was a prick. He wouldna let ya go in with him. C'mon. I'll buy ya a coffee.*

Interior. Diner. Corsetti and Driskell sit in a booth, Driskell faces the door.
Waitress: *Anything other than the coffee?*
L. Corsetti: *No, hun, this is fine.*
The door opens and two cops in dress uniforms enter the diner. They look around, and when they see Driskell they saunter over to the booth. They're surprised to see Corsetti with her.
Detective 1: *What are you doing with her, Corsetti? She killed Drummond.*
L. Corsetti: *Lay off her. Drummond got himself killed.*
Detective 1: *So she says. Why would he go into an abandoned house without backup?*
L. Corsetti: *Because he was a hardheaded prick who wouldn't listen to anyone. Me included. She was doin' what he told her to do. Give her a break.*
Detective 2: *Why don't you give us a break and hire her?*
L. Corsetti: *That's the plan.*
Detective 2: *Your funeral. At least you won't have to worry anymore about what you eat. She'll get you killed long before your heart gives out.*
The cops walk away. Driskell picks up her coffee mug, then puts it back down when her hand shakes.
Driskell: *They hate me.*
L. Corsetti: *Yeah.*

Driskell: How can I get them to trust me again?

L. Corsetti: They never trusted you, and now they never will. Drummond fucked you over and there's nothin' you can do about it.

Driskell: So what do I do? Transfer? I wanted Homicide.

L. Corsetti: Nah. Transfer won't do ya any good. You're the cop who got her partner killed.

Driskell: So what am I supposed to do?

L. Corsetti: Quit. Come work for me. I got my own agency, and I got more business than I can handle. You're a good cop who had the bad luck to be partnered with an asshole. You got screwed. That's life. If you come work for me, you can start over. It won't be the same, but it's better than the alternative.

Driskell looks up and sees the two cops leaving the diner. One of them points a finger at her and makes a shooting motion before leaving. Driskell buries her face in her hands.

As they turned the page, Abby peeked at Mika. She looked pleased. In fact, everyone did. If the first few scenes were any indication, Sara Silver could carry a show. Abby hoped she could keep up.

It's four year later. Open with an exterior of a building sign, "Corsetti and Driskell Investigations."

Interior. Corsetti and Driskell's office. They sit behind desks, reading files.

L. Corsetti: Where are you taking Noelle tonight?

Driskell: I got reservations at that new Italian place.

L. Corsetti: Whaddya get her? Second anniversary is it?

Joey pulls a wrapped package out of her desk drawer. It is long and rectangular—a jewelry box for a bracelet.

L. Corsetti: That's not a ring box. I thought you were going to propose.

Driskell: Why do I have to be the one to propose?

Corsetti picks up a picture of his wife.

L. Corsetti: Because you don't want to waste one moment. You don't know how long you'll have her.

Corsetti dusts off the picture, then turns it over and makes sure the back is secure. He looks up at Driskell and smiles.

*L. Corsetti: You know, if you are ever in doubt, the key to everything is right here, **(he touches his heart)** and here **(he touches the photograph)**.*

The door opens. Noelle Prado enters. Corsetti has a big smile for her.

L. Corsetti: Noelle! 'Bout time you got here. Did you bring me anything?

Prado: You know I did.

Driskell: Baby…

Noelle puts a container in front of Corsetti and kisses him on the cheek. He grins at Driskell in triumph.

Driskell: You spoil him. He's supposed to lose weight.

Noelle crosses the room and kisses Joey on the lips.

Prado: I'll spoil you later, honey.

The room went silent. No paper rustling or throat clearing. Rather than being seductive or playful, Christina read the line like she was in a high school English class. Abby looked at Mika and saw the barest of frowns.

* * *

They were nearly two-thirds of the way through the script. Sara and the actor playing Leo Corsetti had read several scenes, and most of the dialogue between the two was working. There were a few lines that Mika felt didn't fit the personality of the character or the tone of the scene, but overall, the script was good.

What wasn't good was Christina Landis. Her reading in the first scene had been stiff, but Mika thought she would be able to work through it. Unfortunately, the restaurant scene was even worse. The playful banter between the characters came across all wrong. With Christina's flat affect, every teasing note Sara tried to hit sounded sarcastic rather than loving.

They were reading the scene where Corsetti and Driskell were on a stakeout. Mika forced herself to relax and pay attention to the nuances that needed to come across.

Exterior. Corsetti and Driskell are in a car, Driskell in the driver's seat. Around them are coffee cups and food wrappers.

L. Corsetti: *I gotta pee.*

Driskell: *You just went. It's like I'm on a stakeout with a five-year-old.*

L. Corsetti: *Yeah? Wait 'til you get old. You won't be such a smart ass.*

Corsetti's phone buzzes, and he struggles to pull it out of his jacket pocket. When he sees who's calling, he declines it.

Driskell: *You can answer. I won't listen.*

Corsetti gives her a look, then sits up and points out the window.

L. Corsetti: *Is that our guy?*

Driskell pulls up the photo on her phone and holds it between them.

Driskell: *That's him.*

They burst out of the car. The man sees them and takes off running. Driskell runs after him, and Corsetti gets in the driver's seat and starts the car. A chase ensues. The man runs into an alley. While he's looking over his shoulder at Driskell, Corsetti drives into the alley and hits him with the car. Driskell catches up and bends over the body.

Driskell: *Leo, you gotta quit hitting them with the car. We needed to talk to this guy, and now he's out cold.*

L. Corsetti: *If you were faster, I wouldn't have to hit 'em.*

Corsetti's phone buzzes again and he pulls it out of his pocket. He takes a quick look, then silences the call.

Driskell: *What's going on with you? Who are you avoiding? Girlfriend?*

The man on the ground moans and the detectives bend over him.

L. Corsetti: *Where's the money?*

Man: *Fuck you. I wanna lawyer.*

Mika made a note on her script, then braced herself for what was next. It was the intimate scene between the two women. She'd left a lot of the details out of the script, planning to choreograph it with the actresses, but she knew what she wanted: romantic, sensual, loving. Joey and Noelle had to be a couple the audience was excited to watch. She contemplated skipping the scene, but knew she had to get a sense of how the actresses approached intimate dialogue.

Interior. Joey and Noelle's apartment. Noelle's studio. Joey enters carrying a bottle of wine and two glasses. Noelle is painting a landscape at her easel.
Prado: *You're early. Good news?*
Driskell: *We got him. He blamed his wife, but the money was in his bank account.*
Noelle wipes off her brush and walks to where Joey is seated on a stool, holding the wine and glasses.
Prado: *So, we get to celebrate tonight?*
Noelle kisses Joey deeply. When she pulls back, Joey touches the bracelet.
Driskell: *You're wearing it.*
Prado: *I love it.*
Driskell: *Are you disappointed I didn't get you a ring?*
Prado: *No, baby. Are you disappointed I didn't get you a ring?*

Mika had written the line to show insight into the relationship, but it didn't sound right. She scribbled a note beside it. "Actor or line?" She missed Sara's next line, but caught Christina's response.

Prado: *I love you too.*

She'd had enough. The scenes between the two would need work. She made a note to talk with her director. "Okay, let's skip two scenes. Sara and Christina, we'll work out the dialogue when we choreograph the sex scene." Papers rustled as everyone flipped ahead.

Interior. Corsetti and Driskell's office. Joey sits at her desk, alone in the room. Two men in cheap suits enter. One carries a file folder.

Driskell: *What do you want?*

Detective 1: *Driskell. So, he really did hire you.*

Driskell: *Is there something I can help you with?*

The detectives sit in the visitors' chairs in front of her desk.

Detective 1: *When was the last time you saw your partner?*

Driskell: *I'm not going to answer any of your questions until you tell me why you're here.*

Detective 1: *You can answer here or downtown. Maybe you'd like to come and visit your old friends at the precinct.*

Joey stands. The second detective who has so far remained silent pulls a photograph out of the file and lays it on her desk. She picks it up. When she sees the image, she collapses in her chair.

Detective 3: *Leo Corsetti was found this morning with a single gunshot wound to the head. When did you last see him?*

Joey stares at her desk, unable to speak. The first detective shifts in his chair angrily. The second gives him a look and retrieves the photo from the desk.

Detective 3: *I know it's a shock. It would help if you could tell us anything about the last time you saw him. When was it?*

Driskell: *Yesterday afternoon. We…we closed a case and had a beer to celebrate.*

Detective 3: *What time was that?*

Driskell: *Um, maybe three thirty? We stayed for over an hour. I was home by five.*

Detective 1: *Can anyone verify that?*

Driskell: *Yeah. My girlfriend.*

Detective 1 snorts. Detective 3, clearly in charge, gives him a look.

Detective 3: *Did Corsetti say where he was going when he left?*

Driskell: *No. I assumed he was going home.*

Detective 3: *How did he seem? Was he upset, agitated? Anything bothering him?*

Driskell: *No. He was happy. It was a big case. We were celebrating.*

Detective 3: *What was this case?*

Driskell: *Insurance fraud.*

Detective 3: *Could it have had anything to do with his death?*

Driskell: *I don't see how.*

Detective 3: *Who hired you?*

Driskell: *I can't tell you that.*

Detective 3: *Okay, give me the specifics of the case.*

Driskell: *C'mon. You know I can't tell you that either.*

Detective 1: *So you won't help us find your partner's killer? Just like Drummond.*

Joey stands.

Driskell: *That's all I have to say. Did you call his daughter?*

Detective 1 starts to protest, but Detective 3 silences him and stands, extending his hand to Joey. She takes it.

Detective 3: *We haven't.*

Driskell: *I'll do it.*

Detective 3: *Yeah, that's fine. If you can think of anything that will help us, call me.*

He leaves a card on her desk. Joey watches them leave the office. When the door closes, she collapses into her chair and buries her face in her hands.

CHAPTER TEN

The first AD read, "Fade to Black," and everyone applauded.

Out of the corner of her eye, Sara saw Abby relax into her chair, then suddenly sit bolt upright and arch her back. "The back of my dress is soaked," she groaned.

Sara laughed. "Why do you think I tossed the sweatshirt halfway through? Thanks, by the way. I almost flashed the room."

"You should get used to it," Abby teased. "I think most of the people in this room, no, most of the people in the country, are about to see you in your bra."

Sara dropped her head. "I know. I hired a trainer to work on my abs, but nothing good is happening."

"That was great," Mika said to the room. "We'll have a production draft to everyone later today. Renee has the hard copies of call sheets for shoot day one. You also have it in your email. New call sheets will go out by seven p.m. daily." She paused. "Let's hope this is the first day of many. Thank you, everyone."

"Are you here tomorrow?" Sara asked.

Abby looked through the pages until she found the section marked "Talent." She scanned the list of names. "Looks like I get to sleep in tomorrow. But you"—she pointed to Sara's name—"will be here bright and early."

"I know. All those years of playing concerts has my internal clock screwed up. Mornings are tough." She heard a sound next to her and glanced at Christina. "Hey. You doing okay?" she asked.

Christina had her purse over her shoulder and her script held tightly in her hand. She looked like she was about to run from the room. "I'm fine," she mumbled.

Sara looked back at Abby. "I'll see you soon. It was great to meet you." She turned so her body blocked Christina from Abby's view. "Are you sure? Sit down for a minute." Christina hesitated, and Sara was afraid she would refuse, but she dropped her purse on the table and sat. "What's wrong?" Sara kept her voice soft.

Christina shook her head. "I was so stiff."

There was no point in denying it. "Are you uncomfortable? Do you want to get together and run lines?"

Sara wasn't sure, but she thought Christina flinched. "No." She scooped the purse and script off the table. "I'll be fine. See you in a couple days." She was gone before Sara could say anything else.

"Did I miss Christina?" Sara turned back to see Dani standing in front of the table.

"Yeah, she just left." Sara gestured over her shoulder. "I don't know where Abby is, either."

"I just talked with her," Dani said. "Do you have a couple of minutes so we could talk about social media?"

Sara nodded.

"How much do you interact with your fans on Twitter?"

Sara frowned. "What do you mean? Are you asking if I respond to their comments?"

"Yes."

"Not usually. I don't reply unless it's something from a friend. Honestly, I don't even read all of the comments. Do I need to?"

Dani turned so she was looking at Sara. "Yes." When Sara widened her eyes, Dani continued, "For a while. You don't need to answer many, just interact with a few fans. Show them you care about them, but don't be fake. People can see through it." Dani handed her tablet to Sara. "Here, pull up your feed and retweet the photo I posted on the *Corsetti's Will* page. Make sure you add a comment."

Sara opened the page and looked at the picture. Then she enlarged it. She was sitting on the desk, holding Christina's hands. "Wow," she said to Dani. "It looks like I'm gonna rip her clothes off."

"Check out the comments."

Sara read through about half of the forty responses. Most, whether by emoji or words, were some variation of "hot." When she looked up, Dani asked, "How will your Range Street fans respond to the picture?"

Sara thought for a moment. She'd never shied away from queer content, but neither had she displayed her own gayness so vividly. "It won't surprise anyone. I may have some fans who will stop following me." She shrugged. "But that's okay."

"Let's find out. Don't forget to add a comment."

Leaning back in her chair, Sara looked up at the ceiling. She thought back to Mika's first description of the couple and how she wanted them portrayed. Sara typed, then flipped the tablet to show Dani. "What do you think?"

"It's great. Go ahead," Dani replied.

Sara posted, *Joey loves Noelle*, and set the tablet on the table. "Okay, what else?"

Dani pointed to the tablet. "This is where you need to change the way you think. It's not a one-way street anymore. Any responses, yet?"

Sara looked. "Five."

"Pick one and reply."

She scrolled through, amazed as more comments appeared. "Can I answer this?" she showed the question to Dani.

"Yeah. That's good. They're looking for a name for your 'ship.' By the end of the day, something will stick."

Sara typed, *Joey Driskell loves Noelle Prado*.

Dani pointed to the post. "And that's how a fandom begins."

* * *

Mika rubbed the spot between her eyes, trying to get some relief from the headache.

She was tempted to start the meeting with the easier but more time-consuming task of reviewing notes on dialogue, but that was counterproductive. Plus, many of the people in the room had already been on one of her writing staffs. They would know she was avoiding the problem.

"All right, then. As most of you know, we start by evaluating the talent we brought in for the week. Since this is the pilot, we'll talk through all of the actors in order of appearance. Comments on Drummond, our dead homicide detective. Any concerns?" She looked around the table at the shaking heads. "That's my feeling too. He makes an excellent misogynist." She got some half-hearted laughter and appreciated their effort. "Next, Sara Silver as Joey Driskell. Any concerns?"

David Stamper spoke. "No concerns. A pleasant surprise, actually. I thought she might have been typecast in *Enough*, but she's got a lot of range. It's going to make it easier for us to write the character." The others nodded or made sounds of agreement.

The read hadn't surprised Mika. At the Globes, she'd cornered the director of *Enough*, who assured her Sara was a natural. "Yes, I thought she did quite well. I don't think she'll disappoint us when we need her to tap into deeper emotions." She waited a few seconds for anyone else to speak. When no one did, she asked, "Alan Fletcher as Leo Corsetti?"

One of the new writers spoke up. "I wondered if we could use him for more than the pilot?" She was tentative. "Maybe some flashbacks? He and Sara had good energy together."

"Yes," Mika said. "They did. We may also want to build a backstory with him and Bria. We were originally going to reveal their relationship as a conflict between Bria and Joey, but we should consider using flashback rather than straight exposition. Good thinking, Aniyah." She looked to Renee, who was taking notes.

"Let's do the detectives together. Detective 1. Thoughts?"

"Um," Aniyah said after a few moments of silence. "What about having a cop as a recurring character? Either Detective 1 or Detective 3 could be antagonists for Joey and Bria."

One of the writers she brought over from *Malice Aforethought* answered. "It's a good idea, we just have to check with the line producer on budget. Maybe the weeks we don't have a location shoot."

Mika liked that Aniyah had ideas and that she wasn't afraid to share them. "We planned to bring in different cops depending on the crime in the B storyline, but whenever possible, we should use these characters. It would be good to have a primary foil for Joey." She took a deep breath, looked around the table, and said, "Christina Landis."

David didn't hesitate. "Recast. I didn't hear anything today that convinces me she can handle the role."

Another writer from *Malice* said, "She couldn't identify the tone of the scene. She interpreted the character incorrectly every time."

"It may be as simple as that," David said, "but I don't think so. She was flat in every scene. She doesn't have the talent."

Mika listened without comment while they dissected the performance. After several minutes, she stopped the discussion. "We are not recasting. Christina Landis comes with an audience, not as big as Sara's, but certainly as committed. I can't recast without backlash, and I don't want negative press before the show even premieres. You are a talented group of writers. You've seen her limits. Do the best you can to work with them. Moving on."

They discussed the actors in the fraud storyline and quickly agreed everyone else was fine. Mika jotted a note to acknowledge her casting director for the diverse and talented actors she'd brought together. They were at the last character introduced in the script. "Abby Farina as Bria Corsetti."

"Another pleasant surprise," David said. "Unlike Christina, Abby could read the tone and deliver it. She and Sara worked off each other well, which is good considering she's the other lead."

"I agree. She'll be strong. Okay, last thoughts before we take a break and move on?"

Everyone knew the question was a formality, and she was about to call the break when Aniyah spoke. "Sara and Abby have chemistry. What if we switched their parts? Does playing Bria require less range than Noelle?"

The others stopped shuffling papers and shifting in their chairs. They looked at Aniyah, then turned as one to gauge Mika's reaction. She closed her eyes and let the idea roll around. Sara's icy blond and Abby's warm Mediterranean. The visuals would be stunning, but as appealing as it was, it would just make the situation worse. The relationship between Joey and Noelle would be no more than three scenes per week. Most of the action of the series centered on Sara and Abby investigating cases. She opened her eyes and looked around the room. "You're right again, Aniyah. They do have chemistry, but there are a couple of problems with switching parts. From what we saw today, I don't think we can trust Christina to handle a bigger role. Secondly, and equally as important…" She paused, needing to emphasize this point. "As far as I know, Abby Farina is straight. Our target audience expects queer roles to go to queer actors." She smiled at the young woman. "But keep thinking, and keep paying attention. Twenty minutes, everyone."

David followed her out of the room and into her office. He watched while she shook four ibuprofen tablets into her hand and swallowed them. "We're fucked," he said.

"Did you watch her today? Not just when she was reading? She was caved in on herself." Mika sank into her desk chair. "No, something's going on." Mika closed her eyes and leaned back, thinking. What happened to the actress she'd seen in *Night in Time*? The director, Luciana Raithman, had raved to Mika about how Christina took direction, how quickly she'd developed the character.

"What are you going to do?" David asked.

She'd almost forgotten he was in the room. She kept her eyes closed. "Talent doesn't just disappear."

"Well, it'd better reappear or she'll tank us."

CHAPTER ELEVEN

They were starting the second week of production for the pilot. It was unusual to film chronologically, but Mika wanted to get the crowd scenes and the guest talent done by the end of the first week. The benefit was that most of the first hour of the pilot was already in editing.

Today the set was closed as they filmed the intimate scenes between Joey and Noelle. She'd hired Celia Edwards to direct the pilot before she realized Christina's weaknesses. As she watched the director work with the actresses, she was grateful for the soothing presence the older woman brought.

"This is an intensely emotional scene," Celia was telling them. "Joey has just learned that Leo Corsetti is dead. All of her guilt and uncertainty from Drummond's murder has returned. She promised to call Bria, but she wants Noelle beside her when she does. Christina, even though you're confused, you know something is terribly wrong. You want to comfort Joey, but you can tell she's barely holding it together. Okay?" Celia waited for their nods. "Let's try it. Whenever you're ready."

"Is that you, babe?" Noelle puts down her paintbrush and picks up a rag, wiping her hands as she walks out of her study toward the living room. She stops when she sees Joey standing frozen inside the door. "What happened?" she asks.

"I have to make a call." Joey hesitates, barely looking at Noelle. "I have to call Bria."

"What happened?" Noelle reaches for her, but Joey stops her with a hand.

"I can't. If you touch me, I'll fall apart, and I can't" She lifts her phone and touches the screen. Her eyes are on the floor.

"Bria? It's Joey." There's a pause while Joey listens. Then she looks up into Noelle's eyes. "Bria, I have to tell you something." She takes a shaky breath. "Your dad was found this morning. He'd been shot. I'm so sorry, Bria, he's gone…" Joey sinks to the floor, her back against the door, hand over her eyes. She starts crying.

Noelle kneels beside Joey and takes the phone from her hand. "Bria? It's Noelle, Joey's girlfriend." She listens as she pulls Joey against her. "I don't know anything. She just got home, and I heard it when you did. Do you know anyone he worked with in the department?" Noelle listens for a few moments. "Do you have someone to stay with you? Okay, yeah, we'll talk soon." Noelle hangs up the phone and wraps herself around Joey.

"Cut. Yes. That's what I want." Celia stepped closer to the actresses. "Christina, give it a few more beats when you're on the phone listening. Sara, think about what Joey's body would be doing while she's crying. Your body expresses emotion as much as your face does."

They talked through the scene a bit more while Mika watched. The rehearsal had been better than expected. Christina's rote delivery was gone and her movement was more natural. Mika stepped over to where Hair and Makeup were touching up the actresses. "That's going to be a beautiful scene on camera." Even though her words were directed toward both women, they were intended to bolster Christina's confidence.

Celia joined them. "Let's try something different this time. Change the dynamic of the relationship. These characters don't play into gender roles, so don't be limited because Noelle wears flowy skirts. Play against the preconceived ideas of how these women would act. How could Noelle be stronger, more dominant in this scene?"

Mika saw Sara and Christina's eyes light up. This is why you hire a good director, she thought. She also made a mental note to talk with the writers about watching gender stereotypes. She didn't want them to automatically assign certain characteristics to Joey because she was in a historically masculine profession. The scene went on, and Celia's suggestion resulted in Noelle cradling Joey in her lap, holding her head against her chest. Mika knew she would use the image in the trailer too.

They broke for lunch, and Mika and Celia found their usual table to talk through the afternoon and evening shoots. "That was good work this morning," Mika told her. "You've gotten Christina to understand Noelle. I think she's starting to feel the character."

"She's coming along," Celia agreed. "This afternoon will be the measure of how far."

"How are you going to approach the scene? You turned everything on its head this morning when you forced them to rethink Noelle. Are you going to stay with that?"

"I've been thinking about what to reveal about the women in the scene. It's a key emotional moment in the story, and the audience's first introduction to the intimacy of their relationship. That being said, Joey's your main character, and frankly, Sara's the better actress. She'll have to be the emotional anchor."

"I think so too," Mika said. "But while we're figuring out Christina's limitations, we're going to have to be flexible. Maybe she'll respond better to taking an aggressive role in the scene. Ultimately, it's going to have to be up to the two of them and what they feel comfortable doing."

* * *

An hour later, they were on the set of Joey and Noelle's bedroom. The room felt strange with so few people around, but it was a good strange. Sara couldn't imagine taking off her robe and exposing her breasts, despite the nipple pads, for the crew. "I flossed, brushed my teeth twice, and gargled. No garlic or onion for days," she whispered to Christina. They were seated behind the cameras, waiting for the lighting crew to finish.

Christina gave her a side-eyed look and the barest smile. "Me too," she said. Then she looked back at the bed with the same unfocused stare she'd had since lunch.

"You okay?" Sara turned her body so her knees almost touched Christina.

"Yeah. Fine." No eye contact.

"Really? Because you're the expert at this, and if you're nervous, I'm going to freak out."

"I'm not an expert. I've done a few scenes in one film. That was different."

Genuinely curious, Sara asked, "It was? Why? What made it different?"

When Christina looked at her, Sara saw the shimmer of tears. They held eye contact, then Christina shook her head, causing the tears to spill. "It just was," she finally answered.

Sara was at a loss. She placed her hand on Christina's forearm and leaned toward her, ensuring that no one could hear them "I'm sorry this is upsetting you. If you don't think we should do the scene today, or any day, just say so. I'll back you up, I promise."

Shocked eyes turned to hers, but before Christina could speak, Celia called for them. Sara stood blocking Christina from the view of Mika and Celia. "Say the word, and I'll stop it," she whispered.

Christina's watery eyes were full of gratitude. "No, I can do it. It's…well, just sad memories." She shook her head as if she were shaking away the thoughts. In a stronger voice, she said, "I can do it."

They walked together to the set and Sara watched as Mika and Celia took in Christina's tears. Mika moved toward her, but Sara spoke with forced cheer. "Okay, we're ready." Her words drew Mika's attention. Sara moved a step closer to Christina so their shoulders were touching.

Mika seemed to understand the unspoken message. "Okay," she said. "As you know from the script, there is very little written about this scene. We will not do anything on *Corsetti's Will* that makes you feel unsafe or uncomfortable. The four of us together will choreograph the scene, but I want you to be very clear about something." Mika paused to emphasize her point. "You can say no to anything we propose. It ends there. On this set, no means no."

Sara released a breath and her shoulders relaxed. "Thank you."

Mika nodded to her and looked at Christina. "Okay?"

"Yes," Christina answered.

Celia took over. "The scene before this takes place in the living room where Joey tells Noelle she needs to be close to her. They start to kiss, and Joey becomes overwhelmed with emotion. The kissing becomes passionate, and one or both of you will disrobe the other. We'll work that out depending on this scene." Celia checked to see that the actresses were with her before continuing, "We want to convey the deep love these women have for each other. Simulated sex acts are not as important as bringing out the emotional intensity of the moment. Joey is lost and Noelle is her anchor."

At Celia's direction, they removed their robes. "Sara, lie on your back." She did, and Celia handed her a thin pillow. Sara started to put behind her head, but Celia stopped her hand. "That goes between you." She took the pillow back and placed it on Sara's pelvis. "It will be more comfortable for both of you." At Celia's direction, Christina straddled Sara's hips and hovered over the pillow. Sara wanted to tell her it was okay to sit, but she was afraid it would elicit more emotion.

Celia looked at the monitor, then returned to adjust the sheets to her liking. She walked to the side of the bed and knelt down so only the actresses could hear. "Have you two talked about how you want to be touched?" They stared at her, both at a loss for words. "Sara, are you ticklish?"

"Not really," Sara answered, then looked up at Christina. "Are you?"

Christina touched along her rib cage. "Don't run your fingertips down my side. You can use your whole hand, but I can't stand a light touch."

"Christina, could you show her, please? Take her hand and place it how you want it." Without hesitation, Christina took Sara's hand and placed it flat on her rib cage. "That's good," she said, then moved Sara's hand down her side and over her stomach. "Use your whole hand and a little pressure, and I'll be fine." For the first time, Christina's eyes matched her smile.

"Good," Celia said. "Sara, how do you feel about Christina touching your breasts?"

"Fine," Sara said.

"Kissing them?" Celia asked.

Sara lifted her head and looked at her breasts. "How will you do that without the nipple pads showing?"

Celia put her hand over her own breast. "Christina will cover your nipple with her hand, or we'll use her hair. Then she can kiss the sides of your breast."

Sara looked up at Christina. "That's okay with me," she said. "You?"

Christina gave a little laugh. "In the film, we kissed a lot more than the side of each other's boobs. I'm okay with that."

"Last thing for right now. Have you discussed what parts of your body you'd like your partner to help hide from the camera?"

Christina understood the question and answered by taking Sara's hand again and putting it on the lower part of her stomach. "I hate this pooch." Sara wanted to look under her hand but held Christina's eyes.

"So whenever possible, I should have my hand here?" Sara asked.

"No," Celia answered. "When that part of her body is in a camera shot and we can't avoid it, that's when you cover her. Otherwise it will look awkward."

"Okay." Sara looked at Christina. "For me, it's my breasts. I don't mind showing a little, but less is more."

While they'd been talking, Christina gradually relaxed until she was resting on Sara. She popped up when she realized what she was doing. "Oh my God, I'm crushing you."

Sara laughed and pulled her back down. "You're not. Relax." They shared a smile and Sara patted Christina's thigh.

Celia's knees creaked as she stood. "I'm too old for kneeling," she groaned. "How would you feel if we filmed rehearsal? Since most of this scene will be small clips anyway, we might get something we can use."

The actresses agreed and Celia nodded for the camera to start rolling. "Let's start with kissing." The rehearsal went on like that for several minutes with Celia giving instructions off-camera and Christina or Sara responding. Sara could feel the tension in Christina's body. At one point, Celia went to look at the monitor and Christina rolled off Sara, stretching her legs.

"What's wrong?" Sara asked quietly.

"I can't relax. I don't know what it is, but everything feels wrong."

"Let's tell them." Sara started to sit up, but Christina stopped her with a hand on her arm.

"No, it'll be okay."

"Should I be on top? Would that help?"

Christina considered the question for a minute. "Yeah, I think so," she said.

"What about the kissing? Is my breath okay? Too much tongue?"

As hoped, Sara got a laugh from her question. "No, your breath is great and you didn't use your tongue."

"So, not enough tongue?" Sara winked at her, pleased when Christina laughed again. "Look, I have an idea, and I can't believe I'm going to propose it." Sara explained what she had in mind, and when Christina agreed, Sara playfully scowled at her. "You better have your hands covering my boobs the whole time."

CHAPTER TWELVE

Sara couldn't stop laughing. Abby Farina was recounting tales from her days as a preschool teacher to a crowd of extras and crew. "No, that's not the worst one," she said. "Once I asked if anyone had a pretend microphone I could borrow for a play we were doing. One sweet little boy raised his hand and said, 'My mom does.'" Abby started laughing, which made the rest of them laugh. "And hers does this." Abby moved her hand rapidly and made a vibrating noise. The group roared.

"Oops, we gotta get going," someone said.

Sara looked at her watch. "Oh," she said and stood abruptly. "I didn't go over my lines." The dispersing crowd laughed again. She looked at them in confusion. "Why are you laughing?"

"Like you don't already know your lines. You probably knew your lines the day after you got the script," one of the camera crew teased.

"You're just saying that because you're afraid she'll go all diva on you," Abby said.

"She's got a long way to go before she becomes a diva."

"What, no special requests in her trailer?" Abby gave Sara a mischievous grin. "Like her own personal microphone?"

The group laughed and wandered away. Sara nudged Abby. "The set's a lot more raucous when you're around."

"Really?" Abby looked at the departing group. "They're fun. Do you guys usually work through lunch or something?"

"No. We just didn't have anyone to entertain us. It's nice to have you here."

"It's good to be here." They started walking toward Makeup. "We haven't had a chance to talk," Abby said. "How's it been?"

"Good. I really liked working with Alan—"

"That's Corsetti, right?" Abby interrupted.

"Yeah, he's a great actor. It was easy to work off of him, you know?"

"I do. I once did a play where my costar stared at me without expression while I delivered my lines. So weird." She laughed a little. "I tend to overcompensate in situations like that. At one point the director asked me what I was doing with my face. According to him, I looked constipated. I wanted to say, 'At least my face moves!'"

They walked to Makeup and fell into conversation with the two women inside. Sara watched Abby in the mirror and marveled at how she made everyone feel at ease. "Sa-ra," Abby called. It was clear it wasn't the first time she'd said her name.

"Sorry, I was zoning out," Sara said. "What did you say?"

"What are you doing when filming finishes? We have a couple weeks off. What are your plans?"

Sara smiled. "I'm going to buy a house."

"Really?" Abby said. "I love house shopping. Who's your realtor?"

"I don't have one. I was going to ask around. Any recommendations?"

"Why do you think I asked? I have a really good friend who's a realtor. You'd love her. And she works in your price range."

Sara raised her eyebrows. "And what is my price range?"

Abby waved her hand at her. "It depends."

"On?" Sara raised an eyebrow.

"Well, since I'm going with you. It depends on what house I like best."

"Oh, you're going with me?"

"Absolutely. Didn't I just say I love house hunting? Plus, I like spending time with Katie—that's my friend. Win-win for me."

Sara shook her head and looked at the other two women. "What just happened here?"

Abby grinned back. "Just wait 'til I pick out your house."

* * *

Mika looked up at the knock on her door frame. "Are you ready for me?" Dani asked.

Mika walked around her desk to the table in the corner of her office. "I am." She flipped to a blank page on her legal pad and uncapped her rollerball. "What do you have?"

"A few updates," Dani began. "We've got approximately two thousand followers on most of the platforms. That's a good start considering how little content we've given them. Most of our followers came after the preproduction photos posted."

Mika wrote a few notes on her paper, then looked up. "What's your plan for improving those numbers?"

"Can we talk about the premiere, first, then work backward?" Dani asked. She pulled a document out of her portfolio and passed it to Mika.

"What's this?" Mika asked as she scanned the document.

"Remember when I talked to you about a panel at ClexaCon?" Dani asked.

"Yes, I said we'd make sure we're available. If all goes well with the executive screening, we'll be shooting, but I can build the schedule around it." Mika put a note on the top of her paper and starred it. "What are the dates, again?"

"Late April in Las Vegas. The exact dates are on the bottom." Dani pointed to the document next to Mika. "This is a proposal to premiere the pilot at ClexaCon."

Mika looked up, her forehead creased. She dropped her pen and leaned back in her chair, hands resting on the table. "Before it premieres on Binge?"

"Yes."

Mika continued to look at the woman sitting across from her while she thought. "Say more," she said at last.

"ClexaCon exists for fandoms like the one we're trying to create. Look at their vision." Dani read from her copy of the proposal. "'ClexaCon provides a platform to build community, bringing together a diverse group of LGBTQ fans and content creators from around the world.'" Mika made a note on the page as she listened to Dani.

"The convention draws just over four thousand loyal, involved fans. Fans who are active on social media. If they see the show before the Binge premiere, word of mouth will reach a more targeted audience than any other advertising we could do."

"I'm not sure the network will approve it," Mika said.

Dani pulled out her tablet and tapped the screen. "This is a page on Tumblr called 'Joelle Forever.'" She handed it to Mika who scrolled through the posts.

"Joelle, huh? I do love a good portmanteau."

"It's a good name for their 'ship.' Sexy," Dani said.

"What am I looking at other than the posts?"

"This is an involved fan who, before the show even premiered, created a fan page that already has eighty followers. That might not sound impressive, but even if only half the women who attend ClexaCon draw in just forty followers each…"

Mika didn't let her finish. "That could be eighty thousand subscribers we wouldn't have otherwise."

"Right, and that's on the low side because we'll put out more content before the pilot, which in turn will draw more followers to pages like this," Dani said as she flipped a couple of pages in her presentation. "Then there's merchandising. I suggest we hold off on selling anything until the premiere. Then, as the fans exit the convention hall, we have a limited number—say, a thousand—T-shirts available for sale. I'm thinking a shirt with a picture of the Corsetti and Driskell Investigations sign. Nothing Joelle because we need to get the show's name out. It's not *Corsetti's Will*, but it's close enough. If we limit the number of shirts available, anyone who gets one will wear it at the convention. And on the Vegas Strip."

Mika sat back, letting the idea sink in, then asked the question she expected from the network: "Why do we need to show the pilot? Won't the panel be enough?"

"I don't think it will. Right now, there's nothing for the fans to connect with. They don't know Joey and Noelle. The audience at the panel will be there to see Sara, and that's what they'll emphasize on their social media accounts—Sara Silver, not Joey Driskell."

"Do you think you can convince the organizers to let us do the premiere during their convention?" Mika asked.

"I have no doubt. It might even increase registrations."

"Get me confirmation of that and a guarantee we get to pick the day and time. I need a detailed proposal by the end of the week, and I'll take it to Binge. Anything else?" Mika asked, gathering the papers.

"Yes, and I'm not sure she'll go for it, but what if we have Sara do a concert to benefit LGBTQ+ charities? Ideally, it would be away from the convention site—maybe at Caesar's. Our fans will attend, but so will Sara Silver fans. Maybe we have some Joelle merch there."

Mika was shaking her head even before Dani finished. "I don't think that will work. When would she have time to rehearse a concert? She'll be filming."

"That's true. I didn't think about what Sara needed." Dani frowned.

"It may be the only thing you didn't consider. Excellent work, Dani."

* * *

A week later, Mika stood next to Larry Rand, shaking hands and making small talk with network executives as they arrived for the screening of the *Corsetti* pilot. The last exec had entered the room when her father made his entrance. He reached around her to shake Rand's hand and clapped him on the back.

Mika struggled to hide her disdain, but he saw it and pulled her into a hug full of false affection. Rather than make a scene, she allowed his charade. "Hello, Father."

She started to pull out of the embrace, but he grabbed her forearms before she could completely break free. In a voice that was too loud for the small room, he said, "Mika, I'm excited to see this little show of yours." She wondered if his condescension was obvious to everyone, and if it was, whether they judged him or her for it.

Forcing a smile, she walked to the front of the room. "Thank you for coming. I'm excited to share the pilot of *Corsetti's Will*. Does anyone need anything before we start the screening?"

She barely avoided swearing when she heard his voice. "I'd like some coffee. Does anyone else want some? You know how I like mine, don't you?" He grinned at her.

She smiled back, fighting the urge to humiliate him with a sharp comeback. Instead, she asked, "Anyone else?" When the others declined, she said, "I'll have something brought to you." He wouldn't be getting any coffee, and they both knew it. "We're ready," she called up to the booth.

Mika had seen this cut twice and was proud of it. The writing was strong, and for the most part, the actors delivered. But watching with an audience had a way of magnifying any problems. And when Christina Landis appeared on-screen for the first time, she realized how big her problem was. So did the executives. During each of Christina's scenes, she heard Rand's voice in the ear of John Belinski, the studio chief. When the lights came up, she steeled herself.

"Mika, this is why we partnered with you," Belinski said. "The writing is outstanding. Your team put together a story I want to watch. Any changes in your Season One plan? The murders are your A storyline and won't be solved until the season finale?"

"That's right," she said. "The B storyline will be introduced and resolved each week. The premise is the characters need to work cases to pay the bills. As the season progresses, some of those self-contained stories will relate to the murders. And, of course, the C storyline is the relationship between Joey and Noelle."

Mike Williams took his opportunity. "I warned you about that, kid." She bristled but maintained her neutral expression. "Most people can't relate to those women. You may get viewers at first, but they'll get tired of your agenda."

Several of the men shifted uncomfortably at his words. Belinski sat forward. "Don't let that concern you. However, it's because of the importance of the relationship that I have concerns."

"Yes." Rand had been nodding as Belinski spoke. "You need to recast Noelle Prado and reshoot her part."

"That girl can't act her way out of a paper bag," Mike Williams added.

Mika's calm slipped. "What does that even mean?" she snapped at him.

Belinski answered, "She slows the pace of the scene. It's uncomfortable to watch her."

"In every scene she's in?" Mika pressed.

He paused to consider her question. "No. Not every scene."

"What if I get her an acting coach?" Mika asked, hoping her plan would be enough for them.

Rand pushed. "Why not just recast? Surely you saw the same thing we did."

Mika sighed. "Let me show you something." She called up to the booth. "Renee, could you play the clip from *Night in Time*?" The lights went down and the group watched a ten-minute scene where an emotional Christina discovers her lover has been unfaithful.

When the lights came up, Mika said, "This is the actress I signed. I know that there is depth in her, and I believe we can help her tap it. Also, she has a loyal following in the LGBTQ community and a strong social media presence. Binge saw a subscriber bump when we announced her signing. If I get rid of her now, I'm concerned the backlash will affect us. If it doesn't get better, I'll write her out of the show."

"What difference will two months make?" Rand asked.

"I'll have time to find a replacement the community will get behind."

"And that's why we wanted to work with you. We'll be ordering a full season of *Corsetti's Will*." Belinski stood and extended his hand. "Congratulations, Mika."

Mike Williams waited until everyone left the room before approaching her. "Belinski may have missed it, but I didn't. You've already fucked this up. You have an actress who can't act, but you can't fire her 'cause the queers will turn on you." He paused. "And then they'll turn on the network. Wanna guess who they'll fire?"

Mika wished she could slap the gleeful look of his face. Instead, she pushed past him to get out of the room.

CHAPTER THIRTEEN

"Don't try to find the perfect house right now. Look over these listings and tell me what you like, and I'll do the rest." The email from Katie included a link to an online inventory of houses.

Sara called Nathan so they could look through houses together. "Oh, do you see the warehouse conversion?" he asked.

"I'm not going to live in another cold, industrial building."

"It's California. Nothing is cold there."

"I want a house…" she started to say.

"Okay. Here's one. Look at the second page, third house. Two pools wrapping around the house. Oh my God, do you see that view?"

"It's sixty-two million dollars!" Sara's voice cracked. "What do you think our budget is?"

"You're so cheap. Here's one for thirty-nine million. Do you see it? It's got a good view."

"Do you like the large abstract sculpture in the middle of the pool? Oh." She swallowed a laugh as she clicked through the online images. "Or is it that photograph of a topless Barbie that has you excited?"

"The artwork doesn't come with the house. Look at the rooms, and the view."

"That house is way too masculine for me. It looks like the guys from *Pulp Fiction* decorated it."

"Have you even seen *Pulp Fiction*? Because I'm not getting the connection."

"I don't want a house that looks like I bought it from a hitman. Even the pool table is black."

"So dramatic. Most of these houses are modern…"

"Here's one. Page four. The one in Laurel Canyon for three million."

"Why are you so cheap? What's wrong with spending sixty-two million?"

"Look at how cozy it is," she said, ignoring him. "Oh, but it only has three bedrooms and three baths. That's not big enough."

"Thank God," he muttered.

That night Sara sent Katie her list. *I want to feel at home. Too many of these houses look like museums. I just want large enough for my family to visit comfortably, but still cozy. A nice pool area is a must. Nathan wants a movie room and a wine cellar, but he's not paying. Maybe one of the two, just to keep him happy.* She put a smiley-face emoji at the end of the email.

* * *

A few days later, she waited outside her executive apartment for Abby and Katie. A white Lexus SUV pulled to the curb, and Abby hopped out of the passenger seat and looked around in confusion. "Excuse me," she said. "I'm looking for Sara Silver. Have you seen her around here?"

"Very funny." Sara pulled her baseball cap lower on her forehead. "You'll really laugh when random strangers belt out 'Street People' in the middle of Starbucks."

"Well, that's a lesson, isn't it?" Abby said. "You should be supporting independent coffee shops. People in independent coffee shops are too busy writing slam poetry to sing your music. You're beneath them."

After a quick hug, they climbed into the SUV. Sara greeted Katie then turned so she could look back at Abby. "What have you been up to? I've missed seeing you."

"Did you hear that, Katie? Rock star Sara Silver misses me. I told you we were friends." When Katie rolled her eyes, Abby added, "Katie thought I invited myself along today."

Sara's mouth fell open. "You totally invited yourself. In Makeup? On the second to last day of shooting? Sound familiar?"

Abby waved her off. "That wasn't self-inviting, that was an offer of support from one friend to another. As I recall, you took me up on the offer."

Sara shook her head and turned around. "How long have you been friends?" she asked Katie.

"Since high school. We met in Geometry. Abby cheated off my tests."

"Of course she did. So, where are we going first?"

"I thought we'd go up to Laurel Canyon to see that little bungalow you thought was cute. I know you think it's too small, but the listing agent contends there's room for an addition. Added bonus, Stockard Channing owns it."

"Really? I love Stockard Channing. I don't think I want to go through construction, but I'd love to see the house."

"Maybe she has a picture of John Travolta," Abby said.

"I always thought Rizzo was gay," Sara mused. "I think she was hot for Sandy all along."

"Puh-lease," Abby said. "Sandy wasn't her type. Marty was definitely her girl."

Thirty minutes and an unresolved argument later, they pulled up to a gate. Katie punched in a code. "Another reason I wanted you to see this house is because it's owned by a celebrity. It has the security and privacy you'll need." They drove down a long road and pulled up in front of a small, wood-framed house. "I name-dropped you so we could get in without the seller's agent present."

They explored the cottage ending under a covered patio overlooking the pool. "This is beautiful," Sara told Katie. "Look at the view of the mountains and the canyon from here. If only the house were bigger, I'd take it." She bit her lip, considering, then shook her head. "I can't do construction. As much as I love it, this isn't the house."

"No pictures from *Grease*. They must have staged it," Abby called from inside the house.

"We better go before she steals something," Katie said.

They drove back down the canyon and into Beverly Hills. On the way, Katie explained the next house. "I'm taking a chance on the next listing, but I think it might be perfect for you and your brother. It's on two acres of land with unobstructed views."

"That sounds expensive in Beverly Hills. How much is it?"

"That's the tricky part. There are two houses. If you want them both, it's thirty-seven million. One of the two is seventeen million."

"It's too much," Sara said. "Let's skip it."

Katie pulled the car into a strip mall and turned to Sara. "It's well within your debt-to-income ratio. I wouldn't put you in a house you couldn't afford."

"That's too much." Sara was adamant. "Even if I can afford it, I don't need a house like that. Let's go see the third one, okay?"

Katie gave her a half-smile. "I don't think that house will be any better." She pointed across the street. "Why don't you guys hang out at that coffee shop for a little bit. I get the feeling you're a Laurel Canyon girl. Let me look through the listings and see if I can find a house bigger than the one we saw."

Sara gave her a grateful smile "Thanks for understanding." She and Abby dashed across the street. As they reached the door of the coffee shop, Sara handed Abby a few bills. "Will you order? I'd like a large iced tea. Unsweetened. And a cookie if they have any."

Abby pushed her hand away. "I'll get this. Any particular kind of cookie?"

"Um, chocolate chip or oatmeal raisin. Oh, if they have peanut butter, definitely peanut butter, but they probably won't.

Any of those three are good. Actually, anything but white chunk macadamia nut is fine."

"You're a little crazy, aren't you?" Abby asked. "I mean, it's not a lot of crazy, but you've got some, don't you?"

Sara pushed her inside the door. "I'll find a table," she whispered.

"Okay," Abby whispered back.

Sara chose a table where her back was to most of the coffee shop. Abby joined her a couple minutes later and placed a paper bag in front of her. "I want you to control yourself when you open that." Sara reached for the bag, but Abby put her hand on it. "I mean it. No squealing, no hugging, and definitely no kissing."

Sara tilted her head to the side and looked at Abby. "Are you done? If you're overselling this cookie, I'm going to be upset."

"Joey," the barista called out.

Sara's eyes narrowed, and Abby feigned innocence. "I didn't want them to know it was you," she whispered. Before Sara could respond, she pushed back her chair and headed to the counter. "Did you say 'Joey?'" she asked loudly.

When she returned, Sara said, "Really? Are you always like this?"

"Did you look at your cookie?"

Sara opened the bag and gave a little moan of delight when she saw the peanut butter chocolate chip cookie. "You're forgiven," she said, taking a bite. "Mmmm, I hope my new house is around here." She chewed happily. "Where do you live?"

"I have an apartment in Studio City. It's small, but I like it."

"You grew up in LA? What was that like?" Sara asked.

"Just like anywhere else. It's not like we had movie stars in our neighborhood."

"Do your parents still live here?"

"No. As soon as they retired from teaching, they moved to Palm Springs."

"Oh, I like Palm Springs," Sara said. "I love midcentury architecture. Too bad there aren't any houses like that around here."

Abby gave her an incredulous look. "There are. Lots of them. Have you told Katie that's what you're looking for?"

"Well, not specifically. I looked at the sample listings she gave me and told her what I like and disliked. None of them were midcentury, so..." Sara trailed off because Abby was concentrating on her phone at her ear.

"Hey. We're sitting here and she just told me she likes midcentury." Abby listened for a second. "Okay, hold on." She looked up at Sara. "You know those houses can have a modern vibe."

"Yes, but they also have a lot of wood and stone. They don't feel cold."

"Did you hear that?" Abby was quiet. "What's the price? Oh. Okay, hold on." Abby looked at her. "How do you feel about ten million? She said she just saw a great midcentury for that."

"That feels better. Can we see it?"

An hour later, they pulled in front of a two-story, midcentury house tucked into a wooded lot. One step inside the door and Sara knew she'd found her home. Stacked stone pillars separated the living and dining areas while dark hardwood floors warmed the space. Against one wall, a large fieldstone fireplace dominated the room. She stood still for a moment, taking it all in. Neither Abby or Katie spoke, nor did they follow when she finally moved. Once Sara saw the large island in the kitchen and the table overlooking the pool, she was sure, but it wasn't until she'd walked all around the backyard that she spoke.

"I'll take it."

CHAPTER FOURTEEN

Filming had begun on the second episode, and after three days of early morning calls, Sara was visibly dragging. Abby was already in the makeup chair with Michelle when she arrived. Tanya, the other artist who worked magic on them every day, held out a smock as Sara plopped into her chair. "Ooh, we've got some work to do today," she teased.

"I know." Sara groaned. "I'm trying to go to bed earlier, but my brain won't go to sleep." She looked in the mirror at Michelle. "How was your date?"

Instead of answering, Michelle stepped away from Abby and reached in her bag. "Look what I found at 7-Eleven when I was buying breakfast." She pulled a magazine out with a flourish.

"Ew." Tanya made a face. "You buy breakfast at 7-Eleven? How did I not know that?"

Michelle sniffed. "Because I don't do it every day. Only when I need to get gas or I'm tired of Egg McMuffins." She held up a finger and shook it at the older woman. "Not the point. Look what I found. I'm going to have Sara sign it, then I'll sell it on eBay." She stopped, looking wide-eyed at Sara. "You don't care, do you?"

Sara shook her head, laughing. "Whatever you want." She flipped the magazine over and Abby leaned in to look. On the front was a photograph of Sara wearing a Range Street concert T-shirt. The shirt was faded and torn, exposing an expanse of Sara's upper chest and a hint of cleavage. "I forgot all about this," she said. "He tore my shirt." She wrinkled her face at the image.

Abby looked at the other women in the mirror. "I forget things like that all the time, don't you?" They laughed, and Abby was about to say more until she saw the stricken look on Sara's face. She reached over to touch her arm. "Hey, what's wrong?" Sara looked like she was going to cry. She turned the magazine so Abby could read the cover. "You look hot. Look at the definition in your arms." Abby pulled the magazine closer, staring at Sara's exposed collarbone and perfectly shadowed cleavage. She wished she looked that good in a torn T-shirt.

Sara tapped the headline. "Sara Silver: I Didn't Deserve an Oscar Nomination."

"What the fuck?" Michelle said. "You totally deserved the nomination!"

"Did you say that?" Abby asked.

Sara shook her head. "Not like that. The interview was the day the nominations were announced. He asked me how I felt about not being included, and I said something like, 'Look at the actresses nominated. Which one didn't deserve it?'"

"Was he trying to get you to badmouth someone? I hate when men do that," Abby said.

Sara took the magazine back and opened it to the story. She visibly cringed and turned the page to Abby. "Is this how I come across?" There was a full-page photo of her leaning against a street sign, the words "Range Street" visible above her head.

Tanya bent down and read the caption below the photo. "*Can Sara Silver ever get out from under the shadow of Range Street?*"

Sara read the first paragraph aloud. "*Sara Silver has always been a reluctant star. Now on the cusp of superstardom, does she have the strength to take the next step?"* She stopped reading and the color rose on her face.

Abby touched her arm. "What's it say?"

Sara took a shaky breath. *"Silver has always faded in the background behind her more gregarious bandmates, often choosing to let them speak for her in interviews and on stage. Her behavior was considered indulgent and shy. But when grainy black-and-white images of the exhausted singer revealed an emaciated frame, the narrative changed. Was she indulgent, or high? Silver responded to the rumors of drug use by releasing a critically and commercially successful solo album. She followed that with her moving portrayal of Bridget Keogh in* Enough.

"Yet questions persist. No longer about drugs. Silver addressed those allegations with a passion rarely seen offstage. 'Those pictures were a gross violation of my privacy. I don't use drugs and I don't abuse alcohol, so I haven't needed professional help to overcome an addiction.' Asked about other health issues, she was equally adamant. 'I don't have an eating disorder, nor am I suffering from a debilitating illness.'

"No, the questions that persist aren't about her health. They're about her fragility. Silver has rare talent, and her Oscar snub was universally decried by film critics. It seems the only person who didn't believe she deserved the nomination was Sara Silver herself. 'I don't look at it as being overlooked,' she said. 'The women who were nominated had outstanding performances.' Her lack of ego may be refreshing, but it reveals a shockingly low self-esteem."

Sara stopped reading and looked at Abby, the anguish clear on her face. "Is that how I come across? Like I'm weak or fragile?"

"No," the three women spoke at once.

"Not at all," Abby assured her. "You are kind, and being kind is not a weakness. He's probably used to interviewing divas and thinks if you aren't bitchy, you must be a pushover. Didn't you make any outrageous demands before the interview? From now on you need to require sparkling water from a Tibetan monastery."

Sara responded seriously to Abby's teasing. "No, I don't do that. I think it's a ridiculous power trip when people behave like that. We grew up in a middle-class, maybe even lower-middle-class family. My mom and dad took a calculator to the grocery store to make sure they didn't spend more money than we had." Sara's eyes welled up. "Why do I have to be a bitch for people to treat me with respect?"

"Oh, honey." Tanya squeezed her shoulders and looked at her in the mirror. "You don't. I told my daughter how good you are to the people around here. Everyone loves and respects you."

The sight of Sara's tears hit Abby low in her gut. She wanted to wrap her in a hug but wasn't sure it would be welcome. "She's right, and I bet that's true when you're on tour as well." She leaned down to catch Sara's eye. "Why are you letting this bother you?"

"They make me sound like I'm not able to stand up for myself. That I can't make it without the guys." Sara's face flushed. "Of course I wanted to be nominated, but the women who were deserved to be nominated, and maybe I did, too, but I wasn't. What did he expect? That I'd cry to him? Throw things?"

"What are you going to do about it?" Tanya asked.

"Nothing." Sara shook her head, tears resurfacing. "And not because I'm a pushover. There isn't anything you can do once something like that is out."

Abby pulled off her cape, making eye contact with Michelle in the mirror. "I'm good. You always touch me up, anyway." She squeezed Sara's shoulders. "Don't read any more of that trash. He doesn't know you. I'll see you on set."

* * *

Sara tried to telegraph her subdued mood by ignoring Dani when she saw her approaching with her ever-present tablet during the lunch break. Dani would not be deterred, apparently, as she promptly sat down uninvited. "People love you."

Sara looked up from the salad she was pushing around. "Really? Why's that?"

Dani opened her tablet and showed Sara the trending page on Twitter. "Look at this." She pointed to the number-three trending topic: #womensupportingwomen. Then Dani scrolled down to number twelve, #belikesara.

"Hmm." Sara went back to her salad.

"No, Sara. These are about you. This is from your fan's response to the *Rolling Stone* article. Look. These are just your friends. There are a lot more." Dani handed her the tablet.

Mika Williams

@real.sarasilver supports other actresses, and she's weak? Congratulations to Sara for her breakout role in @ EnoughMovie, and for honoring the women who were nominated. #womensupportingwomen

Abby Farina

Shout out to my friend and costar @real.sarasilver for being kind, generous, and supportive. Be like Sara. Celebrate women when they succeed. #belikesara #womensupportingwomen

Bridget Keogh

If Rose and I hadn't lifted each other up, Enough would never have been recorded. #belikesara #womensupportingwomen

Range St.

@real.sarasilver has already made it on her own. We're blessed to have her talent. #belikesara

Christina Landis

Women need to support other women. #womensupportingwomen

Sara was taken aback by what she read. "This is all because of that article? How did it happen so quickly?"

"Who cares how it happened?" Dani went back to the trending page. "This is how many people are talking about you today. All of the nominated actresses have commented and most of the men. It's so bad, *Rolling Stone* had to make a statement."

Sara's mouth dropped open. "Really?"

"Yeah." Dani opened a page and read the statement. "*Rolling Stone* regrets that our recent cover on musician and actress Sara

Silver suggested that her humility and grace is a weakness. Even though *Rolling Stone* has a long history of supporting female musicians, we can always do better."

She looked at Dani, stunned. "I don't know what to say."

Dani patted her. "You've got good friends."

CHAPTER FIFTEEN

"I'm out of ideas," Celia Edwards told Mika. "She's not getting any better. If anything, she seems less focused. Her lines are wooden, her movements uncertain. I don't know who she is."

"What does the acting coach say?" After seeing the dailies for Episode Two, Mika knew something had to change. In a half hour, the table read for Episode Three would begin, and Christina Landis was fast becoming her albatross.

"The same. He doesn't think she has the talent."

"Would it be better if we hired a woman to work with her?" Mika tried not to sound as desperate as she felt.

"She doesn't respond any better to me or to you. We hired him to see if she'd respond to a man. Nothing is working."

"I know." Mika took off her glasses and rubbed the spot between her eyes, trying to stave off another headache. "Is there anything you can think of. Anything we haven't tried?"

"Honesty," Celia said. "Have you told her the truth about what the network thinks? Maybe that will have an impact."

Mika sighed. "It's worth a try." She walked to the door of her office and spoke to her assistant. "Renee, would you find Christina Landis and ask her to come in here?"

"Do you want me to stay?" Celia asked.

"No, it's better if I talk to her alone."

Celia gave her a slight nod. "I'll see you at the read."

Ten minutes later, Renee knocked and opened the door. Christina Landis stood behind her. "Come in, please." Mika motioned to a chair and the other woman sat carefully. She got right to the point. "The network and I have concerns about your performance thus far." Mika paused, watching for a reaction, but Christina didn't move. "I want to be brutally honest with you. I'm getting pressure to recast your role." Christina's head dropped and her shoulders slumped. Mika waited to see if she would speak, but she stayed silent, wiping her face. "Christina, look at me, please." When she did, Mika continued in a gentle tone. "That is a last resort, and it is not what I want to happen, but you have to get better. Your performance lacks any believability. The passion you showed in *Night in Time* is nonexistent. Do I need to go on?"

"No," Christina mumbled.

"Then what is it? Why can't you inhabit this character? What's holding you back?"

Christina sat unmoving so long that Mika thought she was refusing to answer. Just as she was about to lose her temper, Christina spoke. "Sara."

"Sara?" Mika's voice rose. "Sara is holding you back? What do you mean?" Mika regretted her tone when she saw Christina flinch. She softened her posture and voice. "I'm sorry. Can you tell me what it is about Sara that's holding you back?"

"She's intimidating."

Mika maintained the even tone. "Sara intimidates you? What about her?"

Again, it took several moments for Christina to answer. "I guess it's that I don't know her very well. It feels awkward when we're together."

"When you're together in a scene, you mean? The intimate scenes?"

"Yes. I can't relax."

Renee knocked and opened the door. "Five minutes."

"Thank you for your candor." She looked back to Christina. "We'll talk more, but for now, I'm going to find ways for you and Sara to get to know each other better."

* * *

"I have a couple of surprises for you this morning. First, the trailer is finished and will be released simultaneously on the Binge website and our social media platforms. We thought you might want to get a peek before it goes out." The group cheered, and Mika gave her team an indulgent smile. "This isn't the best venue, but I think it'll work for today." The lights went out, and the show's title image appeared on the large-screen television mounted to one wall.

Abby's stomach tightened, dreading the moment she'd see herself on-screen. The two-minute trailer was a fast-paced blend of action and humor, but it was the intimate scene that drew Abby in. Sara's naked back filled the screen, her head thrown back, blond hair mussed. She was straddling Christina, whose hand slid over Sara's shoulder and trailed down her back. The whole scene couldn't have been more than ten seconds, but it left Abby breathless. "Jesus," she hissed to Sara. "That's fucking hot."

"Shut up," Sara hissed back.

The next image was of Abby's tear-stained face. Sara as Joey Driskell hugged her while music played softly in the background. "He loved you so much. I promise, we'll find out who did this," Joey told Bria. Abby felt the emotion of the scene rise in her chest, and just like the day they filmed it, she felt drawn to Sara's strength. She closed her eyes, trying to get herself under control.

When it was over, Mika stood as the room cheered their collective work. "Congratulations, everyone. I think our introduction of *Corsetti's Will* to the world is quite powerful." The group applauded again, and Mika held up a hand. "One more surprise. Dani, will you do the honors?" Dani stood, and

Mika continued, "Dani has created a unique opportunity for the premiere, and I, for one, am very excited about it."

"As most of you know, Mika, Sara, Christina, and Abby are scheduled to appear on a panel at ClexaCon in April. There's been a slight change to that schedule." Dani tried to hide her smile, but it burst through as she spoke. "We are going to premiere the pilot of *Corsetti's Will* the first night of the convention." Her words were met with tepid applause.

Mika took over. "ClexaCon is fairly new, but very influential. It draws thousands of women to Las Vegas to celebrate LGBTQ+ programming." She looked around the room. "This is where fandoms go to interact with the shows they support and where they find new shows to love. These people are very active on social media, so if we get them excited and talking about the show, that energy will go out to thousands more in a matter of hours. It is our opportunity to create a massive following in one night."

Dani nodded. "Instead of waiting for word of mouth from existing Binge subscribers, we have local influencers, who may not otherwise have seen the pilot, sharing their enthusiasm with their communities. And, as you know, enthusiasm equals subscribers."

The table read finished an hour later. Abby and Sara were teasing each other about the trailer when Mika joined them. "Sara, are you free to spend some time with Christina this weekend?"

"Oh," Sara said. "Well, I was going to ask Abby if she would go with me to some estate sales. Christina is welcome to join us." She looked at Abby. "I mean, if you want to go."

"I think it would be best if it were just you and Christina," Mika said to Sara. "You don't mind do you, Abby?"

Abby blinked in confusion. What could she say? Her boss just disinvited her to something she would have loved to do. "Of course not. I have plans this weekend, anyway," she lied.

"Excellent. Sara, will you connect with Christina?"

"Sure. I'll send her a text." Sara picked up her phone, and Mika walked away with a wave. A whooshing sound signaled

Sara's text had been sent. She looked from her phone to Abby. "What do you think that was about?"

Abby was afraid her hurt would be obvious, so she looked away. "Who knows?" She shrugged.

Sara touched her arm. "Hey, I'm sorry. I shouldn't have asked you in front of Mika. I put you in an awkward position."

Abby groaned inwardly. Leave it to Sara to think she'd done something wrong. "No, that's fine. Don't worry about it." She bumped Sara's shoulder. "Do you think she's trying to fix you up?" Sara's eyes widened in panic, and Abby couldn't resist teasing her. "I mean, did you see how hot you looked on-screen?" She waved a hand in front of her face.

Sara shook her finger at her friend. "Nice try deflecting. Plans this weekend? Got a date? Did you finally listen to Michelle and sign up for that online dating site?"

The only thing Abby had planned for the weekend was sleep. Now she had to come up with something to do. "I thought I'd go see my folks." Why did she say that? She wasn't up for the drive to Palm Springs or a visit with her parents. She opened her mouth to undo the damage when Sara grabbed her arm.

"Hey, I close on my house in two weeks. I was thinking Palm Springs would be the perfect place to buy furniture. If you get a chance, scope things out for me, will ya?"

"Oh sure." Abby pretended to be put out. "Because you're the center of my world."

Sara winked. "Don't I know it."

CHAPTER SIXTEEN

After looking over the weekend estate sales, Sara texted Christina. *Hey, would you hate it if we went to some secondhand shops instead? The sales don't look great.* In truth, she didn't want to spend that much time in the car with Christina. At Mika's request, Sara ate lunch with Christina the days she was on set, and Sara was running out of conversation topics.

When Christina walked out of her apartment, Sara groaned. Her hair was down and, even from a distance, Sara could tell she was wearing makeup. Anyone who'd seen *Night in Time* or the *Corsetti's Will* trailer would recognize her. Sara frowned. She really didn't want to spend the day taking selfies, particularly when she wasn't wearing makeup and her hair was hidden under a floppy hat.

"Hi," Christina said as she got in the car.

"Morning," Sara replied. "You look nice." She knew her tone lacked sincerity but couldn't seem to stop herself.

Christina eyed her, unsure of how to take the compliment. "Thanks." Then she got it. "Do you think I need a hat?"

Sara gave her a half-shrug. "I think you're going to be more recognizable this weekend than you were last. Maybe you should get one."

When Christina returned wearing a white straw fedora, Sara wanted to roll her eyes. Rather than concealing, the hat drew attention to Christina's striking looks.

"I'm glad you changed your mind about estate sales," Christina said. "You'll pay more in the vintage shops, but at least you know they have pieces in the style you like."

"That's good, because other than knowing I like midcentury, I have no idea what I'm looking for."

Christina proved to be an expert at treasure hunting. In the first store, Sara kept her arms wrapped tightly around her body as she did a quick lap through the main showroom. The musty smell of the old furniture had her rethinking a vintage piece. "Ready to go? I don't see anything here."

Christina put her hands on her hips. "Have you ever done this before?"

"No, but I thought it would be fun."

"It is fun, but you won't find anything unless you dig." She gestured to a sign over her head. "Come on. Let's go up to the second floor."

Sara looked at the rusted metal stairs. "Do you think it's safe? Think how upset Mika will be if something happens to you."

Christina gave Sara a look she couldn't interpret. "Mika wouldn't care. Come on. I want to see what's up here."

What was up there was a flea market of furniture. Along the walls, pieces were stacked in precarious piles three and four high. Crude aisles had been created and then narrowed as more items were added, making it impossible to walk without turning sideways. There was so much wood and upholstery and metal piled up that Sara's eyes couldn't differentiate one piece from the next. She wandered around with her arms crossed, hands gripping her biceps, wondering how long Christina would make her stay. A scream from across the room made her jump and let out her own scream. "Christina, are you okay? Did something bite you? Was it a rat? God, I'm sorry, I shouldn't have made you come here," Sara babbled as she rushed to where she thought Christina was.

"Help me move this stuff," came the muffled reply. "There is an unbelievable table back here."

"You're okay? That was a good scream?"

A dirt-smudged face popped up from behind a turquoise-and-gold upholstered chair. "Get over here." Christina's eyes were bright with excitement.

Sara held up her hands in surrender and shoved the chair so she could get to Christina. She stared down at something just visible under dust and vinyl kitchen chairs. When Christina lifted an end table away from the pile, Sara saw it. "Oh my God. You're right. That's amazing." The mahogany table had two triangular tiers. The lower tier sat on four tapered legs. The upper section was attached on one end, but the other floated delicately over the lower section. "How is that not broken?" Sara whispered, afraid her words might send the precarious pile crashing down.

Together they moved the kitchen chairs and a lamp out of the way. At last, Christina managed to slide the table out, and Sara's heart sunk. While the table wasn't broken, the finish was scratched and discolored. "It's ruined," she said.

Christina had her hands on her hips, looking at the table in triumph. At Sara's words, she laughed. "No, it's not. It just needs to be refinished. Come on let's get it downstairs and see what they want for it."

Even though she had her doubts, Sara dutifully picked up her end of the table. "How are we going to get it down those stairs?"

"You are terrible at this," Christina said, walking backward toward the metal steps. "When we start going down, I'll set the pace. Do not push," she warned. Sara was terrified that either or both of them would miss a step and tumble to their deaths. Christina was unfazed, and in no time they stood in front of the owner, the table between them.

"Five hundred," he said before either woman spoke.

Sara reached for her wallet, but Christina glared. "Two minutes ago, you didn't know this table existed. There's no marking and the original finish is beyond saving. She'll pay one fifty, and that's high. She'll have to pay at least that to get it refinished."

"Two fifty."

Christina turned away from him. "Let's check out the other shops." She headed toward the door with a confused Sara trailing behind. "Don't speak," Christina hissed.

"Two hundred."

"You're our first stop. Maybe we'll be back." Christina reached for the handle.

"Cash," the owner said.

Christina looked to Sara with raised eyebrows. "What are you asking me?" Sara whispered.

"Do you have one fifty in cash?" Sara nodded, still unsure if she was allowed to speak. "Then go buy your table." Christina made a sweeping gesture toward the owner.

"Do you have someone who could load this for us?" Sara asked.

"Don't bother," Christina interrupted. "It's light." Sara paid and the two of them picked up the table, and after maneuvering through the door, walked side by side to Sara's SUV.

They were almost there when Sara heard a voice call, "Christina! Hey, Christina Landis." Sara ducked her head and turned her face to the side, hoping she would remain unrecognized. Two women rushed toward them. "Can we help you with that?" one asked. "Where's your car?"

Christina, still holding her end of the table, gestured with her head. "We're right here. I think we can handle it, but thanks for the offer." They set the table down while Sara searched for her keys.

The women ignored her refusal and picked up the table. Sara was about to protest when one of them said, "Your table has a weird shape. It's not going to fit." On cue the two women flipped the table and Sara gave a little cry. "We need a flat-head," one said to the other. They put the table back down and one woman jogged across the street while the other explained, "Trust me. We do this all the time. It's best to take the legs off and let the top rest flat rather than on its side. You have to be super careful with this kind of construction." She tapped the edge of the table. "Our shop is around the corner. Deb'll be right back with a screwdriver."

Forgoing anonymity, Sara asked, "What kind of shop do you own?"

The woman started to speak, then did a comical double take. "You're Sara Silver." She looked from Sara to Christina. "Oh my God. Sara Silver and Christina Landis."

"Yes," Sara answered. "And, I really appreciate your help with the table. Do you own a vintage shop? Is that how you know so much?"

"No, we refinish and reupholster vintage furniture. This location is perfect for us."

Sara looked at Christina, then back to the woman. "Can you fix this table for me? Refinish it?"

"Sure. Mahogany finishes up nicely. We'll be glad to do it for you."

The other woman jogged back to the group. "Here we go. I brought a blanket so we can flip it over."

Her partner smiled at her. "No need, honey." She hesitated, then said, "Sara Silver wants us to refinish her table." The woman looked at Sara in confusion, then recognition hit, and she took a stumbling step back. Her partner laughed. "Close your mouth. You're drooling." Sara blushed as did Deb, but the other two laughed. "She's been a big fan of yours for a long time." The woman reached in her back pocket and pulled out a card. "Here's our business, Vintage Revival. Do you know what kind of finish you want? Mahogany is a dark wood."

Sara looked to Christina, but all she got was a shrug. She took off her sunglasses and looked at the table. "Can you do this color?" Sara pointed to the original finish visible in one corner.

"We can. It'll take…" She looked to her starstruck partner. "What do you think? A month?" Without waiting for an answer, she said to Sara. "About a month."

"That's great. Should we carry it to your shop? I assume you want a deposit?"

The woman waved her off. "Just give us a good daytime number so we can call when it's done. And, maybe, you could take a couple of pictures with us?"

Once everything was settled and they were back in the car, Sara smiled at Christina. "You were amazing. How did you know all that?"

"My parents. We used to drive all over going to flea markets. You develop an eye for the good stuff. Sometimes the people don't know what they have. Like that guy. He didn't know anything about the table. He saw a couple of women and thought he'd make a sucker sale. I almost walked out on principle, but I knew it was a good piece." She grinned at Sara. "You got a steal."

"Thanks to you. What are you hungry for? I'm buying lunch." They settled on a Mexican restaurant not far from Christina's apartment. After washing away dirt and grime, they ordered margaritas and relaxed into a booth. Feeling closer to Christina following their morning adventure, Sara took a chance. "What's going on? Why is Mika pushing us together?" She paused, realizing her question could be misunderstood. "Not that I mind. Abby thinks she's trying to hook us up..." Her words trailed off. Why did she add that? She was going to kill Abby for planting the idea in her brain.

Christina's eyes flitted away from Sara and she flushed. "It's my fault," she said at last. "Mika's going to recast my role if I don't get it together." She took a deep breath and blew it out. "She asked me why I couldn't 'inhabit' the role." Her blush deepened. "I told her I was intimidated by you."

Sara had been in the process of dipping a chip in salsa. She dropped it in the bowl and gave Christina her full attention. "You are? By me? Why?"

Christina ran her finger around the rim of her glass, knocking salt onto the table. "I'm not. I didn't know what else to say. I couldn't tell her the truth."

"Why not? If something's bothering you, Mika will try to fix it. She wants this show to succeed more than anything."

"She can't fix it. Nobody can." Christina hesitated. "Well, I guess one person could, but she's not interested." She turned her head and dashed a knuckle under one eye.

"Can you tell me what it is?"

Christina pulverized the fallen salt with her thumbnail. When there was nothing left but salt dust, she straightened and met Sara's eyes. "I had an affair with Luciana Raithman."

"How do I know that name…" Sara started, then she lifted her brows, eyes wide. "Oh, shit. The director of *Night in Time.*"

"Yeah. The director. Who's married." Sara was stunned into silence. It didn't matter, because Christina finally wanted to talk. "It started almost right away. The night before the first sex scene, she invited me to her house to go over blocking. We started talking about the scene and how she wanted it to look. She told me she'd set up the spare bedroom like the set, and asked if I wanted to see it. Then she suggested I rehearse the scene in my bra and underwear so I'd get used to working with fewer clothes."

Sara's eyes blazed. "Jesus, Christina. She's a predator."

"No." Christina was vehement. "I wanted her. I was the one who asked if she'd like me to take off all my clothes. I asked her if she could show me what she wanted. I fell in love with her." Sara didn't know how to respond. Christina continued, a faraway look in her eyes, "The sex scenes in that film were reenactments of our lovemaking. After the first time, she told me she wanted the world to see our love even if they'd never know it was us. She said to imagine I was with her. We'd make love at night, and the next day she'd direct the scene so it was exactly like what we shared."

"Oh, Christina." Sara's heart hurt for the woman. "What happened?"

Christina bent her head and started to cry. She covered her eyes with one hand, and Sara reached for the other. They sat like that for several minutes while Christina composed herself. "She told me she couldn't leave her wife. That it would ruin her financially. That was the day of the wrap party. I haven't seen or heard from her since." A sob escaped. "It's been over a year, and

I should be over her, but being on a set again has brought it all back."

The waitress arrived and slid the plates across the table. "Be careful they're hot." One look at Christina, and she turned her focus to Sara. "Anything else?"

"I think we're going to need another round," Sara said.

They ate in silence, Christina picking at her meal as Sara searched for something to say. Luciana Raithman used Christina and discarded the young actress as soon as the movie was done. Sara was furious over the wreckage Raithman had left of Christina's life and career. For Christina, acting and lovemaking were conflated, and Sara couldn't see a way to help the younger woman separate the two. With a sigh, she pushed her plate away. "I think you should tell Mika."

Christina's head whipped up and frightened eyes met Sara's. "No," she said. "I can't. No one can know. You have to promise me you won't tell anyone. Please, Sara."

Reaching for her hand, Sara said, "Of course I won't tell anyone, but does this woman deserve your loyalty? This is hurting your career, Christina. What about you?"

Heartbroken eyes met Sara's. "I love her."

CHAPTER SEVENTEEN

Today was a half-day for Abby. In the morning, she and Sara would finish the Joey and Bria scenes. Then the set would be cleared for the scenes between Sara and Christina. This morning they had more pages than usual to finish, so they had an early call. A bleary-eyed Sara was in Makeup when Abby arrived.

"Good morning, everyone."

Sara eyed her suspiciously. "Why are you so happy? You hate getting up early."

"Truth." Abby pointed at her. "And I couldn't fall asleep last night. I should be biting your heads off this morning, but I'm not."

"Well, the three of us need more time to wake up, so think your happy thoughts, don't speak them." Sara made a shushing gesture.

Abby smirked. "Oh, I predict I can wake all of you just by reading a little story." Tanya and Michelle looked as disinterested as Sara felt. Their grunts made Abby's smile grow wider. "Okay, settle back. This one's called 'Lunch Time in Sara's Trailer.'"

Sara closed her eyes, ignoring Abby, who cleared her throat and shook out the pages in her hand.

"*Christina knocked on Sara's trailer door. She looked around to make sure no one was paying attention to her. Then she opened the door and walked in. 'What took you so long?' Sara asked from the bed.*

"'*The director wanted to tell me how to make our kissing scenes hotter.'*

"*Sara laughed. 'Any hotter and I'll catch on fire. Come here, baby, I'm already wet for you.'*"

Michelle and Tanya burst out laughing. Sara's eyes flew open. "Give me that." She grabbed at the paper, but Abby pulled it out of reach.

"We're not even to the good stuff yet. Wait until your firm, high breasts are revealed to Christina's ravenous eyes."

Sara put her face in her hands only to have them slapped away by Tanya. "Don't mess up my work. We don't have time to start over." She grabbed a brush and dusted where Sara's fingers had touched her face. She looked at Abby in the mirror. "Go on, what happens next?"

"Abby, I'm begging." Sara clasped her hands together. "Do not read that."

"Sara." Abby pursed her lips together. "I've already read it. And although I'm not entirely sure what a strap-on is, you, my friend, are apparently an expert." Michelle and Tanya exploded with laughter. "Not to spoil the end, but you're the best Christina has ever had." Abby waggled her eyebrows. Sara lunged and managed to rip the paper from Abby's hands. In seconds, she'd made confetti out of the pages, glaring at Abby the entire time.

When the laughter subsided, Sara gave Abby a death glare. "I still have money in the bank," she said, her voice emotionless. "I don't need to save up for the hit man. I have enough money, right now." The three started laughing again, but Sara didn't crack a smile.

"I didn't write it," Abby protested, carefully dabbing at her tears. "I just thought you could learn a few things before you film this afternoon."

Michelle grabbed her stomach. "Stop it, you two. I can't breathe."

Sara watched as the women dissolved into laughter again. "That's it. I'm putting out a hit on all of you. I can buy in bulk."

* * *

The morning taping ran long, and Christina had arrived by the time they broke for lunch. As soon as she caught sight of Sara, she pulled her aside and spoke in a low voice. "Can we eat lunch in your trailer?"

Sara took a step back and stared wide-eyed at Christina. "Um, well, I, uh…" Then she put her hands on her hips and squinted. "Did Abby put you up to this?"

Christina shook her head. "What? Abby? No, I have to tell you something and no one else can know. At least not yet." She grabbed Sara's arms and squeezed. "Please, I'm about to explode."

Sara looked around. "Where is she? Did she tell you to say that?" Sara stepped closer to Christina. "Do not let Abby Farina corrupt you."

"Abby's already gone." Then Christina paled. "You didn't tell Abby about Luciana, did you?"

"No, of course not." She turned her head slightly and eyed Christina. "Okay, let me grab something and I'll be right there."

When Sara made her way back to her trailer, lunch in hand. Christina was seated on the metal stair waiting for her. Sara opened the door and dropped her sandwich on the dining table, Christina taking a chair on the other side. "Luciana called me last night. She wants me back. She said all of the pictures of you and me are driving her crazy, and she can't stand it."

Sara wasn't sure this was good news, but she reached for Christina's hand and said, "I'm happy for you."

"I love her so much. I know you think she used me, but it wasn't like that. She told me she loves me and wants us to be together."

"And her wife?"

"Luciana moved out. She said they're getting a divorce, and she doesn't care what it costs her because she can't be without me any longer."

"I'm glad. It was hard to see you so sad."

"Thanks, Sara, for everything. If we hadn't gone furniture shopping and those pictures hadn't gotten out, I don't think she would have called."

"Don't thank me. I tried to get you to be more incognito, remember?" Sara grinned.

Christina looked at Sara, eyes wide with hope. "It was meant to be."

That afternoon, the scenes between the two of them had more energy. For the first time, Sara could see the actress Christina could become. They finished early, a relief after a long morning of shooting, and walked together back to the trailers. Out of nowhere, Christina said, "Now we need to get your love life figured out."

Sara laughed. "My love life? No such thing."

"Really?" Christina gave her an odd look. "What about you and Abby?"

"Abby?" Sara's voice came out in a squeak. "What about me and Abby?"

"Aren't you dating?" Christina stopped and put a hand over her mouth, her eyes wide. She pulled her hand away and whispered, "Sorry. Are you worried about Mika knowing?"

Sara was lost. "Wait." She shook her head, trying to sort out what Christina was saying. "What? I'm confused."

"It's okay. I get it. Luciana didn't want people on set to talk about us." She paused and looked up in the air, thinking. "That was because of her wife, but I guess it could create problems if people knew about you guys."

"No!" Sara reached out and turned Christina so they were facing each other. "No. Abby and I are friends. That's it. There's nothing going on." Sara was worried she was being too vehement, but this idea needed to be quashed. "Plus, Abby's straight."

"Really? Are you sure she's straight?" Christina's brow furrowed. "You're really not seeing her?"

"No." Sara emphasized the word.

"Huh. I guess I just thought after the whole Twitter thing and the way you're always together…" Christina pointed at her. "And you two flirt a lot."

Sara was stuck on something Christina said. "What Twitter thing? You mean the thing about us? The furniture?"

"No. The women-supporting-women thing."

"What?"

Christina laughed. "Okay, you aren't together. The look on your face is hysterical. I'm guessing you also don't know Abby was responsible for the tweets after the *Rolling Stone* article."

Sara was dumbfounded. "She was? I thought that was the studio. Abby did that? How did she get all those people to respond?"

Christina threw her arm around Sara's shoulder. "She texted a bunch of us, and we all posted something. I heard she even got Mika to call people. That's how Bridget Keogh and the *Enough* cast knew about it."

"Abby did all that? How did I not know?"

"No shit." Christina laughed.

* * *

For the first time in weeks, the headache that simmered behind her eyes was gone. Christina Landis had blown them away yesterday. Mika dropped into her desk chair. It felt good to breathe again.

Sara knocked on her open door. "Do you have a minute?"

Mika flipped over her wrist, fighting the urge to point out to Sara that while Mika had a minute, Sara needed to be in Makeup. Instead, she said, "What do you need?"

"I only have a second, but I have a question." Mika watched as Sara shoved her hands in the pouch of her hoodie, pulled them out, and smoothed the front of her jeans. Mika's mind flashed through reasons Sara might be nervous talking to her. She didn't like the answers.

"What is it? Is something bothering you?"

"Did Abby start the women-supporting-women hashtag?" Sara asked.

Mika pushed up her glasses and wondered why the question would make Sara nervous. "Yes. She was very angry at the way the writer characterized you. She felt it demeaned you and all women." Mika smiled. "I wouldn't want her mad at me. You didn't know?"

"I had no idea."

"You've got a good friend."

"Yes," Sara said. "I didn't realize how good."

CHAPTER EIGHTEEN

They were preparing to film the last scene of Episode Four. Since the pilot, there had been several kissing scenes with Sara and Christina, but nothing sexual. This would be the second intimate scene, and it needed to be done well.

Celia was arguing for them to be in Noelle's art studio, but Mika wasn't convinced. "I don't know. It's been done so many times."

"Maybe," Celia said. "But you have two passionate women, one of whom is an artist. Are you telling me that these characters would never make love in the studio? I don't believe it."

"You're right, but as only our second scene, it's too predictable. I don't want our audience rolling their collective eyes." Mika crossed her arms. "Let's go back to what happens right before Joey gets home. She's been on a stakeout with Bria, reminiscing about Leo Corsetti. Lots of laughs between them, but also plenty of emotion."

"That's not quite where it ended," Sara said. "I chased that guy, tackled him. Well, my stunt double tackled him, and then Bria caught up and wanted to kill him."

"Which was tied to the emotion of her father's death." Mika looked to her director. "Joey has to show depth. She can't come home and use Noelle to work out her grief. That's what we did in the pilot. Their relationship is richer than that."

"I think Joey would be reminded how thankful she is to have Noelle. She's seen Bria's grief and realizes that as much as she misses Corsetti, she's not alone like Bria is," Sara said.

"Good. Shall we work from there?" Celia asked.

Mika looked at the two actresses. "I like it. Let's see if we can capture that feeling physically."

Celia moved to the bedroom. "Christina, let's have you in bed reading. Reading?" She looked at the other women, who nodded. "Joey comes home, sits on the edge of the bed, and runs her fingers through Noelle's hair."

"Let's try it," Mika said. Christina climbed on the bed and Sara sat next to her. "Okay, with your right hand, reach up and brush the hair back on her left side, then cup her cheek." When Sara did, Mika continued, "Lean forward and slowly kiss her. Good. Christina, put your hand on the back of Sara's head like you're pulling her into a deeper kiss. Yes. Okay, stop. Where would you go from here?"

"Either Sara climbs on top of Christina, or Christina gets up on her knees and starts undressing Sara." Celia had her chin in her hand as she spoke.

"Okay, Christina, throw the book to the side of the bed, tuck your legs underneath you, and pull Sara to her feet." Mika saw the problem as soon as they started. The sheet covering Christina tangled as she moved. "Let's put you on top of the covers instead of under and try again." This time Christina was able to get to her knees and pull Sara up. "I like how that looks. Christina, unbutton Sara's shirt. Kiss her neck and her collarbone as you go."

Christina looked at Sara and slowly worked the buttons. When the first three were undone, she pulled Sara's shirt back, exposing her neck. She kissed it, then trailed fingers over the kiss before returning to the buttons. Once they were all undone, Christina put her hand flat against Sara's chest and kissed her before pushing the shirt off Sara's shoulders. It dropped to the floor. Christina slid Sara's bra straps off her shoulders, pulling the cups down too.

"Oops." Sara stepped back, laughing as she grabbed her bra. "Almost got a show there." She smiled at Christina, who blinked several times then shook her head as if coming out of a trance. With wide eyes, she mumbled, "I'm so sorry," before scrambling off the bed and running from the room.

Mika looked at Sara, who was still holding the cups of her bra to her chest. "What is that about?" Sara turned from watching Christina's departure. She pulled her bra straps up and bent to find her shirt, never making eye contact. Mika stepped closer to her star. "Sara, do you know what just happened?"

Sara looked up, then busied herself buttoning her shirt. Finally, she seemed to reach a decision and looked directly at Mika. "She confided some things to me that I promised I wouldn't share."

Mika tried to keep any hint of irritation from her voice. "Do you think you can get her back on set?"

Sara's expression didn't give her hope.

* * *

"Clear your calendars. Christina Landis has asked to be released from her contract. I need a plan for the rest of the season, rewrites of the completed scripts, and ideas for how Joey moves forward." If Mika had a sense of humor left, the look of shock on the faces of her writers would be entertaining. It may have been an outcome they wished for, but not midseason. Midseason meant hours of work and good writing lost. Although the Joey/Noelle storyline was only a few scenes each episode, Christina's departure created major issues.

David Stamper asked one of the questions Mika had been wrestling with for the last sixteen hours. "Recast?" His face was neutral, but there was a hopeful lilt in his voice.

Mika sighed. "I don't see how. Christina is too known in the community for another actress to step in without suffering from the comparison."

"How could she suffer? Other than a couple of scenes, Christina's acting was terrible." David huffed.

"It's not the acting. It's loyalty to the actress. Maybe we'll get some goodwill after her episodes air and the audience sees the quality of her performance, but it won't be enough to slide someone into the Noelle role." Mika took off her glasses and sat down. "Which brings me to our dilemma: break them up, or kill Noelle? And before you answer the question, let me illuminate the complexities of the decision. Break them up." She held out a hand, palm up. "What I've promised, and what I will deliver, is a story featuring a lesbian couple in a committed, loving relationship. An infidelity storyline is a nonstarter for me. So, if no one cheated, why are these two women, who we've portrayed as madly in love, breaking up?"

One of the newer writers spoke. "Well, family issues, job move, illness, mental illness? Any of those are possibilities."

"Yes," Mika replied, "and I've thought through all of them. How many of you are married or in a long-term relationship?" Two-thirds of the group raised their hands. "Which of those problems would lead to the end of your relationship?"

Aniyah, the young writer who had continued to impress Mika, sat forward. "What if we give ourselves some time to decide? Noelle could get an artist grant or an opportunity to run a gallery."

Several of the people at the table nodded. "Right, but then we have no relationship to feature, and we've broken a promise to our audience," Mika said.

David rubbed his face. "Fuck. Okay, kill her off. I guess it makes more sense for our show, anyway. We've already had two murders close to Joey. We make Noelle's death part of the conspiracy."

Mika held out her other hand, palm up. "And that brings me to the second problem. As you know, we are premiering our show next week at ClexaCon. Anyone know how that convention began?" A woman at the far end of the table raised her hand. "Care to explain, Cindy?"

"It's from the CW show *The 100*. They teased a relationship between two women, Clarke and Lexa for three seasons. After a lot of sexual tension, the relationship is consummated, then one of the women is killed in the next scene. There was huge backlash, and a lot of negative publicity. But, one of the results was the creation of ClexaCon. Clexa, for Clarke and Lexa."

"It's known as the 'Bury Your Gays' trope," Mika said. "In mainstream television, queer characters have been expendable, and the community is tired of it. Probably the only thing worse than killing Noelle would be to make her straight."

"Fu-uck," David moaned. "We can't win."

"Still, we need to decide. Take a moment to think, then I'm going to ask you to write your recommendation and pass it to me. Consider what is logical for our characters and best for our storyline. Picking the lesser of two evils may not be the right choice. I want the right choice from a storytelling perspective." Mika watched as her group took various thinking positions, then wrote their thoughts one by one. When she had all of the papers in front of her, she said, "I want to be clear. I'll make the decision, but your opinions are important to me." Then she smiled at her friends and colleagues. "Since I know you'll tell each other anyway, I'll read them out loud." Mika pulled the scraps of paper in front of her and opened each one, read it aloud, and turned the flattened paper over. When the last scrap was on the stack she looked up. "It seems we're all of the same mind." She paused, looking at each of them. "No gratuitous violence. It doesn't have to happen in Episode Five, but there's no reason to prolong it."

She pushed her chair back, gathering her notes and the loose papers. "I need a draft story arc by noon." She looked at David. He nodded his reply, then she turned her attention to Aniyah. "I'd like to see you in my office for a few minutes."

Once they were in her office, Mika got right to the point. "After the table read you said you felt Bria and Joey had a connection. Do you still feel that way?"

"Yes."

"Good. I want you to work on that. Look for ways to build an attraction. Joey is going to be grieving for the rest of the season, but she will move on. You're in charge of when and how that happens. Tell the rest of the room that's the direction we're going."

She picked up the phone and asked for Larry Rand. "This can't wait for him to finish his meeting. I need to speak to him immediately," she said to his assistant.

While she waited, she jotted notes. There was so much to consider beyond the story. Announcing Christina's departure would take careful planning.

A full ten minutes later, Rand came to the phone. "What is it?"

Interesting, she thought. The undercurrent of animosity she'd always sensed from him was on full display. "Christina Landis requested to be released from her contract."

"Effective when?"

"Immediately," she answered.

"Be available."

Realizing he'd hung up, she muttered, "Asshole," and carefully placed the receiver in the cradle.

* * *

The conference call with the network executives went better than expected, probably because no one bothered to invite her father. The omission surprised and gratified her. Maybe they were finally realizing he was more liability than asset. After much discussion, they'd agreed not to do a press release until after the premiere. Mika would share Christina's decision at ClexaCon during their panel, and the PR department would put something out an hour later. It was risky, and it was going to be even riskier when Mika shared Noelle's fate.

"If this is our audience," she'd told the group, "and we believe it is, then I need to make the case to them, and trust them to defend us. If I do my part, they'll do theirs." What she was doing wasn't unprecedented. Other shows announced when a character was leaving and highlighted the actor's last episode. Some even teased death scenes. "I trust our audience," she told the executives.

After the call, Mika walked around her desk and pulled open a drawer, searching for an aspirin. She popped the lid and shook two pills into her hand. Out of habit she took off her glasses and rubbed her forehead, then paused. She stood a little straighter and paid attention to her body. A slow smile crossed her features as she dumped the pills back into the bottle and snapped the lid in place.

She didn't have a headache.

CHAPTER NINETEEN

Everyone was moving in the same direction, and if the noise level was any indication, it was an exuberant crowd. Dani followed along, absorbing their excitement. At the door, she stepped out of line and took a photo of the mass of women waiting to enter. She pulled up the Corsetti feed and posted: *Five minutes until the doors open on the ClexaCon premiere of Corsetti's Will!*

"I hope they won't be this noisy during the show," a tall woman griped to the woman beside her.

"Don't worry. If someone talks too much, you know there'll be a dyke to shut 'em up." They laughed, and Dani thought the statement was accurate. She followed them to the VIP entrance and did a quick calculation. The people in this line had spent upward of $150 on their tickets. That bought them reserved seating in the first twenty rows and early entry into the autograph session the next day. When the doors opened, Dani stepped to the back of the room and watched the entering crowd take in the surroundings. The team had done as much as they could to turn a conference center into a movie theater. There was a theater-size screen in the front with smaller screens lining the edges of the room, guaranteeing everyone would have an unobstructed view of the show. Concert-style speakers hung from the ceiling and were interspersed along the walls.

As she made her way to the front of the room, she heard someone say, "These seats are amazing. If Sara Silver gets cold, we'll be able to see her nipples. Turn up the air-conditioning!"

Dani made her way backstage to look for Mika. She found her off to one side, looking at her phone. The black pencil skirt she wore accentuated her thin build. She'd accessorized the limited-edition Corsetti and Driskell T-shirt with a chunky silver chain. She looked up when Dani approached. "How's it look?"

"It looks like a hundred thousand new subscribers."

"Let's hope so. Has Sara arrived?"

"Yes. She's in her room. Hotel security will escort her down five minutes after the show starts." Dani touched her boss's arm. "Just enjoy it. We've got everything taken care of."

Mika blew out a breath. "Let's hope so. All of the equipment was checked, right?"

"Several times. And we have technicians here in case there's a problem. Nothing will go wrong."

The conference chair joined them, and the three women made small talk while they waited for the event to start. A radio crackled to life as another woman joined them. "They're a punctual crowd," she said. "There are only a dozen or so seats at the back still empty. We'll keep the doors open until Ms. Williams finishes her introduction, then close it all down."

"How will Sara get in?" Mika looked at Dani.

The woman pointed to a curtained area off to the side. "She'll come up the electronics walkway. We'll have two people escort her through so she doesn't trip on the cords."

"Thank you," Mika said. "Your team has been great to work with."

The woman blushed, then looked at her phone. "It's time," she told the conference chair.

"Ready?" At Mika's nod, she pushed the curtain aside and walked onstage.

"Good evening. On behalf of the entire ClexaCon team, welcome to the convention…" She continued, thanking the staff and making announcements to the excited crowd.

Dani had worked her way from backstage to her reserved seat by the time Mika was introduced. She joined the other women shouting and applauding the producer.

"Thank you for coming tonight. *Corsetti's Will* has been a dream of mine for a long time, and now that the dream has become a reality, I am so very excited to share it with you." The audience cheered in reply. "Many of you in this room know that the lesbian community has a proud tradition of serving in law enforcement." When the ensuing applause died down, she continued, "I grew up watching television shows featuring police officers and private investigators. Few told the stories of women on the job." She paused. "Not one told the story of lesbians on the job. Thanks to Binge, and those of you who subscribe to the network, that changes tonight." The crowd jumped to their feet, applauding furiously. Mika let the microphone drift to her side until the ovation subsided. "I've brought one of the cast members with me tonight, and I'll introduce her to you after the show. I think you might know her," she teased. "Please enjoy the premiere of *Corsetti's Will*!" Mika walked offstage and the room went dark except for the Binge logo projected on every screen.

While the audience was absorbed in the show, Dani focused on their reactions. When Sara's white-gloved hand saluted her fallen partner, a few sniffles could be heard, followed by teasing giggles. When Corsetti stood up for her in the diner, there were a few cheers, quickly silenced so no one missed a line. Women whooped when Christina appeared and the two women shared their first kiss.

Dani knew there would be excitement about the on-screen romance. She listened to see if Christina's lackluster performance was noticed. A few women shifted in their chairs and someone in front of her whispered to her partner, but other than that, there was nothing.

That wasn't the case for Abby and Sara's performances at Leo Corsetti's funeral. When Bria could only get a few words of her eulogy out before breaking down, Dani heard the sniffles. When Joey stepped forward, there were cheers. "Leo Corsetti was the finest man I knew. He was a loving father who adored his only child, Bria. She was the center of his world." Joey stood taller and stared out at the congregation, many in police blue. "He was a good man who made his own judgments and never let popular opinion sway him from what was right. He stood by me when my brothers in blue turned their backs. When they threatened me, he stood up. It didn't matter where we were or who we were with, he always made sure I knew he was proud of me. He taught me what real loyalty is. To Leo Corsetti, loyalty was earned by people, not a uniform." Then Joey turned and hugged a sobbing Bria. Dani smiled. Bria wasn't the only one sobbing.

When the credits appeared, the ovation was loud and long. Mika walked back on stage and the cheering crowd roared their approval. She allowed the ovation for twenty seconds or so before lifting a hand up and saying, "Thank you. Thank you. I'm glad you liked it." The crowd finally settled down and Mika asked, "How many of you are Binge subscribers?" Loud applause. Dani thought it was most of the room. "How many of you will be subscribing after you leave tonight?" The applause was smaller, but equally enthusiastic. "Wonderful," Mika said. "I hope you'll indulge me a moment. Please, take a seat." Mika waited while the crowd settled. "If you liked *Corsetti's Will*, we need you." She paused. "Binge has been supportive of my vision, but that will only last as long as we bring in subscribers, and those subscribers watch our show. So, I'm asking you to tell your friends, your community, your followers what you thought about the pilot. Encourage them to support us too." The audience applauded. "Now, it's time to take out your phones, because I think you're going to want a picture." She waited while they did, then took a deep breath. "Please welcome Sara Silver, our Joey Driskell!"

An enthusiastic wall of sound greeted Sara as she walked onstage carrying a microphone. She hugged Mika, and they smiled at the audience. All around Dani, cell phones were held out recording the scene. After well over a minute of applause, Mika gestured for the crowd to settle. When they finally did, Sara said, "Thank you for that incredible welcome and your generous response to *Corsetti's Will*. Did you really like it?" She grinned as they reacted. "That's great. We're very excited to be here. We have a panel later in the week and a selfie session tomorrow." She sighed theatrically. "I hope you don't get tired of us." The crowd laughed and shouted back to her. "Great, then once again, please tell everyone you know about the show. We want the world to know the power of queer fandoms. Thanks for coming." Sara waved at the audience, linked arms with Mika, and walked off stage.

* * *

With three devices open in front of her, Dani was simultaneously following Twitter, Instagram, and YouTube. "It's looking good," she said. "We've been trending all day, but down in the twenties. Now we're in the top five. Every mention is positive."

Sara took a sip of Champagne. "How was it being in there?" she asked Dani. "Could you see their reactions?"

"I couldn't see as much as I could hear. They responded to everything. They laughed when we wanted them to, cried when Corsetti died and again when you gave the funeral speech." She laughed. "And, I predict there will be a lot of lesbian sex in Las Vegas tonight. They were into that scene. In fact, I'm seeing several 'Sara's a top' hashtags."

Sara and Mika both laughed out loud. "Too bad we didn't finish the last scene with Christina," she started, then stopped. "Sorry, Mika."

"We're working on it. The casting director is searching for a body double so we can finish the episode. You may have to be a top again."

"Whatever you need." She paused. "Try not to blame Christina too much. She's young, and that woman really did a number on her." When Mika talked with Christina, Sara was relieved the actress shared everything about her relationship with Luciana Raithman. Christina confessed that the sex scene with Sara felt like she was cheating on Raithman. That's when Landis asked Mika to release her from her contract.

Mika frowned. "Sara, that was a bad situation from start to finish. Christina's done irreparable damage to her reputation. I won't talk, but the town is small, and between the crew and her wooden performance, she'll only work in Raithman's films. And I predict Luciana will dump her sooner rather than later. I don't trust that woman."

Dani watched their exchange, looking troubled. "What is it?" Mika asked.

"I'm worried that the panel is the last interaction you have with the fans. You announce Christina, and then we leave."

"What do you suggest?" Mika topped off her glass and lifted the bottle to offer more to the others. Sara nodded and Dani pushed her glass toward Mika.

"Well..." She looked to Sara, then back at Mika. "I know you didn't think it was possible, but what if..."

Mika held up her hand to stop Dani from speaking. "No. It's too much to ask." Her tone was clipped.

Sara looked at Mika. "What is it? Something you don't want to ask me?" She looked at Dani, who looked to Mika. "Hey, I can say no. Just ask."

Mika inclined her head to Dani, who hesitated then turned to Sara. "I thought maybe you could do a benefit concert. We could select a LGBTQ charity and donate the proceeds. It might offset any bad feelings the fandom has over Christina."

"I wondered if that was it," Sara said. "It is too much. Not to ask, but to pull off in a short amount of time. Even if you could find a venue, I'm not prepared, and I won't go on stage with a half-assed show."

"I don't want you to think we're taking advantage of you, Sara. It was just a thought Dani had as part of this trip," Mika said smoothly, then turned her focus to Dani. "I believe we'll be able to handle the situation at the panel. I'm not concerned."

But she looked concerned, Sara thought. They all were. The announcement could destroy the goodwill they'd created with the premiere.

A knock interrupted them, and Sara crossed the room to answer. When she looked through the peephole, all her worries faded to the background. Abby was standing in the hall, and Sara couldn't help her delighted squeal. She threw the door open and wrapped Abby in a hug. "I didn't know you were coming tonight. Get in here and drink Champagne with us."

"The commercial wrapped early, so I got a flight. Tell me everything. How did it go? I got stopped a few times in the lobby and people seemed enthusiastic."

Sara held on to her arm and checked the hallway. "Where are your bags? Did they have a room for you? I thought everything was booked."

"Mika booked our rooms for the entire convention. I'm just down the hall." She gestured over her shoulder. "Probably next to you, so no wild parties." She waved to Dani and pointed at the electronics. "What are they saying?"

"We're trending!" Sara threw her arms in the air and did a little dance.

Abby looked at her, amusement lighting her eyes. "Is that how you dance on stage? What do you people do during the long winters? No dance lessons in Minnesota?"

Sara grabbed Abby's hands, lifted them above her head, and danced with her. When Abby protested, Sara pulled her close and spun them around. After a few turns, Abby put a hand on Sara's shoulder. "You're going to make me sick before I even get a drink. Let me go, crazy woman."

"So, it went well?" Abby asked Dani.

Dani handed her one of the tablets and pointed to the screen. "We've been trending since Mika told them to take out their phones and get a picture of Sara."

"And I suppose you think that's all about you." Abby quirked an eyebrow at Sara. "What was the reaction like?" she asked Mika.

"They were ecstatic. Dani was in the room during the screening. She said they were with us the entire time."

"So, we have a hit? Please tell me we have a hit. I have bills."

The arrival of room service interrupted them, and when Mika went to the door, Dani apologized. "I'm sorry I put you on the spot earlier. I shouldn't have brought it up."

"Brought what up?" Abby asked.

Dani looked uncomfortable, so Sara answered, "Dani thought it would be a good idea if I did a benefit concert. And it is a good idea, but I can't put a show together that quickly."

"I know. I'm sorry…" The pop of the Champagne cork halted the rest of the sentence, and Mika moved around topping off glasses and pouring Abby her first.

"Did we toast?" Abby asked. Before anyone answered, she said, "To *Corsetti's Will*," and lifted her glass. "Cheers." They touched glasses and there was a moment of silence as they drank. "Ooh, that's good," Abby said. "I've never had fancy Champagne. Let's make sure this is a hit because I want to drink more of this."

Sara leaned back on the couch, happy Abby was there. As soon as she walked in the room, everything brightened. Despite a day of work, her dark eyes sparkled and her smile was as relaxed and easy as always. Sara couldn't take her eyes off the stunning woman.

"I've got it!" Abby called out, startling the rest of the group. "Karaoke. Sara can host a karaoke night. She doesn't have to sing, she just has to emcee it."

Dani sat upright, Mika looked intrigued, and Sara groaned. "Karaoke? Really? Are you trying to kill me?"

Abby squinted her eyes at Sara. "Have you ever done karaoke?" At the look on Sara's face, she said, "Aha! You haven't. You've been famous too long. Karaoke is fun. Drunk girls singing 'I Kissed A Girl'? There's nothing better."

Sara tipped her champagne glass to Abby. "Your karaoke nostalgia is moving." She looked at Dani. "Abby's in. She'll be hosting Corsetti Karaoke. If we're lucky, there'll be lots of video."

"Nuh-uh," Abby shook a finger at Sara. "You're the star. I'm the unknown. It's gotta be you." She stood and made her way to the ice bucket. "How many glasses do I need to drink to catch up with you guys? I'm up for it. Just give me a number."

They laughed as Abby filled her glass, waited for the bubbles to recede, then topped it off. Mika looked between Abby and Sara, a slight smile on her face. "If you're willing, I think it's a great solution. But…" She waved a finger between the two of them. "It has to be both of you. Abby, you keep the audience from pressuring Sara to sing. Sara, she's right. You're the star. Like it or not, it's your presence that will soothe the masses."

"Don't give me that smile," Sara said to Abby. "You will pay for this. Somehow, some way."

CHAPTER TWENTY

Mika stood backstage with Sara, Abby, and Alan Fletcher watching a video the production team put together for their panel appearance. When they planned the video, they'd decided to use clips from the pilot and the second episode to emphasize the relationship between Joey and Noelle. Mika hoped it didn't backfire.

Dani stood to the side filming their reactions for social media, so Mika made sure to keep a steady smile as she watched Sara, Abby, and Alan tease each other. She made a mental note to call David Stamper about bringing Alan in for the flashbacks Aniyah suggested. It would give them filler as they worked through the Christina problem.

The video finished to thunderous applause, and the group hugged. The moderator introduced Mika, and she took a deep breath, gave the actors a reassuring smile, and walked on stage. "Hello, everyone," she said as she took a seat next to the moderator.

"Mika has asked to speak with you before we introduce the rest of the panel. Mika?"

Even though the room was packed, Mika could see most of the faces smiling at her. She'd thought carefully about the tone and posture to adopt as she announced Christina's departure. David had suggested she project sympathy for the young actress, and Mika knew despite their tumultuous tenure, that was what she felt for Christina. Her voice regretful, she said, "Just before we left to come here, we got some unhappy news." The silence in the room allowed Mika to lower her voice. "Christina Landis asked to be released from her contract." Mika paused for the crowd to react and to get a sense of the room. It was what she expected.

Disappointment was the primary reaction, but there were flashes of anger too. "Christina made the decision for personal reasons which are hers to share when she's ready. All of us, the cast and crew of *Corsetti's Will*, are sad to see her go." She looked to the moderator, who had been given a heads-up about the announcement. "I'll answer any questions I can while still respecting Christina's privacy."

"Let's put any rumors to rest right now," the moderator began. "Was Christina pushed out?"

It was a question Mika hoped to be asked. It meant that there was talk about Christina's shortcomings in the pilot. She opted for a simple answer. "She was not. We were willing to work with her."

"How many episodes will Christina appear in?"

"We just finished filming Episode Four when Christina made her decision." Mika didn't add that they had a scene that needed to be completed. She took a slow, even breath, bracing herself for the next question.

"What will happen to Christina's character, Noelle Prado?"

"This is a difficult decision. The role was written for Christina, and I can't imagine anyone else playing her." It was a lie, but a necessary one. "We won't recast."

She waited a beat or two, allowing her words to sink in. "That leaves us two options with the character. I think you know from my earlier interviews how important it is to me that we portray a loving, committed relationship between two women. Joey and Noelle love each other deeply. I won't minimize their feelings by creating a story arc that would lead to their breakup. That's not the relationship they have." Mika didn't have to fake the passion she felt for this topic. "That leaves me only one option, and I understand how controversial it will be." She took a deep breath. "Noelle Prado will die in an upcoming episode."

There were gasps and a smattering of boos. Someone shouted, "Clexa all over again," and the comment was met with applause. Mika waited for the noise to die down.

"Believe me, I'm very aware of both the history of this convention and how lesbian characters have been mistreated on television. But faced with an impossible decision, I have chosen love." Mika looked around the room and saw a few women nodding. "Joey loves Noelle with all of her heart and will be devastated by her death. I am not doing this to"—Mika made air quotes—"bury a gay character." She looked around the room, making sure her words were being heard. "I'm doing this to show how deeply two women can love each other. My commitment to you is that Joey Driskell will remain a strong lesbian character." A few women started applauding, and others joined. Mika raised her voice. "And I promise you, Joey will love again." This time more women responded with applause and cheers. She knew she hadn't convinced everyone. That would take time and strong writing. Her bigger concern was how many she had lost.

"Let's bring out Joey Driskell, Sara Silver!" the moderator said.

Sara came out wearing her usual jeans, and a Corsetti and Driskell T-shirt under a black blazer. She waved at the crowd before sitting next to Mika. "Thank you. It's nice to see you all, again. I love this convention." The audience responded with loud cheers.

The moderator got right to it. "Sara, how do you feel about Noelle's death?"

"I have a little different take on it than Mika." She gave Mika a side-eye and smiled. "Or, as I like to call her, my boss." The audience laughed. "I would have been upset if the writers had chosen to have Noelle be unfaithful or suddenly leave Joey. It would be inconsistent with the character they wrote in the first episodes. She's not a flake, and like most of you, she's not the kind of person who would choose her job over her love." Mika was impressed with how natural Sara was in front of the crowd. They responded to her words and her authenticity.

"Let's bring out the rest of the cast. Abby Farina who plays Bria Corsetti and Alan Fletcher who plays Leo Corsetti." The audience applauded and cheered, but not to the level they had with Sara, who was clearly the star of the panel if not the whole convention. When Abby and Alan were seated, the moderator moved to questions about the show. "Leo Corsetti's will specified Bria can't sell the business until all open cases are closed, and Joey is the one who decides what's closed. What happens when the last case is solved? Do you have to change the name of the show?" Mika breathed a sigh of relief when the audience laughed. Maybe they hadn't lost that many fans.

"Well, at the end of the pilot, there is a pretty big case open in front of them. Joey wants to find Leo's killer, and there's a possibility that this killer has gotten away with murder before."

"You mean Joey's partner on the police force?"

"Yes. It won't be an easy case to solve."

"Will we ever find out who killed Leo?" the moderator asked.

"I'm tempted to be coy and say you have to watch the show to know that, but I won't. Yes, we will resolve Leo's murder, and no, we won't change the name of the show. We still have a rather strong-willed Corsetti." There was a pause before the audience gave a collective "ah" of understanding, then laughed at themselves.

The moderator leaned forward. "Abby, what's Sara like on set. Does she sing a lot?"

"No," Abby said. "And I try." She looked at the audience. "Sara and I are in Makeup together every morning with our artists, Tanya and Michelle. The three of us sing, but Sara refuses." In a stage whisper she added, "Truthfully, she's a little grumpy in the morning."

"Hey!" Sara protested. This time she looked to the audience and gestured to Abby with her thumb. "She's out of control. If there's chaos anywhere on the set, you can bet Abby's responsible." Sara shook her head in mock irritation.

"She's still bitter," Abby said. "Ever since I…"

Sara turned wide eyes on Abby. "Don't you dare," she started, but was drowned out by shouts from the crowd.

"First, I'd like to thank those of you who are writing fan fiction." The roar of laughter spurred Abby on. "I may or may not have found a story that I shared with Sara. And Tanya. Also, Michelle." The laughter continued, the audience delighting in their teasing banter. Sara's face was in her hands. "I think I have the story with me." Abby pretended to search her pockets.

With a screech, Sara jumped up and lunged at Abby, who laughed and threw her hands in the air, shaking her head. "I didn't," she told Sara. "It's so fun to mess with her," she said to the crowd. Mika watched the exchange, wondering how she'd missed the obvious affection between the actresses. A relationship between their characters would sizzle on-screen.

They continued answering questions from the moderator and eventually the audience. They were getting to the last few minutes when a woman asked, "Sara, who would you like to play your new girlfriend?"

Before she could answer, someone yelled out, "Abby," and the audience laughed, then applauded. Sara and Abby looked at each other with wide eyes, then joined the laughter.

"I'll be happy to work with anyone," Sara said. "Even Abby." She waited for the laughter to fade before adding, "But thankfully, that's Mika's department."

Not missing the opportunity, the moderator asked, "So what about it, Mika? Bria and Joey?"

Mika laughed with the crowd, then said, "Stranger things have happened." The audience whooped their approval, but Mika held up her hands. "For example," she drawled and gestured to Sara to pick up the thread.

"This will be definitely be strange," Sara said, "but I hope you'll consider joining us. Tomorrow night, Abby and I are hosting Corsetti Karaoke. All proceeds from the evening will be donated to charities that support LGBTQ youth. If you're interested in attending, raffle tickets are for sale on the Corsetti website. The drawing will take place tomorrow morning and the winning names will be posted online. Each winning ticket is good for two people, so you won't have to attend alone."

With that, the group stood, posed on stage for a photo, then waved to the crowd as they left. Dani met them backstage. "I think we're going to be okay. I posted your announcement in its entirety. So far, the responses are positive. Look at the hashtag." She flipped her tablet so they could all see it.

#chooselove

CHAPTER TWENTY-ONE

Most days Sara liked that mornings were now a part of her life—a much different life from when she toured with the band. Today wasn't one of those days. It was four a.m. and she was wide awake.

Growing up, she had one close friend—Jeff. When the other girls talked about their best friends and sleepovers, Sara didn't get it. Playing Barbies and talking about boys didn't interest her. In middle school, when other girls formed cliques, she and Jeff played their guitars. High school was more of the same, but now they had the band to take up their time. Without any close female friendships, it was a wonder she ever figured out she was attracted to women.

The tiny Minneapolis apartment the band shared after high school was a magnet for all kinds of artists and musicians. One night Lacy was there, playing guitar and singing in a smoky, coffee-house voice. That night Sara had her first meaningful kiss. Less than a week later, she lost her virginity on a twin bed. Lacy didn't stay around, and Sara's heart was broken only as long as it took for another girl to come along. That set the pattern for her dating life. She had short, intense affairs that sputtered out with minimal heartache.

She hadn't dated since the backstage pictures were posted. For a while, everyone new was a threat to her privacy, so she got in the habit of keeping to herself and her small group of friends and family. Last night, she'd spent hours thinking about how it felt to fall in love, what it meant to have a friend, and what happened if you, God forbid, fell in love with a friend.

Abby was the first woman friend she'd had. It wasn't comfortable to admit that—like there was some mystery of life she missed out on—but there it was, and she was loath to ruin it.

They still hadn't talked about how Abby had stood up for her when the *Rolling Stone* article came out. Sara was deeply touched, so much so that she wasn't sure how to even bring it up.

Now, Mika's answer to the question of Abby as her new love interest was wreaking havoc on her emotions. Sara liked having Abby as a friend, and she had no interest in falling for a straight woman. But she knew she was starting to crush out on her straight friend, and that wasn't good. There was no such thing as a harmless crush. What if Mika made Bria and Joey a couple, and Abby figured out Sara had deeper feelings? She loved their friendship. No. Not loved. She valued their friendship. Abby was good for her.

With a groan, she turned on the light and got out of bed. She'd take a shower, order breakfast, and then maybe put on a hat and sunglasses to wander the Vegas Strip. She could walk off all this energy and get Abby firmly back in the friend zone.

An hour later, she was tucking her hair under a baseball cap when her cell rang. "Nathan," she answered, thrilled at the distraction her brother would provide. "Are you packed?"

"Do you realize you have asked me the same question every day for the last month?"

"Not true," she said. "I don't talk to you every day, so that's an impossibility. Why are you calling me so early? It's five thirty here."

"And yet, you're awake. Did the panel crash? Is that why you're up?"

"No. Mika's a genius. This was the perfect place to announce it. You know I had my doubts, but she really sold them on it."

"That's good. How's social media responding?" Nathan's words were garbled.

"Are you chewing? Because that's gross, and you know how much I hate eating sounds."

She heard Nathan take another bite and say, "Sorry," through a mouthful of what she guessed to be toast.

"Yeah, but you're really not, are you?" Even gross chewing sounds couldn't diminish the affection she felt for her brother. "Social media is better than expected. Dani posted the video of Mika's announcement and that's gone over well. I think we're going to be okay. Even better, Mika heard from the network and subscriptions are up significantly since the premiere."

"That's great, Sar. So, what's going to happen with your character? Will she have a girlfriend this season?"

Leave it to Nathan to find her sore spot. "We-ll," she drew out the word. "Someone in the audience suggested Abby, and people seemed to like it. Mika said, and I quote, 'Stranger things have happened.' I'm not sure what that means. She was probably stringing them along."

"That's good, isn't it? You like her." He took another bite of toast and crunched in her ear. "Didn't you say she's a good actress? You won't have to tiptoe around her like you did Christina."

There was no way Sara would tell him about her possible crush. "That's true, but don't you think it could be awkward? I mean, Abby and I are friends. At least with Christina it was acting. We were just colleagues." She decided to get off the topic before he figured out there was more to her concerns. "Anyway, enough about that. Are you ready for the move?"

"Yep. Everything's all set. I'll be there the day of the closing, and the truck with our stuff is coming the next day. Are you ready? You haven't lost the down payment at the craps table, have you?"

"Not yet. I can't wait for you to get here. You're going to love LA."

"Me too. I gotta go. See ya soon." Sara felt calmer after they hung up. Once Nathan was here, and they were in their new house, this thing with Abby would be put in perspective. She flipped on the TV and poured herself another cup of coffee.

* * *

"We're going out to lunch, so be ready in ten. You won't need the hat and glasses. I'll pick you up." Abby hung up before Sara could respond, smiling as she thought about her friend grumbling. Sara Silver was almost the best part of this job. Obviously, the best part was the paycheck, but Sara was a close second.

Abby knocked on Sara's door, and when it opened she was grabbed and pulled inside. "Where are we going?" Sara demanded. "Am I supposed to look nice or dress down?"

"Dress like you always do. Wear that black blazer, but a plain shirt or T-shirt. Wear a hat if you want, but you won't need one. We're going to eat at the Bellagio and watch the fountains."

"Be right back," Sara said, disappearing into the bedroom of the suite. "Have you ordered a car?"

"Yes, my queen. You don't have slum it in the cab line," Abby called back.

"I thought by now you'd have gotten enough fangirling, but if not, my escort and I will meet you in the lobby. I need to put my hair up, then I'll be ready."

There was a knock on the door, and Abby answered. "Hello," she said to the man. "Are you our escort?"

"Yes, ma'am. I'll wait out here until you're ready."

He took them down the express elevator and out a back door where a town car waited. The driver took them on a meandering route behind the Strip before pulling up to a side entrance. An official-looking man greeted them. "Welcome to the Bellagio, Ms. Silver and Ms. Farina. We'll escort you through the casino to your restaurant."

Three men in suits walked with them, one in front and one on either side. Sara didn't look around as they walked, but Abby did. She was new to this life and enjoyed watching people, trying to guess who they were. A couple of times she heard Sara's name, but Sara never reacted.

Inside the restaurant, they were seated in a private alcove with floor-to-ceiling windows overlooking the fountains. "This is nice," Sara said. She leaned forward, taking in the expanse of water below them.

Abby checked her phone. "We've got a while before they start. Hungry?"

"Starving. I had breakfast at five." Abby made a face, and Sara shrugged. "I don't know what it was. I just couldn't sleep."

"Are you going to need a nap? You better not be grumpy tonight. I expect Happy Sara at karaoke."

Sara's brow furrowed. "That's the second time you've said that. Am I really that grumpy?"

She sounded so hurt, Abby was quick to reassure her. "No. You're never grumpy, but you get quiet when you're tired, and you can't be quiet tonight."

"I won't be. I'll take a nap if I need one." Sara puffed out her cheeks. "I may also need a couple of drinks."

"Deal," Abby said. "Now, let's talk about a plan. The doors open a half hour before we start. That gives the crowd just enough time to loosen up, but not enough time to get obnoxiously drunk. Still, we'll need to warm them up."

Sara cocked her head. "Warm them up? Like, tell jokes?"

"No, no jokes. We'll have to sing two or three songs while they sign up to perform."

Narrowing her eyes, Sara said, "I thought I wasn't singing."

"You'll be singing, but singing karaoke is different. And, good news, you'll be singing with me." Abby grinned at her.

"I didn't know you sang." Sara paused. "Actually, I know you can't sing, unless you've been faking tone deafness."

"What you hear in the makeup chair is a tad worse than my normal singing voice. That's the joy of karaoke. Although some people have good voices and think they're going to get discovered at karaoke, most just go up and have fun." Abby waved a finger between the two of them. "Which is what we'll do. Do you know 'Goodbye Earl' by The Chicks? That's a good one to start with. The vocals are easy, and the chorus is a good sing-along."

"Yeah, I know it. I don't think I've ever sung it in public, but I can probably do it."

"You're overthinking this. Have fun. Try to sound like Natalie Maines." With that, Abby broke out her best Chicks impression by belting out the first lines of "Goodbye Earl" at the top of her lungs.

Sara started laughing and held up her hands. "Okay, okay, I get it. Please don't sing any more. I'll watch the video this afternoon and practice my twang. What else? You said two or three songs."

"We can't take any of the songs we think the audience might want to sing. Nothing too current. And none of your music." Abby tapped her chin. "How about something from the eighties?"

Sara thought. "Madonna? 'Like a Virgin'?"

"Possible. 'Girls Just Wanna Have Fun'?" Abby countered.

Sara looked up, her head bobbing to an imaginary beat. "This is weird, but Cyndi Lauper and Natalie Maines kinda sound alike. Let's pick something different." Their food came, and they stopped talking as they fixed their sandwiches.

"Here you go." Abby pointed out the window at the fountains just beginning to bubble. She reached for the volume and turned it up, so they could hear the music playing outside. Abby watched Sara as the synchronized water danced below them. When the largest of the fountains boomed high in the air, Sara turned to her with a huge grin.

"That is so cool," she whispered. Abby thought it was cute that she didn't want her words to disrupt the music. They watched until the last of the water dropped back into the lake. They sat quietly for nearly a minute before Sara spoke. "Can I tell you something?"

"Sure."

"Right before she quit, Christina told me you started the women-supporting-women tweets." Sara cleared her throat, and Abby thought she might be fighting back tears. "Other than Nathan and Jeff, no one has ever stood up for me like that. I've been trying to find a way to thank you, but I owe you more than a thank-you. It meant so much to me."

"Cars are nice," Abby deadpanned.

Sara laughed. "You think I'm made of money?"

"I happen to know you're buying a ten-million-dollar house. So, yes, I think you're made of money."

Sara's face reflected an emotion Abby couldn't quite identify. "This is going to sound stupid, but why did you do it? Why go to all that trouble for someone you'd just met?"

"It didn't feel like we just met," Abby said.

"No. It feels like we've known each other for a long time."

CHAPTER TWENTY-TWO

Sara had played in sold-out arenas and iconic concert halls, but she couldn't remember a better evening. When she and Abby started singing "Goodbye Earl," the crowd joined in even before the chorus. They performed three songs, finishing with a cheeky version of "I Got You Babe." Although Abby was a better singer than she let on, her real talent was doing impressions. Her Sonny Bono had Sara laughing so hard she couldn't sing her part, so Abby sang the entire song, switching easily between the voices of Sonny and Cher. As the crowd screamed their approval, Sara threw an arm around her and said to the people hidden behind their phones, "I hope someone got that." They laughed, and she added, "Be sure to tag me!"

If there was backlash from Christina's departure, it wasn't from this crowd. The women were fun and seemed intent on making Sara and Abby laugh. Toward the end of the evening, a woman who had sung a Barry Manilow classic asked the DJ a question. He shook his head. She clasped her hands together and gave him a pleading look, but he shook his head again and mouthed, "Sorry."

Sara looked at Abby, who was dancing along with the current group of singers, not paying attention. She hopped off her stool and called out, "Hey." The woman turned, her eyes widening when she saw it was Sara. "Everything okay?" Sara asked.

After a short conversation, Sara walked back to the stage, spoke to the DJ, and took the microphone from the group of laughing women who had just sung "Girl Crush" to each other. She waited a moment for the crowd to quiet before speaking. "Linda—you know her as 'Copacabana.'" The crowd cheered. "Made a very special request on behalf of her best friend. EJ just lost her amazing father who loved and supported her unconditionally." To the woman seated next to Linda, she said, "EJ, this week, Abby and I have learned that *Corsetti* fans are kind and supportive people." She made a wide gesture encompassing the crowd. "You won't find a better group of friends." She paused while the audience cheered. "Linda said you're a fan of my music and asked if I'd sing something for you. Abby was supposed to make sure I didn't hog the microphone and turn this into a concert, so I promise this is the only song I'll sing." She grinned when they booed. "This one's not mine, but I wish it was. She nodded at the DJ and the opening piano notes of "Songbird" started. "For EJ and her dad."

Sara concentrated on getting the opening notes right. The crowd would be forgiving, but she knew Twitter wouldn't. When she felt comfortable, she looked out to the crowd for a moment, then turned her gaze to Abby and saw a shimmer of tears. Sara gave her a soft smile, and Abby smiled back sheepishly, wiping her eyes. Sara wanted to reach out to Abby, to pull her in and hold her. The thought shook her, and she forced her eyes back to the crowd, reminding herself they were being recorded.

As the last notes faded, Sara gave the mic to the DJ and worked her way to Linda and EJ. She pulled the crying woman into her arms and said, "I'm so sorry." They stood like that for a moment, then Sara stepped back and reached for Linda's hand. "You're a great friend. Take care of her."

At the end of the two-hour show, security escorted Abby and Sara to a side room while the crowd cleared. "You should do comedy. When you were both Sonny and Cher? I couldn't stop laughing." Recalling the moment, Sara started laughing again.

"Nah," Abby said. "Comedy's not as much fun."

"Isn't that an oxymoron or something?"

Abby held up her hand and ticked her fingers. "No punching, no car chases, no hot sex scenes."

Sara wasn't sure she'd heard correctly. "Did you say sex scenes?"

"That's right. There aren't many sex scenes in comedy."

Sara's mind immediately went to the scenes she'd done with Christina. What would it be like if that were Abby? She blinked away the images. When she found her voice, she asked, "How many sex scenes have you done? Because the ones I've been in were not fun."

Abby leaned in and whispered, "Maybe you haven't done them with the right people." Sara caught her breath. Was Abby flirting with her? Shit.

Before she could respond, Dani walked in. "There you are. Come on, the car's here."

They left the room and were joined at the door by two security people who escorted the group to their car. Although there was plenty of room in the back seat, Abby insisted on sitting up front with the driver, whom she immediately engaged in conversation that Sara couldn't hear. Dani was talking to her, but Sara couldn't focus on what she was saying. Was Abby uncomfortable or embarrassed by the flirting?

This time the driver took them around the front of the Bellagio. When the car stopped at a light, Abby yelled to the back seat, "Quick! Get out," then jumped out of the car before Sara or Dani could respond.

"Shit, Abby," Dani yelled and followed after her. "I'm responsible for you."

"Sorry," Sara said to the driver as she opened her door and ran to where Abby stood grinning on the sidewalk. Next to her Dani was talking and waving her arms, but Abby wasn't paying attention to her. Her eyes were focused on Sara.

"Hurry," she said, reaching for Sara's hand. "We have five minutes." Sara just managed to get hold of Dani before they were weaving in and out of the crowds. Sara turned back to apologize to a group of women holding giant daquiris when Abby pushed her against a decorative concrete fence and squeezed in next to her. She made room for Dani on her other side.

In front of them, a black pool of water reflected the lights of the Bellagio. Abby threw her arm around Sara's shoulder as the first notes of "The Prayer" played. Like the song, the water moved slowly in graceful arcs. As the music built, more fountains were added and a light spray blew back on them. When the chorus soared, geysers shot into the sky and collapsed back on themselves, adding to the power of the music. Sara didn't move until the last dancing streams slipped back into the lake and the song faded out. She hugged Abby to her side. "Thank you. That was amazing. This whole night has been amazing."

The drive back to their hotel was slowed by the heavy traffic of the Vegas Strip, but Sara didn't mind. Abby was in the back seat next to her, their thighs touching. The lights and the crowds were new experiences, and she wished they could jump out again and disappear into the excitement. Impulsively, she asked, "Do you guys want to come to my room for a drink? I'm too wound up to go to bed."

"Only if you order fancy Champagne," Abby said.

"You can't have good Champagne after drinking beer. It's a waste. You can have mediocre Champagne. Dani, want to join us?"

"No, thanks. I'm beat. You two have fun."

* * *

"I'm going to get out of these clothes. I'll be back in a few minutes. Order the Champagne," Abby called over her shoulder.

Abby was just closing her own door when the room service attendant rolled a cart up to Sara's door. "Here, I'll take care of that." She plucked the bill from the woman's hand.

"Um, we're really not supposed to…" the woman started, but Abby had already added a tip and was scrawling Sara's signature. She knocked on the door and called, "Room service." Sara opened the door, and Abby spread her arms wide. "Here we are," she said before pushing the cart through the doorway. As she passed Sara, she whispered, "Your tip made her very happy."

"It's fine," she heard Sara say to the attendant. "Thank you." The door closed and Sara leaned against it. "Why are you always spending my money?"

Abby furrowed her brow. "I'm not really sure, but I know I have fun doing it." She pulled the bottle out of the ice bucket. "I didn't have her open it. That might have been a mistake."

Sara let Abby struggle for a few moments before reaching for the bottle. "Give it to me. You'll have Champagne everywhere."

Abby stepped back, her hands in the air. "By all means. Show off your superior skills." In seconds, Sara had eased the cork out with the lightest of pops. Abby sighed. "Fine. Your skills are superior."

When they were settled onto the couch, Abby pulled out her phone. "Let's see if Dani posted anything." She set her glass on the table and found the *Corsetti* page. "Hmm. Not yet. She probably went right to bed."

"Even Dani has to sleep sometimes." Sara took a drink of the Champagne. "This isn't bad." She put her glass on the table. "I don't think she had as much fun as we did."

"It was fun, wasn't it? We'll definitely do that again." She'd had just enough to drink that she felt reckless. It felt like Sara had been about to respond to her flirting when Dani walked in on them. She gave Sara a salacious grin. "I know what we can do." A couple of taps, and the site came up, but Abby pretended she was still searching. When she thought it was believable, she turned the phone for Sara to see.

It took several seconds before Sara realized what Abby had found. "No." She groaned. "No more fan fiction."

"Come on, these are fun."

"These?" Sara raised an eyebrow. "How much time do you spend reading this stuff?"

It was a fair question, and even though Abby ignored it, she was afraid her face gave her away. The first time she searched she'd been pleased that there were any stories since the show hadn't even aired. It was a testament to the power of the trailer and the fandom Dani was building on social media. But when she read through the archive, she saw few stories were actually based on the show's characters. Most were about Christina and Sara.

That night, she'd spent an hour picking out the perfect one to read in Makeup. A couple nights later, she'd gone back. There weren't many new stories, but there were more views. Two hours later, she had to admit what she was really doing: she was drawn to the intensity of the descriptions of physical and emotional intimacy between Christina and Sara.

She tried to be nonchalant. "I haven't looked at many. Most of it is RPF."

"RPF? You even know the lingo?" Sara eyed her. "Are you secretly writing fan fiction?"

"Real people fiction." She looked up at Sara. "Or in this case, Sara and Christina fiction."

Sara's eyes were wide, and her voice rose a notch. "Really?"

Abby laughed. "Oh yeah. Want me to read one?" She lifted her eyebrows in challenge.

With a quick movement, Sara snatched the phone and jumped off the couch. "This time I get to pick."

"You won't embarrass me. Go ahead. Do your worst." Embarrassment wouldn't be the issue.

"We'll see. Drink your Champagne. I'll just be a minute here."

Abby laughed and reached for the bottle. She couldn't remember the last time she'd had such a fun evening. As Sara scanned the phone, Abby watched emotions play across her features: laughter, surprise, shock.

"We have a winner!" Sara lifted both arms over her head in triumph.

"Okay, give it to me. I'm ready." Abby beckoned for the phone.

With quick flicks, Sara scrolled to the scene she wanted. "Just so you know, I'm being very kind. I should make you read this in front of Tanya and Michelle." She handed the phone to Abby. "Check out the description."

Abby looked at the top. "RPF *Corsetti's Will*?"

"No, the description." Sara leaned over and pointed.

"Abby finally admits her feeling for Sara."

Sara clapped her hands in delight. "You can start with the line, 'Sara, I've wanted you for so long.'"

Abby reached for her glass and took a big swallow. "Am I losing my virginity in this scene?"

Sara dropped back on the couch and handed Abby the phone. "I don't know. Have you slept with a woman before?"

"Not yet." She took a deep breath and read. "*I've wanted you so long, Sara. Why won't you kiss me?*" Abby looked at Sara, who was practically bouncing with excitement. "Is this all about me?"

"It's all about how you worship me." Sara batted her eyes, then gestured with her hand for Abby to continue reading.

"*You have to know how I feel about you.*'

"*How do you feel about me?' Sara whispered, drawing closer to Abby. 'It's okay to say it.*'

"*Abby took a deep breath. 'I'm in love with you.' Sara pulled Abby into her strong arms and Abby got lost in her pale blue eyes. 'I'm in love with you,' she repeated before lifting her hand to stroke Sara's cheek. 'I've never met anyone like you.' She looked to Sara's mouth, unconsciously licking her lips. Sara moved closer and Abby couldn't take it any longer. She closed the distance. The kiss was a revelation. It was soft and gentle, yet insistent and demanding. Sara wasn't just kissing her, she was possessing her. When Sara's tongue demanded entrance, Abby whimpered and she opened to her.*"

Abby cleared her throat and looked at Sara. "Satisfied?" She put the phone down and picked up her glass. She was sweating. Why did the damn story have to be so close to her fantasies?

"Oh, there's a lot more. Sara is a very good teacher." Sara's big smile faded when she looked at Abby. "What's wrong?"

Abby forced her best smile. "Whew." She fanned her face, looking anywhere but at Sara.

She could feel Sara studying her. "I'm sorry," she said. "I thought, when you brought in the other story…I didn't think it would make you uncomfortable. I'm so sorry." Sara put her hand on Abby's arm and then pulled it back quickly. "Sorry," she said again, shaking her head.

"No." Abby sat up and reached for Sara. "No. It's not like that. That's not it."

Sara looked at Abby's hand on her arm. "Then what is it? What's wrong? You're clearly uncomfortable."

Abby groaned, furious at herself. She'd started this. "It's nothing. Can we leave it at that? Please? Here, I'll keep reading."

Sara shook her head. "Abby, I did something. Tell me what happened."

Abby put her head in her hands. What was she doing? She felt a gentle touch on her shoulder. She lifted her head and looked into those eyes, and just like the story, she said, "Why won't you kiss me?"

Sara blinked several times and withdrew her hand from Abby's shoulder. She started to slide back, but Abby stopped her with a hand on her forearm. "Oh, fuck it," Abby said under her breath. Then, louder, "I'd like to kiss you."

Sara still didn't seem to be absorbing her words. "You want to kiss me?"

For some reason, Sara's confusion gave Abby the push she needed. "Yes. That's what's wrong. I want to kiss you." She reached out to cup Sara's face and closed the distance between them.

She leaned forward and placed a soft kiss on Sara's lips. When Sara still didn't move, it crossed Abby's mind to accept the message Sara was sending, but she couldn't. Now that she'd voiced her feelings, she didn't want to go back. She moved closer, sliding a hand under Sara's hair to the back of her neck.

Sara's eyes went wide at the touch, and she took Abby's face in her hands, searching her eyes before finally kissing her back. And just like in the damn story, Abby whimpered. When had a kiss ever felt like this? Abby opened her mouth and Sara captured her lips. A barely there touch of tongue on her upper lip excited her with possibility, and she pushed further into the kiss. When their tongues met, Sara's blue eyes opened again, and she pulled back, breathing hard. "Abby, is this..." She moved her hand from Abby's face to her collarbone. "Are you okay with this?"

"So okay," Abby whispered before kissing her again. Sara responded by pulling her even closer. Abby made another little sound she didn't recognize and wrapped her arms around Sara's neck. "You are an amazing kisser."

Sara's hand returned to Abby's face. "So are you." She pulled back a fraction. "When did you decide you wanted this?"

"I don't know. It feels like I've always wanted this with you."

Sara searched her eyes. "We've never really talked about anything like this. Are you…"

"Gay? I have no idea. I'm ridiculously attracted to you. And I keep reading those stories. Does that mean I'm gay?"

"Have you been with a woman before?" Sara shook her head when Abby opened her mouth to answer. "Sorry, that's not any of my business."

Abby leaned in and kissed her again. "No, I haven't been with a woman before, but I have definitely been attracted to women. Just not enough to act on it."

"That's different, now?"

Abby took the phone out of Sara's hand and moved closer. "Very different."

CHAPTER TWENTY-THREE

Keys in hand, Sara pulled through the gate and up to the garage of their new home. She stood, one hand on the roof of the car as Nathan pulled in beside her. He opened his door, a huge smile on his face. "I can't believe it. This place is incredible."

She turned to look at the six-thousand-square-foot home. "Do you think it's too big? Five bedrooms seems like a lot until you figure one for you, me, and a suite for Mom and Dad. That only leaves two guest rooms, and you know the guys and their families are gonna want to stay."

"I don't think it's too much, and who cares if it is? You can afford it." He put his arm around her shoulder and they walked together through the front door.

"Wait 'til you see the fireplace," she said. "In fact, the whole house. We have some serious furniture shopping to do, but we need a decorator."

"Afraid I'm going to shit it up?"

"No, because you and your horrible taste will not be allowed outside your room."

Sara's phone rang, and she grinned when she saw who it was. "Hello, Abby."

"Open the gate," Abby yelled. "I have some fancy Champagne to celebrate your new home."

"Hold on, I have to remember how to do it from inside the house." After several minutes of fruitless searching for the magic conduit to the gate, she finally went out to her car, activated the remote, and waited for Abby to pull up into the driveway.

"You forgot about me," Abby said as she got out of her car.

Sara pulled her into a tight hug. "Trust me, that would never happen." Since returning from Vegas, she hadn't seen Abby, but they'd talked and texted every day. Sara had worried that their night of Champagne-buzzed kissing would lead to awkwardness or regret—Abby's, not hers. But Abby had dispelled that worry on the plane back to LA.

"So we kissed last night," she'd said when they were settled in their first-class seats.

Sara had been relieved that Abby broached the subject, but at the same time, she wasn't ready to hear it was a mistake. "We did," was all she said.

Abby had squeezed her hand briefly and whispered, "We should do it again."

In the few days since their return, Sara had been busy packing her LA apartment and finalizing the purchase of the house. Abby had gone to visit her parents in Palm Springs and had only just returned. Sara couldn't believe how good she looked. "I didn't forget about you. I just can't figure out how to open the gate from the inside."

"Well figure it out, because I'm not waiting out there every time I come to see you."

"I have an extra opener I can give you." Abby pulled a cooler out of the back of her car, and Sara couldn't resist giving her a kiss on the cheek. "I'm so glad you're here. Come on, you have to meet Nathan."

They walked into the house, Sara calling her brother's name as they went. "Did you bring glasses?" she asked as they walked through to the kitchen.

Abby opened the small cooler and pulled out two bottles of Champagne and plastic flutes. "Don't worry, I thought of everything. There's even orange juice in here if, God forbid, you want to dilute fancy Champagne."

"Did you buy this?" Sara asked, looking at the bottles of Dom Perignon. "What are you, suddenly made of money?"

"I'd like to take credit, but Katie sent it as a housewarming. She said she got you something too."

"That was nice of her. Let's have a glass now, but don't let me have more than one. I'm so happy I could easily drink a bottle myself."

Abby laughed. "Why is that a problem?"

"The truck is coming soon." She looked around for Nathan. "Where is he? Didn't he hear me yell?" Sara walked to the edge of the kitchen and called through the house, "Nathan Silver, get your ass down here!"

"Sara, is your brother blond, buff, and pasty white?" Abby asked.

Walking back in the kitchen, Sara followed Abby's gaze. "Good God," she said when she caught sight of a shirtless Nathan dangling his feet in the pool. "I guess I should be thankful he's not down to his underwear." She walked over to the door and slid it open. "We have company. Put your shirt on and come and meet Abby."

"Come out here, Sara," he said in response. "It's incredible. We are going to have the most amazing parties."

"And who will we invite? The only friend I have is currently opening a bottle of Champagne in the kitchen."

"Nope, she's right behind you. Take one of these glasses from me." Abby extended her hands toward Sara, who grabbed the flute closest to her. She walked to the pool and handed another to Nathan. "Hi, I'm Abby. Also known as the only friend Sara has."

"Nice to meet you, Abby. Thanks for taking the pressure off of me."

Sara gestured between them. "You two. Hysterical. Abby, that's Nathan—my freeloading brother."

"Freeloading?" He looked to Abby. "You know she begged me to move here."

"Only because I was afraid you would waste away without me."

Abby kicked off her sandals and plopped down next to Nathan. She dropped her legs in the water, sighing in contentment. "Pools are the best," she said to Sara. "Come here." She patted the concrete next to her.

Sara obeyed but left a foot of space between them. Abby slid closer, entwining her leg with Sara's. "Congrats on your new home." She lifted her glass in a toast as she swung their joined legs through the cool water. Sara felt a thrill at the close contact.

"Is it going to be a relief to have her gone?" Nathan asked.

Abby stopped swinging their feet. "I didn't work with her much. I usually film with Sara early in the week. Christina came in Thursday and Friday to do their sexy scenes." She waggled her eyebrows at Nathan.

"What are the rest of the people like?" he asked. "Mika Williams was kind of a snob when I met her at the Golden Globes."

"Listen to you." Abby affected a posh accent. "When I met her at the Golden Globes." She pushed him lightly. "You sound like you've been in Hollywood for years."

A sound from Sara's phone interrupted their conversation, and she popped up. "The truck's here. Come on, Nathan. This is where you earn your keep."

"I'm not carrying anything," he said. "That's why you hired movers."

"Quit whining. You're helping direct them. Gonna stay out here and bask in the sun?" she asked Abby.

Abby was already pulling her feet out of the water. "Nope. I'm here to help, then drink. Mostly to drink. Do you have anything we can dry our feet on?"

Sara looked at Nathan's T-shirt and lunged for it, but he grabbed it out of her hand and quickly threw it on. "Still too slow," he mocked, leading her into the house.

It was after seven when the truck finally pulled out of the gate and disappeared down the street. Sara threw herself onto the sectional now set up facing the fireplace. "That's it. No more." Nathan plopped down beside her.

Abby appeared out of the kitchen. "Are we drinking now? I'm ready for the rest of the fancy Champagne."

"God, yes. We are drinking all of the fancy Champagne you want." Sara pulled herself up and walked toward Abby. "You are the best friend ever. I cannot believe you made both of our beds and unpacked the kitchen." She wrapped her arms around Abby. "For that you get a big, sweaty, stinky hug."

"Ew." Abby pushed against Sara, but Sara only pulled her tighter. Abby gave in and hugged her back. "It's my dad's rule. Always set up your beds first. That way when you feel like this"—she squeezed Sara—"you can collapse into them."

"Your dad's a genius. Tell him that next time you see him."

"He'll be glad you think so. Now let go of me, so I can get our drinks. And since I unpacked the kitchen, I know where the champagne glasses are. We will be drinking our fancy Champagne in fancy glasses."

"Anyone still hungry?" Sara asked as she followed Abby into the kitchen. "There's a whole pizza in there." Sara took the Champagne out of the refrigerator, and Abby grabbed glasses. "That's a yes, then?" She eyed her brother, who had followed them and was hovering.

"Yes. Please tell me it's not vegetarian. I need real food." He rubbed his stomach.

"I only got one vegetarian and one cheese. It should be…" She opened the box. "Yep. Pepperoni." Sara turned with the box and bumped Abby, who was carrying the glasses. "Ope," she said. "Sorry 'bout that."

Abby placed the glasses on the island and looked at her. "What did you just say?"

Sara pulled squares off the paper towel roll while Abby poured Champagne into their glasses. She looked up at Abby. "I said, 'Sorry 'bout that.'"

"No, you said some strange Minnesota word before that. Is it Norwegian?"

Nathan and Sara stared at each other blankly. "No idea," he said. "Did you say 'uff da'?"

"No, I never say 'uff da.'" She looked at Abby "Did I?"

"It sounded like 'ope.' Like you were starting to say 'open,' but just stopped."

"Oh. Ope. Yeah, like oops. Everyone says ope." She sipped her Champagne and reached for the open pizza box. "Want one?" she asked Abby.

Nathan took a huge bite of his pizza and halfway through chewing—but long before swallowing—said, "You've never heard 'ope'?"

"God, Nathan, you're disgusting. You can't do that when we have company." Sara crinkled her nose at him.

Nathan took another bite, tucked it in his cheek, and said, "I heard you say you were going to give her a gate opener. That makes her not-company."

Abby eyed the siblings. "Are you two always like this?"

Sara, who had just taken a bite of her own, nodded. With a wicked grin, Nathan looked at his sister, took a bite, and said, "Awways."

"Okay, I'm weighing in," Abby said. "First." She made a circling motion around Nathan's face. "I'm with Sara. That's disgusting. No more." He started to protest, but when both women scowled, closed his mouth. "Second," she continued. "'Ope' is a made-up word than no one says. At least no one I know." This time they both started to speak but stopped when she held up her hand. "But, I like it, and as your first California friend, I give you permission to continue using it."

Once the pizza and Champagne were gone, Abby stretched and said, "It's time for me to head home. I'm beat."

"I'll walk you out," Sara said. "The extra opener is in my car." Abby hugged Nathan, told him he smelled, and followed Sara out. Sara stopped at her car to retrieve the opener while Abby unlocked her car and waited for her.

"It's a great house," she said, accepting the opener and putting it on her visor. "Call me if you want help tomorrow. I don't have anything going on."

Sara pulled Abby into a hug. "I won't call you for help, but you should come over. Nathan and I will just be unpacking. We can hang out by the pool."

"Sounds fun," Abby answered. "I'll call you when I get up." With that, she turned her car around and drove out the gate.

* * *

"I feel like a margarita," Nathan mumbled. They were sluggish after hours reading and dozing by the pool. Sara was drifting in and out of sleep but roused at his words.

"If you go to the store, I'll make them." She turned her face away from him, pretending to be indifferent to his answer.

He barely moved his lips. "Going to the store is women's work."

Sara opened one eye and said, "Not if you want a margarita."

"Fine." He sat up "What do we need?"

"Everything," she told him. "And don't forget to get ice."

He made a grumbling sound but shoved his feet into shoes and tugged a T-shirt over his head. "I'll be back."

"Don't forget the chips and salsa," Abby called after him.

Sara rolled her head to Abby and grinned. "Nice try, but couldn't you think of something that would force him to make two stops?"

"Short notice. It's all I could think of."

They watched his car drive through the gate before turning to each other. "I feel like we haven't had a moment alone since we got back," Sara said. "Are you sure you're okay with everything?"

"Yes, I'm very okay. I thought I was pretty clear about that."

"Yes." Sara wanted to say more but didn't know where to begin.

Abby frowned. "Do you wish it hadn't happened?"

"No," Sara said quickly. "That's not it at all. We haven't really talked since the plane. I know you said you were okay, but I'm a worrier. Maybe you realized you had too much to drink and regretted it. I was worried we'd be awkward around each other and that we ruined our friendship. I was worried about the show…"

Abby laughingly put up her hand. "Whoa, I get the picture. You went to extremes. Let's see." She ticked off on her fingers. "I drank just enough to finally tell you how I've been feeling for weeks, and our friendship is as good as ever." Abby hesitated. "I really like you, Sara. A lot."

"But." Sara looked away, not wanting to reveal how much the rest of Abby's sentence mattered even though she also had her own reservations.

"How do you feel?" Abby asked.

"I like you too," Sara said. "But…"

"The show. Would we be putting everything at risk if we…I don't know…whatever?"

Sara laughed. "If we 'whatever'? What does that mean?"

Abby flushed, something Sara had rarely seen. "If we dated."

Sara reached a hand between the chairs. Abby grasped it. "Have you really thought about this? About being with a woman?"

Abby pulled her sunglasses down her nose and gave Sara a once-over. "Are you asking if I've had fantasies about you?"

"Why do I feel like you're deliberately misunderstanding me? You know what I mean."

Abby threw her head back and laughed. "I find men and women attractive."

Sara shook her head. "This isn't like that, Abby. I find men attractive, but I don't want to have a relationship with a man. Attraction for me is much deeper than how someone looks."

"Well, no shit. It's that way for me too. In answer to the question you are so obviously trying to ask, I have had sexual attractions to women but I've never acted on them." Abby rolled to her side so she could look directly at Sara. "Haven't you wondered about why I never mentioned a boyfriend? After the first couple of conversations in Makeup, you never asked."

"I thought you were private. Either that or you were seeing someone and didn't want to talk about it."

"I wasn't being private or avoiding the conversation. There was nothing to talk about. I haven't dated anyone since I met you." Abby shifted on the lounger, and Sara hoped her sunglasses were dark enough that she couldn't see Sara's eyes drift over her body. They must not have been because Abby pulled off her own glasses. "Sara, are you checking out my boobs?"

There was no sense denying it. "They're practically in my lap. What do you expect me to do, pretend they're not there?"

Abby sat up and moved from her lounger to sit next to Sara. She reached for the glasses and deftly removed them. "Thanks for noticing." She leaned in and kissed Sara. Sara closed her eyes, enjoying the feeling of Abby's lips on hers and Abby's hand on the back of her head. Abby pulled back a little, her eyes searching Sara's. "Is this okay?" she whispered.

Sara reached for her. "Yes," she whispered back.

CHAPTER TWENTY-FOUR

"ClexaCon was a huge success. Thank you, Dani Copeland, for recognizing the potential of the conference and for making our presence possible. The latest numbers from Binge corporate show an increase of seventy-five thousand subscribers since the night of the premiere." She looked around the room. "That means your hard work—the work that every one of you has put into creating this show—is being recognized." Applause and a few whoops, followed by laughter, greeted the news.

Mika's face grew serious. "As I'm sure you've heard by now, Christina Landis has decided to leave the show." She held up a hand when the muttering started. "Her departure has left us with a major plot turn which will happen this week. We're bringing in a few familiar faces. Welcome back our two detectives from the pilot." People smiled as the two actors waved. "We'll be seeing more of them, and of Alan Fletcher playing Leo Corsetti in the coming weeks." More applause. When it faded, Mika lowered her voice. "The script in front of you is everything I could ask for in a pivotal episode." She looked around the room. "Now, it's our job to bring that story to life, and it won't be easy.

Anytime you film a major character's death, it's emotionally challenging for the actors. Sara and Abby have a difficult week in front of them. Let's make sure we're all at our best and avoid any unnecessary takes." There were nods of agreement from the seated cast and crew. "Okay, let's get started."

Mika listened as the actors read through what they were unofficially referring to as "The Death Episode." It was lighthearted and almost entirely taken up with the B storyline—a case of marital infidelity. She liked that the suspense wasn't created by the story, but by the audience knowing what was coming. Tomorrow she'd find out if it played as well on film as it did on paper.

* * *

Dani was dressed in a hot pink blazer with black cigarette pants and a graphic black-and-pink T-shirt. Where most women would pair the outfit with heels, Dani wore silver monk strap loafers. It was this very ensemble that had convinced Mika to hire her over a dozen other candidates. At the small conference table in Mika's office, Dani unloaded her bag. When her notepad and folders were arranged in their usual order, she opened her tablet and tapped the screen.

"Dani, I wanted to bring you in on where we're going with Joey's love life." Mika looked up at the sound of a knock. "Come in, Aniyah." The young writer took the open chair and pulled out her own notebook. Mika folded her hands on the table and looked at Dani. "Bria will be Joey's love interest next season. Tell me what I can expect from the fans."

Dani uncrossed her legs, tucked her feet under the chair, and crossed her ankles. "They've already begun lobbying for their favorite actresses to be cast. Several fan sites want someone butch to represent the diversity of the community. There isn't a consensus on anyone, yet." Dani tapped her pen while she thought. "What can you expect? It's hard to predict. Although you had the ClexaCon fans cheering for Abby, the people who were in that room are only a small part of our audience. Most viewers haven't seen what they saw and what we watch every day—their insane chemistry. So, you can expect some social media blow-up, maybe sniping directed at Abby." She paused. "You know the community. They expect a queer actor in this role. If Abby is the love interest, they won't give her a grace period."

"Because she's straight?" Aniyah asked.

Mika held up a hand to stave off any discussion of Abby's sexuality, but it was Dani who clarified the problem. "At this point, Abby's sexuality doesn't matter. Even if she is queer—"

"Which we absolutely cannot ask her," Mika interjected.

"Right, but if she were, it wouldn't matter. She's not out. If she came out for the role, it would look too convenient. No one would believe her, and being fake queer would be far worse than being straight."

"Does that mean we find another actress?" Aniyah looked confused.

"No." Dani opened her tablet. "We make sure the writing and the acting appeal to the fandom."

Mika's irritation flared. "What does that mean, 'appeal to the fandom'?"

Dani flipped through a couple of pages on her pad. When she found what she was looking for, she handed it to Mika. "There are forums where fans go to lobby for storylines. I wrote down the most popular ones." She looked between Aniyah and Mika, then tapped the paper. "If you include one of these ideas or something similar, the fans will see you being responsive to them. In turn, they'll be supportive of you."

Mika wasn't sure she'd heard correctly. "Are you suggesting we take story ideas from an Internet site?"

"No." Dani held her gaze. "I know that would be plagiarism. But there are trends in this list. We've worked to build a fandom, but it doesn't go one way. They expect to be heard and appreciated. Giving them a story they like and letting them know it's for them will show you're listening."

Mika leaned forward, her voice steely. "I won't allow the studio or the fans to determine the narrative arc of *Corsetti's Will*.

I'll give them everything I promised—a queer main character in a stable, loving relationship. But I will not compromise my integrity or the quality of the show for anyone."

She stood. "I'll be on set. Aniyah, go over the storyline with Dani so she knows what to expect."

* * *

"Why aren't you on the set?" Nathan asked as he slid into the booth across from Abby.

"They're filming the scenes where Joey finds Noelle, and then the police arrive at the apartment. My call time is after lunch."

Nathan rubbed his hands together. "Will they haul Joey down to the station and handcuff her to the bar in the middle of the table?"

Abby laughed. "You are creepily excited about your sister in handcuffs. I might be afraid to be alone with you."

"I'm harmless to everyone but Sara. Thanks for meeting me. Sara said your parents live in Palm Springs?"

"Yeah, but I'm not sure how much help I'm going to be. I can give you hotel recommendations for your boss, but I'm not up on golf courses and there are a hundred of them. Literally. One hundred," she emphasized.

"That's okay. He already has his tee times scheduled."

Abby leaned back into the red vinyl of the booth. "It feels good to have a day off. I don't know how Sara does it."

He shrugged. "She likes it. It's been a while since I've seen her this happy."

"Really? Sara is always so Zen. I can't imagine her unhappy. Or sad."

Nathan laughed out loud. "Sara? Zen? I wonder what the guys in Range Street would say to that." He shook his head. "No. Sara's not Zen. I've had plenty of tearful phone calls from her." He sipped his coffee. "Hot," he said, putting the mug down and shaking out his hand.

"See that little half-circle thing?" Abby pointed to his cup. "That's called a handle. If you hold the mug by that, you won't burn your hand."

"Oh, really, smart ass?" Nathan said. "Handles are made for small-hand people. Big-hand people get their fingers stuck in that tiny hole."

"So many things I could say to that, but I shall leave it alone." Abby took a drink of her coffee. "Damn it. All right. That is hot." Nathan laughed, and she gave him a dirty look.

He put one hand on top of hers and the other over his heart. "I am truly sorry I laughed at your misfortune."

He pulled his hand away as the waitress arrived. When they'd both given her their orders, she whispered, "You sure have attracted the interest of that table over there." She gestured with her chin. They both looked up and caught two teenage girls watching them. "You famous?" she asked Nathan.

"Nah."

"Well, enjoy. And if they bother you, let me know."

"They're fine," Nathan said. "No worries."

They talked about Palm Springs for a while, then Nathan told her about his work. Abby studied him while he talked. He was handsome. It was no wonder the girls thought he was a celebrity. Tall and lean, he had the same light hair and eyes as Sara. She cocked her head to the side and considered her lack of attraction to him. He was her type. Smart, funny, handsome, and a great body, at least what she'd seen of it that day at the pool. But she had zero chemistry with him. Now, Sara…

Her thoughts were interrupted when the girls approached the table. Dressed in cargo shorts and baseball caps, they shifted shyly in front of Abby. "Are you Abby? From the karaoke video with Sara Silver?"

Abby laughed out loud. "You watched the video? Where'd you see it?"

"YouTube. You're really funny."

Nathan snorted, and Abby fake-scowled at him. "Thank you," she said to the girls. "Please ignore him."

"Can we get a picture with you?"

"Sure." Abby stood, and Nathan took the phone. He snapped a couple of quick pictures and returned the phone to girls. When Abby sat back down, they continued to linger but didn't speak. Their waitress hurried over, and her disapproving look sent the teenagers scurrying away.

"I'm sorry about that. I was helping another table and didn't see them bothering you."

Abby waved away her concerns. "It's no bother, really. They were very polite. But thanks for watching out for us."

* * *

Sara took slow, even breaths, emptying her mind. Her left hand held three plastic grocery bags. Her right was on the door handle, keys already in the lock. She waited.

"Action."

Joey opens the door, fumbling to pull the key out of the dead bolt while calling out, "Noelle, I'm home." After finally getting the key out of the lock, she looks up, a smile on her face, then freezes. Carefully, she puts the bags down and reaches to her waist. With the slightest tremor, Joey lifts her gun and calls again, "Noelle?"

She moves sideways past overturned tables to the door of the bedroom. Using her left hand, she turns the knob and gently pushes the door, letting it swing open fully. Seeing nothing, Joey moves through the room, checking behind the door and in the closet. All of this takes less than fifteen seconds.

With a steadying breath, she moves back through the wreckage of the living room to the door of Noelle's studio. It's open just enough for her to see Noelle lying facedown on the floor.

"Noelle," she screams and drops to her knees beside the body.

"And cut," Celia called.

Sara dropped her head, then moved it side to side to loosen the tense muscles in her neck. "The pacing was good this time," Celia said. "You got through the bedroom in under twenty seconds. One more take, then we'll move on. Did you stay out of the blood?"

They all looked at Sara's clothes. "I'm good."

Celia called to the woman lying on the floor. "Okay?" The woman, careful not to change her position, gave a thumbs-up. Celia nodded and said, "Places."

As promised, they finished the take, then set up for the next scene. Sara slipped away to change from the blazer and jeans she was wearing to the identical outfit stained with stage blood.

Celia and Mika were waiting for her, as was the body double for Christina wearing a long, blond wig. The script called for Joey to cradle Noelle's body to her, but Celia and Mika weren't sure about the staging of the scene. It would be difficult for Sara to pull the woman to her while keeping the wig in place and her face concealed. Celia had questioned whether Joey Driskell, former homicide detective, would contaminate a murder scene. Mika, on behalf of the writers, argued that in this moment Joey was a loving partner and would react as such. "What's your opinion, Sara?" Mika asked. "You know Joey as well as anyone. What would she do?"

Sara didn't have to consider her answer. "She would touch her. She would pull the woman she loves into her arms one last time."

Celia tapped her chin with her fingertips. "You're right. That's a good motivation for the scene." She turned to the body double. "Could you lie down so we can work on it?" When she was in place, Celia pointed to the floor. "Sara, take your place, please." Her arms were crossed and she continued to tap her chin. "Sara, do what comes naturally. Don't worry about anything, just approach it as if that were Christina."

Sara looked down, considering what she would do. Then she stood back up and walked several steps away. "It would be a continuous motion." She took three large steps, sinking to her knees beside the body. "Noelle? Baby?" she said and lifted the shoulder closest to her, bending lower as she did. "No," she cried. "No." She slid her other arm under the body and used both arms to pull the actress to her.

"Cut," Celia said. She looked over to the camera operator. "What did you see?"

The woman stepped from behind the camera. "If I film from just below the midline of her body, I can keep her face obscured."

"Did the wig stay on?"

"Not a problem," the actress answered.

"Let's do it for real, then," Celia said. They moved to the set of Noelle's studio. Celia turned to the script supervisor. "What do we need for continuity from the last scene?"

Without looking at her notes, she pointed to Sara's wardrobe. "She needs to change back. If she walks in the room and kneels beside the body, there shouldn't be any blood on her until she picks up Noelle. As long as Joey cradles Noelle close to her, we should be good with the clean outfit. And she yelled 'Noelle' in the earlier take. Do you want to keep that or the softer version?"

"I like the softer version." Celia looked at Sara. "Do it just like that."

It only took a few takes for Celia to be satisfied, and the scene wrapped before lunch. Mika had been right about the emotional stress the episode created for Sara, and this would be the easier of the two scenes they were filming today. This one was all movement, her character slipping into cop-mode as she searched the apartment. Even when Joey found the body, she didn't have to make a lot of decisions on how to portray the moment. Joey would be shocked, not yet processing her loss.

The scene they would film after lunch was more difficult, and she wasn't sure how to play it. She needed Abby. Of the two of them, Abby was more experienced and a better actress. Sara found her at her usual lunch table surrounded by crew members. When Abby caught sight of her, she said, "I just left your brother."

"I need help. Can we meet in my trailer?"

Abby got up and followed Sara across the lot. "Do you really need help, or do you just miss me?"

Sara was too desperate to tease back. "How do I play Joey in this scene? It's a couple hours after she found Noelle. Would she be crying? Numb? Angry? I don't know what makes sense. I've never experienced grief like that." She blew out a breath.

"Last night I studied the funeral scene to see how you played Bria's grief."

"Did it help?"

"No, but it made me realize how talented you are."

"The funeral was different from the scene you're doing. Bria had to be inconsolable so Joey could take over the speech." Sara opened her trailer and they sat at the table.

"Do you want something to eat?"

"No, I ate with Nathan. Let me think." After nearly a minute of silence, Abby said, "You're only thinking about how Joey feels about Noelle's death. There's another dynamic you have to reveal. Joey's at her most vulnerable in this moment, and who is she surrounded by? The police. The people who turned on her. She doesn't trust them." Abby made a humming sound. "Wouldn't she be closed off?"

Sara sat upright. "You're right. And that's so much easier to do than crying." She smiled broadly. "Thank you."

"Uh-huh," Abby said. "Don't get lazy. Joey's trying to control her emotions. That's different from not having any. Reveal her grief to the audience, not to the other characters."

"I hate you." Sara groaned.

"But do you? Do you really?" Abby laughed.

* * *

Sara and Abby stood in front of Celia Edwards and listened to the logistics of the scene. "Bria rushes to Joey's side to support her. She asks questions while the police and crime scene techs move around them, and then the gurney. Ready?"

Bria enters the open apartment door and kneels on the floor in front of Joey. Joey is seated on the couch staring at the floor. She looks at Bria, then back to the floor. Her jaw clenches.

"Joey, what is it? What happened?" Bria leans closer and gasps when she sees the blood on Joey's clothes.

"Joey, are you okay? Where are you hurt?" She touches Joey, searching for an injury. "Why aren't they helping you?" Joey looks at her.

The coroner enters from the studio. "Miss Driskell? We're taking her now. The crime scene team will be here for a few more hours. They're going to need the clothes you're wearing."

Joey looks down at her stained blazer and T-shirt. She starts to remove the jacket but freezes when the gurney comes into view. There's a black body bag on it. She closes her eyes and her shoulders slump.

Bria turns and lets out a cry.

"Oh my God. No, not Noelle."

CHAPTER TWENTY-FIVE

Abby was in Sara's kitchen making a pitcher of margaritas when she got the text. She filled the blender with ice and pressed "crush" before picking up her phone. It was from Michelle to Abby, Sara, and Tanya. *Who's the hottie? And why haven't we heard about him?* There was a link to a Twitter page where two photos of Abby were posted. One was of her standing between the teenagers from the diner. The other was of Abby and Nathan sitting in the booth. He had one hand over his heart, the other covering hers. Abby enlarged the picture. They looked like they were on a date.

She turned off the blender and quickly typed a response. *That's Sara's brother, Nathan. Do you think he's hot? I think he looks like Sara.* After adding the winking emoji and sending it, she glanced out the window to see if Sara was on her phone. She and Nathan were floating in the pool.

With the pitcher in one hand and her phone in the other, Abby used a foot to slide the door open. "'Bout time." Nathan paddled his float toward the deck. "Please serve me at the swim-up bar."

Sara was right behind him on her float. "Why did we wait so long to leave Minnesota?"

Abby filled two glasses and carried them to pool's edge. "Maybe because you're Scandinavian and your ancestors migrated to the only place cold enough for them to feel at home?" She looked them over. "How long's it been since you two put on sunscreen?" The siblings gave her identical shrugs. Abby walked back to the table with their drinks. "No more margaritas until you do."

"We got a text from Michelle," she said over her shoulder. "Nathan and I were photographed at breakfast the other day."

"I took the pictures. How can I be in them?" He dried his hands on a towel. "Let me see."

Abby pulled up the text. "Where's your phone, Sara? Michelle sent it to both of us." She handed hers to Nathan. Sara leaned over his arm to look with him.

The crease between her eyebrows deepened. "I'm sorry. I didn't think about this when I asked you to move here."

"It doesn't bother me." He touched her hand. "I just know how upset you get." A look passed between them, then he pulled his hand away and his usual goofy grin was back. "The waitress thought I was a star."

Abby was glad to see Sara's smile come back. "And, I suppose you didn't mention that Abby is actually a star?"

"I can't help it if I'm beautiful."

Sara ignored him and typed something on her phone. When her text tone sounded, Abby read it aloud. "Take a look at Abby's face. Notice the look of sheer panic? She's trying to figure out how to escape!" Abby laughed and Nathan reached for the phone. He enlarged the picture and looked from it to Abby.

"That's not your 'I want you' face?" he asked, pointing at the phone.

She gave him a sympathetic look. "Sorry."

* * *

"You two were a hot topic this weekend," Dani said to Sara and Abby as they stood at the coffee machine Monday morning.

"First, there was your date with Sara's brother." She looked at Sara. "I didn't know it was your brother, but the fans did."

"I'm not dating Sara's brother. We went out to breakfast, and he—" Abby stopped herself. "Never mind. We're not dating."

"You should post that."

"Why?" Sara asked.

"What?" Dani frowned, distracted by her screen.

"Why should Abby post anything about her personal life? If she wants to date my brother, it's her business."

Dani looked up. "Sorry. The picture just came at a bad time. Have you been on your social media this weekend?"

Abby wondered if she looked as guilty as Sara did. "Uh, no. Is there a problem?"

Dani passed her tablet to them. It was open to an online gossip site.

Abby Farina to Play Sara Silver's Love Interest

A source close to *Corsetti's Will* showrunner Mika Williams has revealed that Abby Farina's character will become the new love interest of Sara Silver. Fans of the show are already expressing their displeasure, citing the lack of opportunities for openly gay actresses in Hollywood.

"Is this true?" Sara asked.

"Which part?"

"Has Mika decided Bria and Joey are going to be a couple?"

"You have to ask Mika." Dani held her tablet against her chest and turned to Abby. "The timing of the picture was bad. The hashtag gay-play-gay has been trending."

"I could put something out. We're not dating."

"I've got a better idea." Sara crossed her arms. "Let's make Abby date a woman. That's what they want, and the fans should always get what they want."

Abby and Dani stared as Sara stormed away.

* * *

Renee knocked and opened the door. "Ms. Copeland here to see you." She stepped aside to allow Dani to enter the office.

Mika got right to the point. "What's the reaction?"

"There is a hard-core group opposing the ship. I don't think there's anything we can do about it. They want a lesbian actress."

Mika made a frustrated sound. "I hired a lesbian actress, and her poor performance jeopardized the show. Now all I want is a quality actress capable of playing a loving partner to Joey." She sighed. "Does the fact we originally cast Christina have any sway with them?"

"No. They say it proves you know the importance of casting a lesbian and that you must be getting pressure from the network. They think they're helping you by speaking out."

"Why would the network want Abby to play Joey's lover?"

"She's pretty, and"—Dani hesitated slightly—"feminine."

Mika stood and walked to her window, trying to keep her anger in check. How was it possible she was being accused of the very wrong she'd set out to correct? She didn't want Abby because of her look. She wanted her because of the chemistry between the two actresses. Given the chance, she knew Abby would deliver the emotional intensity Mika wanted portrayed.

She turned back to face Dani. "What else?"

"They want someone butch."

Mika leaned back in her chair. "You're kidding. They want an actual butch, or they want someone who looks masculine of center? Do they even know the difference? Christina doesn't look butch. Where was this outrage when she was cast?"

"Christina is gay."

"But now someone like Christina is too feminine for the role?" Mika took off her glasses and rubbed the deepening crease between her eyes. "What is happening?"

"They're tired of lesbians only being represented by the most feminine of the community, like they are the only ones palatable for television. They want the whole of the community represented." Dani paused. "And, there is the suggestion that we are using feminine actresses to play to male viewers."

Mika shook her head. "I get it. But, in real life, not considering butch-femme identities, where would someone like Joey find a second love?" She didn't wait for an answer. "It would be in her own small world. With someone who feels the pain she does. Someone who also grieves Noelle and Corsetti. There's one logical answer, and it's not about representation. It's about storytelling."

"It is. Yes. But you told the fans you wanted a show with a lesbian main character, and now they're asking you to prove you know what that means."

"I'm not sure I do. Before, women were excluded from television because they were too masculine. Now, they're too feminine?" She took a deep breath. Dani was right; the fans were owed *something*, but she'd be damned if she let fan fantasy casting hijack her show. "Do you have any idea how many people we're talking about?"

Dani pursed her lips and shook her head. "There's no way to know. I can tell you how many followers a certain page has, but does everyone on that page agree? Doubtful. If you're asking me if they have enough support to damage the show, I'd say no."

"Then I've got to make sure the writing and the acting connects to them emotionally. I believe that's what we all want to see—our own love represented. And if great writing and acting isn't what they want to see, then maybe I'm too far out of touch with the community."

CHAPTER TWENTY-SIX

Abby pulled through the gate, disappointed to see Sara's car wasn't in the drive. She knocked on the back door and walked in. Nathan was sitting at the kitchen island staring at his computer, an ice-filled cocktail halfway to his mouth. His hair was disheveled, his sleeves rolled up, and one shoe was under the stool. He looked up when he heard her and responded to her laugh with a grin of his own. "Thank you for rescuing me," he said.

"I'm not sure I want to rescue you. What have you done?" She walked to him and gave him a side hug. He put an arm around her waist and pointed to his screen.

"Do you see this? I'm supposed to have this figured out before tomorrow, and I can't think because I'm starving. Let's go out."

"I thought Sara was stopping for something on the way home."

"She was, but she called and said there were problems on set and she'd be late."

Abby frowned. "Problems? Did she say what?"

"Something about the wig she had to wear for flashbacks...I don't know. I really wasn't listening. She said she texted you."

Abby stepped back. "My phone's in my bag. I didn't hear it. I don't want go out. Maybe I could make us something?"

"Don't bother opening the refrigerator. There isn't anything in there. I've searched the whole house, and there's nothing to eat anywhere."

"Why don't you order something to be delivered?"

"Nooo," Nathan whined. "It takes too long. I'm starving. Come on, you need to eat. We'll go out, have a drink and dinner. We'll find someplace quiet."

Abby sighed. "This is a bad idea. The whole world thinks we're dating."

"There's a small mom-and-pop Italian restaurant around the corner. In this fancy neighborhood, you'll be beneath their notice."

"Fine." Abby was too tired to fight. She'd agreed to dinner with Sara because they hadn't been alone in days. Now she wished she could go home and curl up with a bowl of microwave popcorn.

Nathan hit a couple keys on his laptop and stood, looking around the room. "Do you see my other shoe?"

The restaurant was crowded when they arrived, so they chose a high-top table in the tiny bar. "Can't reach the ground?" Nathan said after watching Abby struggle to scoot her chair closer to the table.

"I would be weirdly proportioned if I could."

"Your proportions are just right," he said, then looked at her with wide eyes. "Pretend I didn't say that. My sister would kill me for noticing her girlfriend's proportions."

Abby lurched forward. "What did you just say?"

He gave her a smirk and lifted the menu to cover his face. "Do you want an appetizer?"

She pushed the menu down. "Huh-uh. No food until you answer the question."

"Okay, okay. Yes. You are nicely proportioned."

"Nathan," she growled, leaning closer to him, her hand squeezing his arm.

He laughed and leaned in before whispering, "My sister has the hots for you." She gave him a baleful look, and he added, "I think you're hot for her too."

The waiter walked up and they pulled apart, ordering wine and fried calamari. When he walked away, Nathan asked, "Has she kissed you yet? Never mind, I know she has. I think it happened the weekend we moved in. I had to go to the liquor store to get away from the two of you." Abby made a little sound of protest, and he laughed. "So, have you and my sister…" He let the words hang as he waggled his eyebrows at Abby.

She was about to scold him, but a glance at the bar stopped her. Four women had turned on their stools to look at them. "Shit," she muttered. "Stop talking about Sara. There's a group of women at the bar staring at us. They don't look friendly."

He frowned. "They need to leave you alone. I doubt they'd be happy even if they knew you and Sara are dating."

Nathan was leaning even closer to her so he could see the women. Abby wrapped her arm around his shoulder and whispered, "Stop talking about Sara."

The calamari arrived, saving Nathan from Abby's wrath. They were filling their plates when one of the women approached the table. "Are you on that new Binge show, *Corsetti's Will*?"

"I am," Abby answered with her biggest smile. "I'm Abby Farina."

"Could you take a picture with us?" The woman gestured over her shoulder to the group at the bar. "We saw the premiere at ClexaCon. We loved it."

Although Nathan's expression was wary, he didn't say anything. Abby slid out of the chair. "I'd be happy to." When they got to the bar where the other women were seated, she said, "Hi, I'm Abby. You guys were at ClexaCon?"

Three of the women spoke at once. All Abby got from their excited chatter was they loved the show and loved Sara. "Sara is really talented," Abby agreed. "And she's a really nice person."

"That your boyfriend?" This was from the one woman who hadn't yet spoken.

The others protested, but Abby shook her head. "No." She considered adding that she wasn't dating anyone or that Nathan was Sara's brother, but she was irritated by the woman's rudeness. "Who wants to be in the picture?" They all gathered around her, even the negative woman, and posed. After a few selfies, she stepped away from the bar. "Have a great evening." With their thanks following her, she returned to Nathan.

"What did the cranky one say to you?"

"She wanted to know if we're dating."

Nathan shook his head, eyes flashing. "Did you tell her to mind her own fucking business?" He started to turn, but Abby put a hand on his arm and pointed at the food that had arrived while she was gone.

"Don't. Let's eat."

"It's the same thing Sara goes through. She gives the fans some of herself, and they think they should get it all. Pisses me off." They ate in silence for a few moments, but Nathan couldn't let it go. "It's worse for gay celebrities. I know that's stating the obvious, but it's not just homophobia that makes it harder."

Abby watched him shovel a bite of pasta into his mouth. He chewed for a few seconds, then acted like he was going to speak. She held up a finger. "Huh-uh. Do not open your mouth until you've swallowed your food." He finished chewing, then washed his pasta down with wine.

When he looked back to her, she could see pain in his eyes. "Before Sara came out, people were obsessed with finding proof that she's gay. They stalked her. Not just one person, but hundreds. Everything she did, everyone she was around, ended up on Twitter or Instagram. People spent hours dissecting her. If someone spoke out about the constant invasion of her privacy, they got attacked too."

"I had no idea she went through that. Was it the religious right? Some anti-gay group?"

"No," he said. "Well, after she came out, there was some of that, but, no. They weren't the problem. Her gay fans were." He took another bite and chewed slowly. Abby ate, too, puzzling over his words.

"They said she was ashamed of her sexuality, and the only way to prove she wasn't ashamed was to come out. Sara was never ashamed. She's private." He waved his fork. "You wouldn't believe the lengths they went to—harassing my parents, following me to work." He shook his head, his mouth in a tight line. "Someone even tried to hack my cousin's online wedding album to see if Sara brought a date. So, she came out. We thought everything would be better, but it hasn't been, not really. It was like once they got her to come out, they thought they had a right to know everything about her life.

"That's one of the reasons she struggles so much on tour. Everyone wants a piece of Sara Silver. There isn't anywhere she can go to get away. At the end of their last tour, the stress affected her health, and she lost weight." He shook his head. "Then those fucking photos were posted."

Abby flushed and looked away. She knew exactly what photos he meant. During a backstage costume change, someone took pictures of Sara and posted them on social media. By the time the band got off stage, they'd gone viral.

She could barely look at Nathan, ashamed that she, too, had looked at the grainy images. "Now I understand why you two reacted the way you did to the picture at the diner. What seems like an innocent fan picture to me must feel so invasive to you and Sara."

"Yeah." He nodded. "Touring was always brutal for her, but she sucked it up for the guys. But that did it. She was done. She asked the guys for a break, and they agreed to three years. Then everyone thought Sara was going to rehab. That's why she went right into recording her solo album. Then the offer to do *Enough* came, and all of a sudden no one talked about drugs anymore."

"Did she ever get an 'I told you so' moment?" Abby asked.

"No, and no one ever apologized, either. Some even had the balls to tell her she was looking much better."

"Is she better? Our schedule is brutal. I'm with her every day, and she doesn't seem exhausted, but is she okay?"

Nathan bumped her shoulder. "You're the one kissing her. Did she seem okay?"

She laughed and punched his arm. "Shut up."

CHAPTER TWENTY-SEVEN

Mika relaxed back into the first-class seat. They'd left LA in the early morning, bound for New York and a series of television and print interviews ahead of the Binge premiere of *Corsetti's Will*. This was the kind of marketing she understood—appearances on morning shows, clips of the actresses in compelling moments. She'd done it all before, but now she wondered how effective their time in New York would be compared to what they'd accomplished in Las Vegas.

The network execs were ecstatic with the numbers that came out of ClexaCon, and Mika credited Dani for all of it. If not for her young social media manager's idea to do a soft premiere, they would have missed the opportunity to dramatically expand their fan base. And, although she had nearly nixed the karaoke idea at the time, Dani's instincts on that were also right on. The Christina Landis announcement became old news as soon as Dani posted the video of Sara and Abby singing "I Got You Babe." Already it had been viewed more than 200,000 times. Sara's video of "Songbird," posted a day later, was on track to get over a million views.

Which led her to thoughts of her other new hire, Aniyah. Watching Sara and Abby sing together, Mika saw what the writer had spotted immediately: affectionate looks, lingering touches, easy banter. And the way Sara looked at Abby while she'd been singing? Mika doubted Sara realized how exposed she was in that moment.

Then there was her current problem. Damn her father. Nothing could convince her that he wasn't responsible for the leak about Bria and Joey. Mika wasn't averse to a little controversy; it often increased viewership. But this situation had her unsettled. Even though her logical mind knew it was nothing like what happened with Meg Foster on *Cagney & Lacey*, she was still questioning herself and her responsibilities. What was most important: furthering the career of a queer actor—*any* queer actor, according to some of the fans—or providing viewers with what she knew would be a beautiful portrayal of two women in love? If she chose the first option and hired someone new, she risked not getting the second. And she couldn't afford another Christina Landis.

This morning, Dani showed her the latest pictures of Abby and Nathan Silver at dinner. From the way Abby draped her arm around him and whispered in is ear, it certainly looked like they were a couple. "How are our fans taking it?" she'd asked.

"About what you'd expect. Could be the same fans who've been commenting all along. It's hard to tell."

"Something to drink, Ms. Williams?" The flight attendant pulled her out of her reverie.

Mika had no place to be until tomorrow morning, and she felt a little reckless, which was highly unusual for her. "If I said surprise me, what would you bring?" she asked.

"A mimosa," the woman answered promptly.

Mika smiled. "Surprise me."

* * *

Sara had a blanket pulled tight under her chin. Their morning flight meant she had to be at the airport two hours earlier than even her earliest call times. Getting up two hours before that to make sure she was on time and presentable in case they were photographed basically meant she had to get up before she went to bed. Or at least that's what it felt like. Still, she liked to fly. She liked the floaty feeling of drifting in and out of sleep while the engines hummed around them. Today, she liked that Abby was next to her, and even though they weren't touching, she was very aware of her presence.

But Abby must have thought she wasn't aware enough because her hand was on Sara's thigh, shaking her out of her peaceful state. "Are you ever going to wake up? I've read half of my book, had two cups of coffee, and now I have to go to the bathroom."

Sara opened one eye. "I'm in the window seat. Did you need to wake me to go to the bathroom?"

"No, I need to wake you because when I get back, you are going to be alert and entertaining. Do you need coffee? A Coke? I'll ask our flight attendant to bring you something."

"Fine. Could you have her bring me a coffee?"

"I'll ask *him* if he can do that. Stereotype, much?"

"I'm still asleep. You can't judge my social awareness when I'm groggy."

Abby unbuckled her seat belt. "Should I judge you for sleeping with your mouth open?"

Sara smacked her lips. "No wonder I have cotton mouth. You failed in your responsibilities as a seat partner. You are supposed to gently nudge me when that happens. Jeff does."

Abby raised her eyebrows. "Really? Gently nudge, does he?"

"Well, sometimes he punches my arm, but thanks to him, no one has a picture of me with my mouth hanging open."

Abby stood and stretched. Sara watched as she walked up the aisle and spoke to the flight attendant before she went into the bathroom. He gave Sara a smile, then disappeared into the tiny alcove. A few minutes later, he delivered coffee, water, and cookies.

By the time Abby returned, Sara was feeling more awake. "What would you like to do this afternoon? Want to shop or go to a museum?"

Abby gave her a look she couldn't decipher. "No, I don't want to go shopping or sightseeing."

Sara was embarrassed. "I'm sorry, did you have plans with someone else?" They hadn't talked about their free day in New York, and she'd just assumed they would spend time together.

"Oh, I have plans with you." Abby gave her that look again, and this time there was no mistaking what it meant because Abby followed her words by caressing Sara's thigh.

"Uh, you do? What are you thinking?"

"I'm thinking I'd like to stay in the hotel room."

"Oh." Sara deflated. She'd misread Abby after all.

"Yes." Abby leaned closer to make sure they couldn't be overheard. "I think we should spend the afternoon in bed."

The words slammed into Sara. As much as she'd hoped this was what Abby was hinting around, she wasn't sure how to respond. She wanted Abby. Every part of her body let her know that. But was this a good idea? The thoughts raced through her mind as her eyes flicked between Abby's.

Abby looked at her lips and then back at her eyes. "You're thinking too much."

"I know, but shouldn't one of us be thinking of what could happen?"

Abby gave a low chuckle. "Trust me, that's all I've been thinking about."

* * *

Mika handed each of them an envelope. "Enjoy the rest of your day. I'll see you at six tomorrow morning."

Mika and Dani got off the elevator first, leaving Abby and Sara alone. Sara watched as Abby leaned against the back wall and trailed her gaze over her. God, she was making Sara crazy. How was it that Abby was the one who hadn't slept with a woman? "After the bellman brings your luggage, come to my room." Abby showed Sara the envelope with her room number written in black marker on the outside. All Sara could do was nod as the elevator doors opened and Abby walked away. She didn't look back.

"Jesus," Sara said aloud. After the last two hours of Abby's casual touches and teasing innuendos, Sara was a mess. How could she possibly be this aroused and this uncertain?

She opened the door to her room, walking past the ornate furnishings to the windows overlooking the park. It was a beautiful late spring afternoon. Sara pictured them walking arm in arm past the museum and in and out of the park. They could sit at one of the coffee shops and watch the dog walkers and nannies corral their charges. That's what they'd do. They wouldn't sleep together, they wouldn't risk their friendship or the show. And she wouldn't risk her heart.

At a knock, she stepped away from the view and opened the door for the bellman. After assuring him she didn't need directions or ice, she picked up her phone, ready to tell Abby they should go out. She hesitated, and rather than calling, texted. *I need a shower.*

Bubbles appeared while Abby typed her response. *Good idea. See you in 30.*

Sara placed her toiletries on the shelf of the shower, laid out the towels, and stepped into the spray. She told herself she was washing off the flight, not preparing for an afternoon of sex. She kept telling herself that even as she reached for her razor. Yeah, like that didn't mean anything. Once out of the shower, she blew her hair straight and put the lightest touch of perfume on her neck. "Who are you kidding?" she asked her reflection.

Abby opened the door wearing a white button-down shirt, yoga pants, and no bra. She reached for Sara's arm and pulled her into the room, letting the door close behind them. Without a word, Abby pushed her against the wall, cupped her face, and kissed her. Sara didn't have time to think because Abby enveloped her. Her tongue was in Sara's mouth, her hands moved from Sara's face to her neck to the inside of her shirt. Abby pushed her lower body farther into Sara while she moved her mouth from Sara's lips to her neck, then her earlobe, and back again. The frenzy of Abby's movements should have signaled to Sara to take control, but the intensity overwhelmed her.

Still, when Abby reached for the hem of Sara's T-shirt, she managed to pull herself out of the haze of lust. "Abby, wait," she whispered, putting one hand on her stomach to hold the shirt in place. She studied the beautiful woman in front of her. "Abby, I want this. I want you, but more than that, I need you to be sure." Once again, Abby moved without answering, but this time Sara placed a hand on her chest. She felt the heart pounding under her palm. "Abby. Let's take a minute."

Abby leaned back with a groan. She pressed Sara's palm firmly against her chest and braced a second hand on Sara's shoulder. "I don't need a minute. How can you think I need a minute? I practically jumped you on the plane. I know what I want. I may not know exactly how to touch you, but I know I want you." She rubbed her hand over Sara's, her voice dropping into a whisper. "I feel so much with you. I want to know more."

Sara studied Abby. "I want to feel you too, but I..." She didn't know how to tell Abby what she felt without scaring both of them.

"No, Sara. It's not your body." She let out a little laugh. "Well, that's not true. I definitely want this body." She placed her palm on Sara's chest. "I want to feel your heart." She moved her hand back to cover the hand Sara had on her chest. "And I want you to feel mine."

The words sent a thrill through Sara. She hadn't realized how much she needed to hear them. Wherever this was going, they were both in it. Her nerves were gone. Sara pushed off the wall and took Abby's hand. "Have you looked out yet?" Not waiting for an answer, she led Abby to the window and reached for the remote that opened the sheers.

"It's beautiful," Abby whispered, looking down at the expanse of trees in their early green. Sara stood behind her and reached an arm around Abby's waist, her mouth next to Abby's ear. She kissed below the ear, and Abby shivered. She moved down to Abby's neck while running a hand under her shirt and over her abdomen. With the slightest pressure, she pulled Abby in to her and turned them away from the window.

Sara kept Abby in this position, letting her feel but not see the woman behind her. With care, she unbuttoned Abby's blouse until it hung open. She moved her hand from Abby's stomach to her chest, gliding over smooth skin. A small step back gave her enough room to slide Abby's shirt down her arms and drape it on the bench at the end of the bed. Before Abby became self-conscious, Sara pulled off her own T-shirt and bra and closed the space between them, pushing her breasts into Abby's back. Abby moaned and reached behind her to grasp Sara's thigh and pull her closer.

Sara moved Abby's hair and began to kiss the other side of her neck while her hands wandered over Abby's body, across her stomach, between her breasts. She slid a hand over a breast, loving the feel of a hard nipple under her palm. When Sara's fingers touched Abby's nipple, she hissed. "Jesus, Sara." The words intensified Sara's arousal. She slid her hands into Abby's yoga pants, against her hipbones.

"Can we take these off?" she whispered. Abby started to reach for the waistband, but Sara stopped her. "Let me." She left her hands inside the stretchy fabric and slowly moved them down Abby's body until the pants were puddled on the floor. She knelt, lifting one bare foot, then the other, to pull Abby free. She wanted to turn her, to take her right there, standing at the foot of the bed, but forced herself to be patient. Instead, she stood, undid her jeans, and slid the last of her clothing to the floor. When she was naked, she rested her hands on Abby's biceps and whispered, "Are you ready?"

"Yes," Abby gasped. Sara returned her left hand to Abby's nipple, first brushing, then rolling, and finally pinching. "Sara," Abby moaned. Sara wanted to throw her on the bed, to slide over her beautiful body. She pictured thrusting into her until they both came. Not this time, she told herself. With a shaky breath, she let her right hand make its way back down Abby's body until she encountered the soft, smooth skin between her legs. She could feel the wetness even without opening her or letting her fingers slide inside. Abby pushed into her hand, and Sara was burning. She couldn't decide how she wanted to make Abby come, but she knew when it happened, she wouldn't be far behind.

Abby made the decision for them. With a cry, she spun in Sara's arms and pushed her whole body into her. Their kiss was wild, all tongue and emotion. Sara slid her hands over

Abby's back and down her ass. She walked them to the bed and whispered, "Lay down." Abby's eyes never left hers as she sat and eased backward. Sara knew she wouldn't be able to hold back if she let her body cover Abby's, but she craved that first touch of skin. Slowly, she crawled onto the bed and positioned herself over Abby. Never making contact, she moved a thigh so it was between Abby's legs. Holding the intense eye contact, she slid her thigh to one side, opening Abby's legs. A light flush passed over Abby's face and she moved her legs farther apart.

Sara took in her full breasts and tight nipples. She let her eyes travel down, taking in the smooth skin between her legs and the sheen of moisture. "You're beautiful," she said, then lowered her body onto Abby's. Abby closed her eyes, moaning as Sara's thigh contacted her clit. When Sara stopped moving, Abby opened her eyes and pulled Sara in for a kiss. This time Sara didn't give in to it. She moved her hand until it rested between Abby's legs and whispered, "What do you need?"

Abby's eyes widened, so Sara flattened her fingers and rubbed slow, broad circles over her. Abby closed her eyes again. "Rub my clit," she murmured. Sara rewarded her answer with a deep kiss before letting her fingers move through Abby's folds until she found her. Then, ever so slowly, she started to circle her clit with the lightest of touches. She knew it wouldn't be enough, and Abby's slight frown registered her frustration. She pushed up, trying to force Sara into more contact. Sara responded with the softest of kisses before adding pressure. The moan of relief and arousal excited her almost as much as the way Abby was moving against her hand. Increasing the speed and pressure on Abby's clit, Sara opened her legs and moved with Abby, coating the other woman's thigh. Abby grabbed Sara's hips at the same time she pushed herself into Sara's hand. Her legs stiffened and she let out a long, low moan, her back and neck arching. She put her hand over Sara's, adding pressure as she continued to shudder.

At last Abby pulled her hand away and ran it through Sara's hair and down her back. Her eyes were heavy. "That was so good," she said, her voice barely above a whisper. "I want you to feel like that." She ran her hand down Sara's back and over her ass. "Your skin is incredible."

Sara moved her hand from between them and ran her wet fingers over Abby's bottom lip. Abby let out a little gasp, and Sara leaned in and took the lip between hers. She pulled away for a moment to look in Abby's dark eyes. She had never been this aroused. As much as she wanted to let Abby wind down from her own orgasm, Sara needed to come. Abby reached between them, trailing her fingers down until she touched Sara's wetness. Sara groaned.

"You're so wet." Abby bent her fingers and let her knuckles rub over Sara's clit. With each contact, Sara became a little more desperate.

She reached for Abby's hand and held it against the bed. The light friction on her clit created little pulse points, and she was so close. Sara arched her back and pushed into Abby's thigh, getting lost in the feeling of Abby's skin and her own arousal. It took less than a minute for her own body to shudder and explode in orgasm.

She collapsed, moving so that most of her weight was on her right hip but one leg draped over Abby. She flattened her palm against Abby's chest, and Abby put hers over it. "Can you feel my heart? It's still racing."

"It feels good." Sara pulled herself closer. "I'm glad we didn't go out."

"Why do you think I kissed you before you could say anything?"

* * *

"Two hours, I promise. Then we can come right back here."

"Fine, but you're going to have to buy me a pretzel or something. I'll never make it to dinner." Abby rolled off the bed and made her way into the bathroom. She looked at her hair in the mirror. Despite having Sara's hands all through it, it looked pretty good. There was something to be said for the just-fucked look.

Sara walked in behind her and reached for the soap. She lathered her hands, then looked pointedly at Abby. "I was just thinking I like this look," Abby said.

Sara placed the soap in Abby's hands. "The look is good, but you're not going out in New York City smelling like sex."

"It would be okay in LA?" Abby called after the departing figure.

"Nope."

Sara stopped at the concierge desk on the way out. When she rejoined Abby, she handed her a map of the park. "I forgot it was Sunday," Sara said as she pointed to the path the concierge had drawn in black marker. "One of my favorite activities happens Sunday afternoon in Central Park. I hope it's not too early in the season."

"Is it a surprise?"

"Softball. I'm telling you, watching native New Yorkers pretend they're big-leaguers is really entertaining. We'll get a pretzel and a Coke." Sara's eyes sparkled with excitement.

Abby leaned closer. "Is this a lesbian thing? Are you trying to make me jealous after we just had the most amazing sex?"

Sara stopped dead in her tracks. "You thought it was amazing?"

"Of course, it was amazing. Couldn't you tell?" Abby reached for Sara's arm. "Which way?"

They crossed the street and entered the park. At the first cart they saw, Sara bought pretzels and soda. Abby bit into hers, then held it up for inspection. She pinched a piece from the center and ate it. "It's stale." She turned to go back, but Sara grabbed her arm.

"Don't bother. They're all stale. You're eating it for the experience, not the flavor."

"Huh." Abby eyed the pretzel in her hand, then looked at Sara. "The experience better improve at the softball fields."

They walked along the path, enjoying the warmth of the afternoon. Even though there were hundreds of people around them, everyone existed in a private world. "There they are." Sara pointed to the open space just ahead. "See how close those fields are to each other? The outfielders end up overlapping. They have to pay attention to their game and the one behind them."

Abby watched the outfield. The players were standing shoulder to shoulder, facing opposite directions. "Someone could get hurt," she said as Sara led them to the bleachers. Abby caught sight of another cart. "I'm getting ice cream." Then she stopped. "Ice cream doesn't get stale, does it?"

"Go with the Drumstick. You never know about Bomb Pops." Abby returned with two Drumsticks and sat close to Sara on the top row.

"Tell me why you like this."

"Just listen. All over the city you see tourists and businesspeople, but here you get to see regular New Yorkers." She leaned in to whisper, "It's better than the zoo."

Abby laughed. They ate ice cream and eavesdropped on conversations among spectators and players. The air smelled like spring and hot dogs, and Abby didn't know if she'd ever had a more perfect moment. Her reverie was interrupted by an argued call on the field. She leaned in to Sara and whispered, "How do you spell that? It sounds like there's a 'w' in it."

"Just like it sounds. F-w-u-c-k," Sara whispered back.

"No, I think it's f-a-w-c-k." She turned and kissed Sara's cheek. "I'm having a great time, but I'm ready to go back to the room."

Sara took her hand and pulled her to her feet. "Let's go then." They found the path and Sara kept hold of Abby's hand. "Is this okay?"

Abby bumped her shoulder. "Very okay." They walked in silence, enjoying the day and the closeness. Abby didn't want to ruin the mood, but there was so much she wanted to know about Sara. "Have you had many relationships?"

Sara stopped. "Wow. That came out of nowhere."

"Maybe for you, but I've been wondering about it for a while."

Sara's smile was teasing. "How long's 'a while'?"

Abby tapped her finger to her chin as if considering the question. "Well, let's see. I think it was before you kissed me in Las Vegas."

"Me? I kissed you?"

"Right. I forget you have zero game. It was before I kissed you in Vegas. It might have been about the time I read the fanfic about you, Christina, and the strap-on."

Sara threw her free hand over her eyes. "Stop. I can't unsee that."

Abby peeled Sara's hand away. "Believe me, that image is seared in my brain." She paused. "And I like it very much." When Sara blushed, Abby couldn't resist teasing her. "So, shall we talk about former relationships, or favorite sex toys?"

Sara shook her head and tugged Abby forward. "Okay, you win." They strolled the wide path for nearly a minute before Sara started talking. "There really isn't a lot to say. The women I wanted to be with didn't usually last long in my life. It's another of the reasons I don't like being on tour. There was a woman in Minneapolis. We met in a coffee shop down the street from my loft. She was—well I guess she still is—a lawyer for one of the big firms in the city. We were in line and started talking. She knew who I was, but she wasn't impressed by it. We dated for several months, and it was good."

"Were you in love with her?"

"Yeah, I was. Kim's a good person, but her hours became a problem for me. I wanted to complain, but what could I say? We had a tour coming in the summer, and I was going to be gone for months."

"What happened?"

"I went on tour. We tried to keep going, but I'd be getting ready to go onstage when she got home, and she was up early. There was never a time to talk. Finally, we both just let go."

"Is that the only relationship you've been in?"

"No, but the others didn't last as long. Kim and I were together for nearly a year. Looking back, it was never going to work out. Our lives were too different."

They were nearing the edge of the park and the crowds were thicker, but Abby really wanted to ask the next question. "What about groupies? Do women throw their underwear onstage?"

"It's happened a couple of times, but it's not really like that."

"So, are you saying you've never slept with a fan?"

Sara shifted uncomfortably. "I have had a few one-night stands, but never after concerts. Mostly women I met when I was home, but it's been a while." They were out of the park and waiting at the light. Sara squeezed her hand. "And what about you, Ms. Farina? It's time for you to share your past."

"Maybe later." Abby grinned. "That's not how I want to spend the rest of the afternoon."

CHAPTER TWENTY-EIGHT

The tall, lithe woman greeted her with a smile and a hug. "Sara, it's great to see you. Love the show." Keisha Armstrong had anchored the top-rated morning show for years.

"Thanks, Keisha. That means a lot coming from you." Sara reached for Abby. "Have you met Abby Farina? She plays Bria Corsetti."

"You had us bawling last night," Keisha told Abby. "I need to hug you."

"Thanks." Abby laughed as she was pulled into Keisha's arms. "That was a compliment, right?"

"Very much so." Keisha smiled and reached for Mika. "Congratulations, old friend. It's going to be a hit."

Mika hugged her back. "I hope so. You know this one is special to me."

"Aren't they all?"

"Two minutes," a voice from somewhere behind the cameras announced. A flurry of activity surrounded them as technicians placed lavalier microphones and Makeup did final touch-ups.

In the midst of the chaos, a staff member handed something to Keisha and spoke in her ear. Keisha scanned the page, scowled, shook her head, then touched her ear as she listened.

When he walked away, Keisha looked at Mika. "Read this," she said, "and be ready to respond. I'll start with Sara and Abby, then come to you. You have about a minute."

Mika opened the folded page.

Christina Landis

> *Thanks to all of you who've reached out to me. No, I won't return to Corsetti. I can't fight a straight person spreading hate so she can win an Emmy for playing gay. Thanks @real. sarasilver for your support & friendship!*
> *#supportqueerfilms #gayplaygay*

Mika closed her eyes, took a deep breath, and focused her thoughts. She'd been too cocky thinking the Christina problem would go away. The *Corsetti* promo played, followed by Keisha's introductions. Mika pasted on a smile and pretended to listen while Sara and Abby answered questions.

She heard the reluctance in Keisha's voice as she started the question. "Mika, Christina Landis, who played Sara's girlfriend, abruptly left the show. An hour ago, she posted this on Twitter." The tweet appeared on the monitor, and Mika heard Sara's sharp intake when Keisha read it aloud. "Mika, what do you say to that allegation?"

Mika leaned toward Keisha, a sad look on her face. "We would have loved for Christina to continue in the role of Noelle Prado. She told me her personal relationship was getting in the way of her acting. I accepted her request to leave the show. As for her allegations, I can only say that I'm stunned."

"Are you saying they aren't true?"

"That is exactly what I'm saying."

"Mika Williams, Sara Silver, and Abby Farina, thank you. *Corsetti's Will* premieres tomorrow night on Binge." Keisha smiled at the camera.

"And, we're out."

Keisha had an apologetic look on her face. Mika just shook her head, removed the mic, and handed it to a waiting technician. "I owe you," she told the anchor. "Thanks for the heads-up."

"I'm sorry I couldn't quash it."

"I'd rather the question come from you than anyone else." She stood and embraced Keisha. When the anchor walked away, she whispered to the group, "Not a word."

Mika held her smile as she led Sara, Abby, and Dani off the set, through the corridors of the studio, and out the back entrance where a limousine waited to take them to their next appearance. Before the door was even closed, Mika started talking. "It was naïve of me to trust that girl." She looked at the three women, ready to give direction but saw none of them were paying attention to her. Abby stared out the window, her usually olive complexion devoid of color. When she reached to push her hair back, Mika saw her hands were trembling.

"Abby," she said gently. Abby's eyes fixed on her. "We'll take care of this." She got a short nod in return. Mika suspected she hadn't heard.

Sara's mouth was set in a tight line and was stabbing furiously at her phone, typing, erasing, typing. Mika put her hand over the screen. "What are you doing, Sara?"

"I'm texting her."

"No." Mika took the phone. "You're not. We have to be very careful about how we proceed. No one responds in writing. We're going to get this question in every interview we have today. Whoever gets it, the response is the same. Christina asked to be let out of her contract due to a conflict with her personal relationship. That's all we know."

"That's not enough." Sara's voice rose. "We need to call her on her lies about Abby. We can't ignore it."

"I assure you, I won't be ignoring it. I also won't respond until I know what she's up to," Mika said.

"She and Abby were hardly ever on set together. Can't you at least say that much? Or, I can say it."

"It doesn't matter." Abby's voice was quiet. "It's done. It's out in the world. Nothing you say will change the perception people have of me." She swiped a hand over her cheek.

Sara reached for Abby, but Abby pushed back against the embrace. "I'm fine," she said.

Sara looked at Mika, her eyes narrow, fists clenched. "We need to do something."

The car pulled to the curb and a voice came over the intercom. "We're at NBC Studios."

Mika reached across the seat to take Abby's chin in her hand. "You are stronger than this. Do you understand me? Don't fall apart." Abby's lip trembled, but she nodded. Then Mika turned to Sara. "And don't lose your temper. I need you to be calm for her."

Once in the studio, Mika spoke to the producer. "If you have any questions about Christina Landis, you need to direct them to me. I've instructed the cast not to respond."

He looked at Mika before looking past her to Abby. "Our viewers want to hear from Ms. Farina. She's the one accused of forcing Ms. Landis off the show."

Mika inhaled, ready to pull the plug on the interview, but Sara stepped forward. "Hey, Sam, good to see you again. Look, I can tell you there's no truth in Christina's tweet. Let Mika answer for the show." She gave him a wink. "Plus, you owe me for last spring."

He frowned. "Fine, but you have to do a summer concert if we need you."

The interview went much the same as the earlier one. The anchor had a few questions, but they were all setups to get to Christina's tweet. Mika responded with the same vehemence as she had earlier, but rather than let it go, the woman pressed. "Are you saying Christina Landis is making this up?"

Mika pursed her lips. "I'm saying that Christina was a valuable part of our team until she violated her contract and left the show."

"I see. Well, I'm sure we'll be hearing more about this controversy. *Corsetti's Will* premiers on Binge tomorrow night."

Mika glared at the anchor. "That was underhanded, and you know it."

"I gave you a chance to deny a hostile work environment. You chose not to answer directly."

"You're a former attorney. You know exactly why I didn't answer directly." Mika tilted her head back as the tech unclipped her microphone.

"Ms. Farina, we'd like to offer you a chance to tell your side of the story. Tomorrow morning in the eight o'clock hour?"

Abby stared at the woman, uncomprehending. Sara grabbed her arm and led her out of the studio without a word. Mika worked to keep her fury under control. "When this is resolved, we will offer an exclusive, but not to you."

Mika's phone was ringing even before they got to the car. Seeing it was Larry Rand, she declined it, knowing he'd call back. She silenced the subsequent ring and waited until the town car was in motion before she answered.

"The PR department has canceled the rest of your appearances. Get back to your hotel and get packed. We chartered a jet to fly you back to LA." Rand's voice was flat, his words clipped.

Mika didn't bother arguing. She didn't want to go through the gauntlet any more than he wanted them to. "What airport?"

"The car will wait for you. Be on the plane in an hour." He hung up without another word.

CHAPTER TWENTY-NINE

"Could I get a diet cola?" Mika asked the flight attendant after sinking into one of the seats around a table. "I don't care what brand." When he returned with the soda, Sara saw her shake migraine medicine out of a small bottle. In a rare show of vulnerability, Mika said, "I've got to get rid of this headache. I'm going to try to get some sleep. We'll talk in a bit." Mika pulled the window shade and removed her glasses.

Sara nodded and led the others to the back of the plane. She took a forward-facing seat and was surprised when Dani, not Abby, sat next to her. Abby stood in the aisle, staring at her phone. Slowly, she turned and sank into a seat behind Mika. Sara started to get up, but Dani stopped her. "Give her a little time."

"She shouldn't be alone." Sara stepped over Dani and went to join Abby. Her face was turned to the window. "Hey," she said. Abby wiped at her cheeks but didn't turn. "Abby?" She touched her arm. Abby unlocked her phone and handed it to Sara. An email from the human resources department at Binge came up.

Dread settled in Sara's stomach when she read the subject line. *Notice of Investigation.* The email was formal notification that Abby was under investigation for sexual harassment. She was advised to seek legal counsel and directed not to discuss the case with any employee of Mika Williams Productions or Binge network.

"This is bullshit," Sara said, her voice loud in the small cabin.

"Please leave me alone," Abby said.

"I don't want to leave you alone. This isn't right."

Dani appeared next to Sara, holding her phone. "Sara, we got a similar email. For Abby's protection, you can't talk to her."

Sara looked at Abby, who had turned back to the window. "I'll get you a lawyer. Don't say anything to anyone." Abby didn't respond.

* * *

Sara and Dani used the flight time to check social media. When Binge canceled their appearances, the fans saw it as tacit acknowledgment of Abby's guilt. Calls to fire Abby dominated the *Corsetti* and Binge feeds. Two hours into the flight, the network released a statement: "Binge takes any report of harassment seriously. As such, we will conduct a full investigation into the allegations of harassment on the set of *Corsetti's Will.*"

"Why are they giving Christina so much power? It was a tweet," Sara said.

Dani handed her tablet to Sara and pointed to a post. "This 'boycott Corsetti' hashtag will be trending by tomorrow." She scrolled down. "This one is their biggest fear." She opened the tweet so Sara could read the hashtag.

"Cancel Binge?"

"Yes."

Sara's voice dropped to an angry whisper. "So Abby gets fired to save a few subscriptions?"

Dani turned in her seat, her tone firm. "Studios can't ignore sexual harassment or homophobia, nor do we want them to." Dani took her tablet back. "Think if you'd heard the same rumor about a different show. You would be outraged, demanding an investigation."

Sara rubbed a hand over her face. "You're right. But this feels like it's about business, not doing the right thing. It's like they don't care about the truth."

"It's always about business."

"I texted my lawyer. She's going to call back with some names for Abby." Sara turned so she could look in Dani's eyes. "Will it matter? Are they going to fire her anyway?"

"They can't. She'd have a case for wrongful termination. But if they find anything, they'll fire her."

"What is Christina up to? Does she think this will save her career?"

Dani shook her head. "Maybe? I don't know."

"I should call her."

"Sara," Dani warned. "If you interfere, it will make it even worse for Abby. Find her a lawyer and answer HR's questions honestly. You can't get involved."

Sara dropped her head against the seat. "I know."

* * *

Three cars waited on the tarmac. When they got off the plane, a man in a charcoal suit stepped forward. Mika watched as he handed Abby a sealed manila envelope. "Ms. Farina, have your attorney contact Human Resources to schedule an interview. In the meantime, you are not allowed on the set of *Corsetti's Will* or any other property associated with Binge or Mika Williams Productions. This car is for you." He opened the back door of the first car and ushered Abby inside.

Sara stormed over to him. "Did anyone consider the possibility that Christina Landis is making this up? It was a fucking tweet!"

He turned cool eyes to her. "Ms. Silver, my office will be in touch. You'll have the opportunity to share your experiences at that time." He looked at the women. "Alex will drop you wherever you need to go." He got into the third car without another word.

Mika's eyes were dulled by pain and medication. "Sara, Dani, I—"

Dani stopped her. "There's nothing to be done tonight except for you to get better." Dani took Mika's arm and led her to the second car where their suitcases had already been loaded. "Do you have what you need at home? Food? Medication?" At Mika's nod, she helped her into the back seat and told the driver, "We'll go to Ms. Williams's home, first."

* * *

Abby opened a bottle of wine and filled a tumbler. No sense dealing with a delicate stem. She was going to finish the bottle, and if she was still standing, open another.

Halfway through her second glass, she convinced herself that the women from ClexaCon wouldn't abandon her so easily. They'd loved Corsetti Karaoke. The YouTube videos had thousands of likes. Sara's words from that night echoed in her mind. "You won't find a better group of supporters than the people in this room and the fans we've met this week." She topped off her glass and opened Twitter. Buried in the handles and the hashtags was so much hate.

LOL! Didn't she know the whole fandom hated her before this?
Like Sara would ever sleep with that fat ass bitch.
Share your ideas for how to kill her off!
Stab her with an Emmy.
Maybe we could just send her instructions on how to kill herself.
Anyone got extra oxy? Never mind, too painless.
Lock her in her house and set it on fire. Then we can all watch the bitch burn.

When the phone rang in her hand, Abby jumped. It was Sara. She touched "Decline" and set the phone down. A minute later a text notice sounded. Sara, again. *Answer your phone. I've got the name of a lawyer for you.* A few seconds later, it rang again.

"I don't think we should talk," Abby said in greeting.

"They can't keep me from giving you information about a lawyer. My lawyer recommended Margaret Zimmer. He said she's one of the top sexual harassment defense attorneys. I just got off the phone with her. She thinks you have a good case. She'll call you tomorrow."

"Sara, thanks, but I can't afford a big-deal lawyer."

"I'll take care of it." Abby started to protest, but Sara talked over her. "I'll take care of it until this is settled. Once you prove Christina lied, Margaret said you can go after her for your legal fees."

"Christina doesn't have any more money than I do."

"Margaret doesn't think it will take long to get this settled. She thinks Christina overplayed her hand, not realizing how big this would get. She doesn't think she'll cooperate with Binge's investigation."

"So, it just gets dropped, but people continue to believe I pushed her off the show?" Abby put her head in her hand. This would never end.

"No, Margaret will contact Christina and let her know you'll pursue action against her if she doesn't retract her statement."

Abby shook her head. "It's a no-win. All she has to do is tell people that my lawyer threatened her, and I'm still the bitch who deserves to burn."

"Burn?" Sara paused. "Oh, Abby. Did you get on Twitter? Don't read that stuff."

Abby choked out a sob. "It's awful, Sara."

"I'm sorry. Promise me you won't read anymore."

"They're so hateful and angry."

"Abby, did they threaten you?" When Abby didn't answer, Sara continued. "If they did, you have to report it. You can't ignore threats."

"That will just make it worse. A straight woman reports lesbians for hate speech?" She gave a mirthless laugh. "Imagine the hate I'll get then."

Sara thought for a moment. "Let me take over your account. I want to respond to them. I want to shut them down."

"There are too many. And what could you possibly say to make a difference?"

"I don't know, but I can't let them attack you without responding." They were quiet, then Sara whispered, "I wish I could be with you. I can't stand that you're alone."

Abby couldn't answer. She felt like her time with Sara happened to a different person. After a moment she said, "I'll send you my Twitter password. Thanks, Sara."

A half hour later, Sara posted on both their feeds:

Hey everyone, you'll be hearing a lot more from me as soon as I can speak out. In the meantime, I'm taking over @Abby_ Farina's Twitter feed. As a community who has experienced so much hate, we must be diligent in fighting it. #nomorehate #waitfortruth #womensupportingwomen

CHAPTER THIRTY

Although Mika still felt like she was moving through fog, she couldn't take any more time to recover from her migraine. She'd received her own email from Binge. As the representative of her production company and the showrunner for *Corsetti's Will*, she was under investigation for failing to protect Christina Landis from sexual harassment.

She was pulling out her lawyer's number when her father called. She wanted to ignore him, but experience had taught her it was better to answer. "Mika, what the fuck have you done?"

She bristled at the words and, with effort, remained calm. "Why are you calling?"

"Because the studio expects me to fix your mess. Jesus, this has been a nightmare from the start."

"Has it?" she replied, keeping a firm hold on her temper. "Because last week this show provided a substantial spike in Binge subscriptions."

He huffed out a breath. "Don't be cute. Rand had to bring in extra security for the Binge offices. There's a bunch of dykes in front of the building threatening to shut the network down. I warned you about this."

She sighed as the tension returned to her shoulders and neck. If she wasn't careful, the headache wouldn't be far behind. "Which is why I assumed you'd be calling to see how you could help. But, as that is not your intention, stay out of my way while I handle the situation."

"Belinski has given you a long rope, and rather than thanking him, you're hanging the entire network. That's gonna change."

Mika stared at the phone. Had he hung up on her? For the first time she felt a prickling of fear. The phone call was her father's way of letting Mika know he was planning something. She needed to end the Christina investigations before he succeeded in ruining her. She called Dani.

"How are you feeling?"

"I've had better days. Have you discovered anything?"

"I think so. I kept going back to one of the hashtags, 'support queer films.' Why that? Why not 'support queer actors'? That's Christina's complaint."

"I've suspected Luciana was behind this somehow, but I can't see her motivation. Surely it's not publicity for *Night in Time*?"

"I don't think so. I think she's trying to finance a new film. It took a little digging, but the primary backer of *Night in Time* was Hager Tech. In fact, Hager financed Raithman's last two films. They were modestly profitable, but not enough for others to show interest."

"I didn't realize Elizabeth Hager was her financial backer as well as her wife," Mika said. "That explains why Luciana wouldn't leave Elizabeth. So, what happened? Did Elizabeth find out about the affair?"

"Neither has made a statement, but they haven't been seen in public in weeks. Elizabeth has been off social media for about a month. Luciana hadn't posted anything until Christina's tweet came out. She retweeted it and commented about Christina's incredible performance in *Night in Time*."

Mika considered Dani's words. "So, Elizabeth finds out about the affair and ends their marriage, which means Luciana loses her funding just as Christina is making a name for herself. Luciana tells Christina she loves her and wants her back, then concocts a scandal to explain Christina's departure from the show. How does that help her?"

"Luciana is crowdfunding the movie. She'll use the controversy to get donations. I'll bet in the next couple of days, she'll put something out about channeling people's outrage into financial support for Christina's career."

"Can you put everything you found in a document for me? I'm meeting with my lawyer this afternoon."

"I'll have it to you within an hour. Anything else?"

"No, Dani, you've been invaluable, as always. Thank you."

* * *

"It's all supposition," Mika's lawyer told her. "Your argument is predicated on a hashtag and a crowdfunding site. We can't build a defense on that." She held up a hand when Mika started to argue. "That's not to say we won't float the information out there to generate doubt."

"It never happened. That's the defense," Mika said.

"Yes, and we'll argue that as long as we can, but it's tenuous. One witness, one piece of video that corroborates Landis, and suddenly you're either lying or incompetent."

"What do you suggest?"

"An affirmative defense. We won't argue whether or not the harassment occurred, but that Ms. Landis did not give you the opportunity to correct the actions of Ms. Farina. You can't be liable for behaviors of which a reasonable person would be unaware. My guess is that Ms. Landis will allege the harassment took place at a time you were not on set."

Mika studied the woman. "Can't she argue she reported it to me?"

"Yes, but we'll counter that allegation by documenting what you have done to create a safe environment for your cast and crew."

"We haven't done any sexual harassment training."

"That's not a problem. Ms. Landis is alleging harassment based on sexual orientation. Document anything that you did or said that demonstrated you would not tolerate homophobia."

"You're joking. The show is my response to homophobia in the industry."

"Who knew that? Did you share that information with the cast? How did you talk about the relationship between the two women on the show? How did you approach the sex scenes? Were they respectful of the relationship? How about the women during filming? I need answers to those questions."

Mika scribbled furiously on a legal pad. "I understand. You want to demonstrate how preposterous it is that Christina didn't report the harassment. And if she didn't report, it didn't happen."

"Exactly."

* * *

Margaret Zimmer wasted no time getting to the heart of the matter. "I know you have two concerns. One is easier to resolve than the other. I don't believe you will face any legal charges based on Ms. Landis's allegations. That is, unless someone comes forward to corroborate her claims." She clasped her hands and gave Abby a hard look. "I need to know right now if corroboration exists."

"No." Abby's voice was firm and she held her lawyer's gaze. "Christina and I weren't even on set together very often. My scenes filmed early in the week, and she filmed Thursday afternoon and Friday. Mika wanted fewer people on set when they filmed the sex scenes."

"Document every interaction you had with her. I need to know what was said, who witnessed the interaction, whether it was personal or professional."

"I don't think I'll remember them all, but I'll do my best."

"Was Christina well-liked? Were there members of the cast or crew who she was close to?"

"Nooo," Abby drew out the word as she thought. "I never saw her with anyone. Well, except for Sara. She went shopping with Sara one weekend, and Sara was protective of her."

"Why was that?" Margaret was taking notes.

Abby looked away. "There were rumors that they brought in an acting coach for Christina. She was stiff, kind of robotic in her scenes. I think Sara wanted to help her be more comfortable."

"Why do you think Christina struggled?" Margaret's head was down, but Abby sensed a tension in her.

"I don't know."

"Would she say it's because of you?"

Abby sat back in her chair, furious. "It wasn't. She struggled during the first table read. We'd barely spoken."

"Why did Sara try to protect her?"

"I don't know. There was a day when Mika asked Sara to do something with Christina over the weekend." Abby's breath caught. "Oh, no." Her mind flooded with memories of the conversation. "Sara was going to invite me to go to estate sales with her. She said Christina could join us, but Mika said it should be just the two of them. She asked me if I minded." Zimmer continued writing after Abby finished speaking. "That sounds bad doesn't it?"

Margaret made a noncommittal noise. "Do you and Sara get along well?" Abby looked away. "Abby, I need to know everything."

Still, Abby hesitated. She didn't know how to characterize her relationship with Sara. They'd had less than twenty-four hours together, but Abby had felt her life changing in that time. Now, she didn't know what was left, if anything. "We had a brief sexual relationship."

To her credit, Margaret didn't change expression, nor did she look away from Abby to write that on her notepad. "How long ago?"

Abby crossed and uncrossed her legs, not sure why she was so uncomfortable. The back of her shirt was damp with sweat, and she was sure her hands were shaking. "Sunday. The day before the tweet came out. When we were in New York."

"Are you still seeing her?"

"No. I was told I couldn't talk with anyone associated with the studio or the show. She called to give me your name."

"How would Sara describe your interactions with Christina?"

"Polite, friendly."

"Would she say you were jealous of Christina's on-screen role?"

"No. I had more screen time. Based on that alone, Bria is a better part."

Margaret reached for her laptop and pulled up a video. Abby recognized it immediately—the ClexaCon panel.

"Sara, who would you like to play your new girlfriend?"

"Abby," a woman yelled. The audience laughed and applauded.

"I'll be happy to work with anyone, even Abby, but thankfully, that's Mika's department."

"So, what about it, Mika? Bria and Joey?"

"Stranger things have happened."

Abby stared at the screen. In light of Christina's accusation, the innocent teasing looked planned. "The audience asked the question," she argued weakly.

"Was there anyone from your staff in the audience? Any friends of yours?" Abby could only nod. "Who?" Margaret asked.

"Dani Copeland, the social media manager for the show." Abby watched Zimmer write the name. "It looks bad, doesn't it?"

"It can be used to suggest there was a plan to force her out. How close are you to Dani Copeland?"

"That's not Dani's voice. You could prove that, right?" Margaret looked at her. "She could have had someone else ask," Abby answered her own question. She took a deep inhale and let it out. "Dani and I are friendly, but no more so than anyone else. I probably know her better because of ClexaCon and the press tour."

Margaret Zimmer finished writing, put her pen on her pad, and sat back. "How quickly could you get me the documentation of your interactions?"

"I've got nothing else to do. I'll start as soon as I get home."

"Good. Email it to me as soon as you're finished. Make sure you include names of any witnesses. In the meantime, I've requested interviews with Mika Williams and Sara Silver. I'll add Dani Copeland, as well. I've also asked for any verbal or written complaints against you." She stood. "I know it's difficult, but try not to worry."

* * *

Lost in thought, Abby pulled into the parking lot of her apartment building. She needed groceries but didn't have the energy to shop. Reaching for her purse, she opened the door and stepped out. She was several feet away from the car before the noise registered in her consciousness. A crowd stood just outside the entrance of her building chanting something she couldn't quite make out. Then she saw the signs. "Fire Farina." "Stop the Hate." "Acting Gay is for Gay Actors." "Boycott Binge."

Shocked, she took a couple of backward steps, but it was too late. "Is that her?" someone yelled. Before she could move, they rushed her. She considered running for the car but was afraid they would chase her like a trapped animal. Not knowing what else to do, she stood frozen while they ran toward her, phones and signs held high. In seconds she was surrounded by women shouting and screaming obscenities at her.

With her purse held tight against her body, Abby tried to step outside the circle, but every direction she moved, they moved with her. It was a strange dance with a clear intention. Abby would not leave this circle until they allowed it. She stopped moving. One woman leaned in until her face was inches from Abby. "How does it feel to be hated? We're going to be here every day showing you the same hate you showed Christina." The women cheered and screamed at her. Phones were thrust in her face.

Abby knew she was going to have to push through the tightening circle. She tried to look above their heads to get her bearings. They were so close she couldn't tell which direction to run. Then the sound changed, and the crowd pushed in on itself. Two people broke through the circle. A woman grabbed Abby's arm. "Come on," she yelled above the screams. "Run for the door." A man stepped toward the women and surprisingly they parted. Together they ran into the building, securing the door behind them. The protestors pounded on the glass of the door, cursing Abby and her rescuers.

The woman still had hold of her arm. She pulled her to the stairs at the back of the old building. "You're on the third floor, right?" she said. Abby was shaking all over. She could barely walk, much less answer questions. "It's okay. We live next to you. Well, he does," she pointed at the man standing behind them. "Come on, let's get you into your apartment, then we'll call the police."

"No!" Abby grabbed her arm. "No, it will get worse. Please don't call the police."

The woman wrapped her arm around Abby's shoulders and looked back at the door. "I don't know how it could be worse than that."

Once she was in her apartment, Abby hurried to close all of the blinds, but she could still hear the chants and laughter. Her hands shook and her legs felt too weak to support her weight. Even though it was early afternoon, she climbed in bed. They were still so loud. She put her phone close to her pillow and drowned out the noise with music.

CHAPTER THIRTY-ONE

The first couple of days, Sara comforted herself with memories of their day and night in New York. They'd gone back to the hotel and made love again. After drifting to sleep in each other's arms, they'd awakened to order room service. Over a bottle of wine, they shared stories, laughed and teased each other, but never talked about what would happen when they returned to LA.

Dani's warning—that it would be Abby who paid the price if Sara violated the HR directive—had the desired effect. Other than the first night she'd called Abby with the name of a lawyer, she'd stayed away, but now she wasn't sure that she should have. It was over a week since Christina's tweet, and nothing was happening. No one from Binge had contacted her to ask questions, set an appointment, or let her know what was going on. She'd taken to calling the network daily, but all she got was empty assurances that they would talk with her soon.

As she picked up her phone to call yet again, Nathan knocked on the door to her room. "How you doing?" he asked when she let him in.

"I feel like this pit in my stomach will never go away. What's going on? Why is it taking so long?"

"Let's go downstairs and talk over coffee. I have an idea." He left the room, and by the time she made it down, he had a fresh mug waiting for her. "You know I never like to encourage your ego, but it's time to use your star power. Call the head of the network and demand to speak with him. Don't take no for an answer."

"Really?" But she knew he was right. Part of her star power, as he called it, was that she actually had the number for John Belinski's office. "Okay," she said. "I'm ready to go full diva on him."

"Atta girl," Nathan said. "Let me know what happens."

A polished executive assistant answered her call. "Binge Network, Mr. Belinski's office."

"Hello, this is Sara Silver. I'd like to speak with Mr. Belinski."

"Hello, Ms. Silver. Unfortunately, Mr. Belinski is out of the country and currently unavailable. Mr. Rand is working with Mika Williams Productions. Would you like to be connected with his office?"

"Yes, and would you let Mr. Belinski know I'd like to speak with him? He can call me any time."

"Certainly, Ms. Silver. I'll make sure he gets the message. Please hold, I'll transfer you to Mr. Rand's assistant."

Sara hoped she wouldn't hear her own music as she waited for the call to connect. When another soothing voice answered, she was told Larry Rand was unavailable but would call her back as soon as possible.

As soon as possible was late afternoon, and Sara was furious. "Ms. Silver, what can I do for you?"

"You could explain why the investigation into Christina Landis's false accusation is taking so long. Why haven't I been interviewed?"

"Not to worry. We have plans in place to get your show moving forward very soon. I think you'll be pleased."

His unctuous tone increased her irritation. "So, you're ready to clear Abby Farina?"

"The investigation is ongoing, but I'm confident we'll be able to start filming in another week."

"How can we resume filming if Abby hasn't been cleared?" Sara ground her teeth. Something was going on.

"By chance have you been on Change.org recently?" Rand asked.

"What?"

"Change.org is a website where people create and share petitions."

"I know what Change.org is," Sara growled.

"*Corsetti's Will* is the focus of one of the petitions. Over ten thousand people have expressed a desire for Abby Farina to be fired." He smoothed his voice, becoming even more irritating. "Ms. Silver, you're the star. You bring in the viewers. As long as we have you, we can proceed."

"I will not proceed, as you call it, with a company that allows false accusations to ruin someone's career." She took a ragged breath. "I expect to be interviewed tomorrow."

"I admire your loyalty to Ms. Farina. I'll contact HR and make sure they schedule an appointment with you. In the meantime, I look forward to seeing you next week."

* * *

Mika sat in the empty conference room, fuming. The summons to appear at Binge had come from Larry Rand's executive assistant. She'd arrived promptly at 11:00, and it was now 11:20. She'd just decided to leave when she heard a laugh she knew too well. "Absolutely not," she said aloud.

The door opened and Larry Rand walked in, followed by Mike Williams. "I hope you haven't been waiting long, Mika." Rand extended his hand.

She took his hand, holding it while she spoke. "Of course I've been waiting, but that was your intention, wasn't it?"

Rand looked stunned, but Mike Williams laughed. "Your manners haven't gotten any better, Mika." The two sat, Rand at the head of the table, Williams across from his daughter. She took in his smug expression and felt a tingle of fear down her back. When he noticed her eyeing him, he winked.

"We're just waiting for one more," Rand said. "He's making copies of the script changes." Mika refused to rise to the bait. "Ah, here we go." David Stamper entered the conference room and placed a stack of papers in front of Rand. He didn't look at Mika.

She was too stunned to control her reaction. "David? What are you doing here?"

Williams answered, "I'll give you this, Mika. You hired a helluva head writer. David here has taken my ideas for a reboot and put together a damn fine script."

"What?" Mika looked across the table to David. "You wrote a script for him?"

Rand cut in. "Let me explain, Mika. We're in deep with this Abby Farina mess. You saw the numbers for the pilot. They weren't good. About half of what we expected. This petition is getting traction, and it's just a matter of time before Binge loses subscribers. When Mike called me with an idea for a reboot—more of a reset, really—I got hold of David and had him put together a script." Rand looked at David. "I've got to agree with Mike. He did a masterful job meshing what you have with this new direction."

"And Larry knows good writing," Williams said. He turned to Mika with mocking smile. "Larry was one of the finest writers on my team."

Mika turned her head to stare at Rand. "You worked for him?"

"You didn't know?" Williams slapped a hand on the table. "You probably remember him as LJ. Imagine my surprise when I found out he was a network bigwig."

Mika barely heard him. Everything was becoming clearer. "You've been planning this all along." Even though she'd always known what he was capable of, she still couldn't believe he'd gone this far. "Did you put Christina Landis up to the tweet?"

"Now you're just being paranoid. Your stubbornness with that girl is what got you here. We told you to recast, but you had to have her. Were you hot for her, Mika? Is that what it was?"

Rand flushed, recognizing Williams had gone too far. "This unfortunate situation provided an opportunity to broaden the appeal of *Corsetti's Will*. I think you'll like the direction, Mika. David, give her an overview of your script."

David shifted in his chair, still not meeting Mika's eyes. "Yes, David," Mika said. "By all means, share your ideas."

He looked at her. "Mika, you have to know, I didn't go looking for this. Mr. Rand called me, and I thought it was important for a member of our team to write the treatment."

Mika pointed to the stack of papers. "Treatment? That looks like a script to me."

"I originally asked David to put together a treatment, but when I read what he'd come up with, I knew it was worth developing a script."

Williams crossed an ankle over his knee and smiled at her. "Kid, you're in good hands. I gave him the direction he needed to save this mess." He looked at David. "Want me to tell her about it? You look like she scares the shit out of you."

"Mike." Rand's voice was surprisingly stern. "Let David speak."

David cleared his throat. "Mr. Rand wanted me to write a script to deal with both Noelle and Bria leaving the show. The only way to do that and stay true to your vision is to kill off both characters."

Williams's eyes flashed. "A massive explosion. The special effects will be incredible. That'll show the audience there's a new sheriff in town. If you want, you can even have Driskell get blown off her feet. Audiences love that shit."

Mika never looked away from David. He rubbed the back of his neck. "I wanted to make sure we stayed true to the name of the series, so after Bria and Noelle are killed, Joey is called back to the lawyer's office where she finds out Leo Corsetti had another child."

"Let me guess," she said. "A long-lost son. A down-on-his-luck loner who's been fighting against the system. He inherits half of the agency, and he and Joey have to learn to work together." He stared at her. "Surprised, David? You shouldn't be." She pointed at her father, but still held David's gaze. "That describes the main character in every one of his shows. Every. Single. One." She stood and looked at Rand. "My lawyer will be in contact with Mr. Belinski."

Mika couldn't remember the last time she'd felt the depth of rage she felt now. David had been with her for years and knew the struggles she'd gone through with her father. Her most trusted friend betrayed her at the behest of her father.

She wondered what that said about her, then instantly shut the thought down. A man would never make betrayal about his own character. He would see it as a declaration of war. So would she. Mika picked up her phone.

"Mika. Any news?" Dani asked.

"No. Are you free?"

"Yes. Shall I come to the office?"

"No," Mika said. "Come to my house. We have a lot of work to do."

* * *

Dani listened to Mika without interruption. When she was done, Dani nodded thoughtfully. "Have you been interviewed about Christina and Abby?"

Mika hid her surprise at the question. "No, not yet."

Dani pushed platinum bangs out of her eyes. "I was wondering why I haven't been contacted by HR, so I made a few calls." She paused. "No one has been interviewed."

They were in Mika's study, facing each other across the antique library table she used for a desk. "Are you suggesting they're deliberately slowing the investigation?"

"After what you just told me, there's no question that's what they're doing."

For the first time in years, she fought back tears. How had she not realized the extent of her father's reach? Or how insatiable his need for power was. If she was going to survive his attempted takeover, she needed help. "Do you have any ideas?" she asked, hoping she didn't sound as desperate as she felt.

"I've been researching California's no-fault divorce laws. Although adultery doesn't have a direct effect on spousal support, there's a loophole. If Luciana spent marital assets on her affair with Christina, that money can be subtracted from the settlement." Dani leaned forward, her eyes fixed on Mika. "Elizabeth may not know the extent of her wife's affair. If she did, she could make a case that any money spent on the movie was, in effect, spent on the affair. Didn't Christina tell Sara that the sex scenes in *Night in Time* were based on their affair?"

Mika felt a surge of energy. "What are you suggesting? That I talk with Elizabeth or threaten Luciana?"

Dani grimaced. "I wouldn't say threaten. Maybe confront her with brutal facts?"

Mika tapped her pen on her desk. "If I were Luciana, I would deny anything was going on, and accuse me"—Mika pointed to herself—"of lying to save my show."

Dani shook her head. "She could say that, except it was Sara that Christina confided in. If Sara goes public with what she knows, she'll be believed. Christina gave Sara credibility when she thanked her for her support."

"Do you know if Luciana's in California?"

"There's one way to find out." Dani pulled out an index card with a name and phone number written on it. "Her agent."

Mika took the card and read the name. "I don't pay you enough."

Dani smiled as she tucked her tablet into her purse. "That's easily fixed."

CHAPTER THIRTY-TWO

In the world of Hollywood lesbians, the degrees of separation were far less than six. With a couple of calls, Mika could get Raithman's number, but she needed to maintain the element of surprise. That meant going through an intermediary.

It took far less effort than expected. When she'd gone down her list of friends and acquaintances, she kept coming back to Betty Montoya, a no-nonsense cinematographer she'd liked from the moment they met. Betty was a small woman prone to dressing in oversized flannel shirts. No one, from extras to EPs, messed with Betty. How her reputation was created Mika didn't know, but the message was clear: whatever Betty said was how it would be done.

"Williams, how the hell are you?"

Despite her fatigue, Mika laughed in delight. "Better just hearing your voice, my friend."

"Like your new show. That Silver girl turned out to be a hell of an actress, but that other one was shit."

Mika groaned. "I know, Betty. She fooled me in that Raithman film."

"Mm-hmm. Wish we'd talked before you cast her. Lots of rumors came off that set."

"I didn't think you listened to rumors," Mika teased.

"Sometimes they're like a great pair of tits. When they're right in front of you, you gotta look."

"Betty." Mika tried to sound outraged. "What will Gracie say?"

"About the rumor or the tits? She likes 'em both." Betty cackled.

"I don't see you often enough. You're good for the soul."

"Lord knows this place can suck the soul right outta you. So, I know you didn't call to chat. How can I help you outta this shit?"

Mika closed her eyes, thankful this was the call she'd made. "I need to talk with Luciana Raithman, but I know she won't agree to meet me."

"Huh," Betty said. "Let me think on that. Can't be me. Too many people know we're friends. Give me a couple hours. I'll get back to you."

"Thanks, Betty. You're a great friend."

"I know. See ya."

It took three hours, but Betty came through. "You know Hayley Kendrick? She's that young kid who got all the attention for the arc on my show."

"She played the sister's girlfriend? Isn't she in her twenties?"

"Yeah, that's the one. The kid." Mika laughed. Betty liked to think of herself as the matriarch of every set. "I had her call Raithman. They're meeting tomorrow afternoon for drinks."

"How did she get Luciana to agree so quickly?"

"Do you listen to any gossip? Raithman likes the young ones. Hayley told her she was interested in being in one of her films, and Luciana did the rest."

"Is Hayley worried Raithman will blackball her?"

Betty laughed. "She can try, but who do you think has more power? You with your development contract or Luciana who has to crowdfund her movie?"

* * *

It was Betty's idea to have Hayley actually show up for the meeting. "When she hits on the kid, you can threaten to tell her wife and Christina."

Mika arrived at the restaurant early and sat in a shadowed corner of the bar where she nursed a club soda and worried. Even if everything went perfectly today, undoing the damage Christina had done to Abby was going to be difficult. Despite Sara's efforts, the fans were angry, and Abby was taking a daily hit on social media.

Luciana arrived first and Mika studied her. She was of average height with short dark hair, expensively cut and colored. Her features were soft—her cheeks and chin rounded. She was maternal looking, but Mika had heard she was also charismatic. She probably emphasized different aspects of her personality to suit her needs. Elizabeth Hager had likely fallen for the charismatic filmmaker, while Christina Landis was drawn to the softer caretaker. When Hayley Kendrick was shown to the table, neither trait made an appearance.

Mika watched her tease and flirt, occasionally reaching out to touch the young woman's arm but never lingering. The subtlety of the seduction was fascinating. This was a game Luciana had played many times, and Mika guessed she was usually successful. When Luciana's gaze dropped to the actress's chest, Mika had enough. She wound her way through the bar until she stood in front of their table. She reached her left hand out. "Hayley, lovely to see you."

Hayley Kendrick took Mika's hand and used it to slide out of the booth and stand. She kissed Mika's cheek. "Nice to see you too." She reached back into the booth for her purse before turning to Luciana. "Nice to meet you," she said before walking away.

Luciana's mouth was slightly open as she watched Hayley exit the restaurant. She kept her face turned after the girl was out the door. Mika guessed she was using the time to regain her composure. When she finally looked back, her color had returned, along with a cold stare. "Mika," was all she said.

Mika slid into the booth and clasped her hands on the table. "Luciana."

"You could have called if you wanted to talk." Luciana leaned back, casually crossing her legs and draping her forearms over her lap. "What can I do for you?"

Mika marveled at the temerity of the woman, but she adopted the same polite tone. "I'm glad that's how we're starting this conversation. There are several things you can do for me." Luciana inclined her head, inviting Mika to continue. "Christina has harmed Abby Farina with her false allegations. That needs to be corrected immediately."

"If that's what you want, this conversation should be between you and Christina. Or, better yet, Abby and Christina." Luciana's tone was regretful. "I'm afraid I can't help you." She lifted her hand to get the attention of a waiter.

"I'm sorry you feel that way," Mika said. She tapped her phone's screen and waited for her call to connect. "Renee, I'm going to need that meeting with Elizabeth Hager after all. Yes, as soon as she's available." Mika disconnected the call and looked at Luciana. "I'd be lying if I said I'm sorry this is the path you've chosen." She slid to the edge of the booth and stood. "Goodbye, Luciana. Good luck funding your movie."

As they both knew she would, Luciana stopped her. "Wait. Perhaps I can be a mediator between Christina and Abby."

"Can you?" Mika couldn't keep the sarcasm out of her voice. "Let's not waste each other's time. Christina needs to completely retract her statement. That means the allegations against Abby Farina and the suggestion of a hostile work environment. It needs to be done in a press release and appear on her social media accounts."

Luciana hadn't lost any of her bravado. "Why would Christina want to do that? She was harmed on the set of your show. I would think you would be here offering other opportunities, not threats."

Mika continued as if Luciana hadn't spoken. "If Christina's statement in any way falls short, Sara Silver and I will meet with Elizabeth tomorrow. Sara will share Christina's confidences about the affair you had on the set of *Night in Time*, as well as the use of your shared home for sexual rehearsals. My lawyers tell me that Elizabeth will have grounds to prove you used marital funds to finance your affair. Under California law, you'll be required to pay Elizabeth back the money she invested in your movie and possibly give up any rights to the house." The anger she'd been trying to hold at bay, rose. "You manipulated that poor girl all so you could make a small-budget film. You're pathetic."

Later, Mika regretted her last dig at Luciana. Living in her father's world of self-preservation and the powerful clawing to possess as much power as possible, she should have known that Christina, not Luciana, would be the one to suffer. The press release came late that night. "After much soul-searching, I'm taking some time away to work on myself. I realize now that my perceptions of what happened with Abby Farina and *Corsetti's Will* were not accurate. I regret the harm my words caused to Abby and the show. I'm deeply sorry. You deserved better."

* * *

As soon as Mika saw the release, she called Larry Rand. "We will resume production of *Corsetti's Will* Monday morning. Neither you, Mike Williams, or David Stamper will be allowed on the lot."

Rand laughed. "Yes, we will resume production on Monday, but it's you, Mika, who isn't allowed on set. I was going to call you at a more appropriate hour tomorrow to update you on the progress of the reboot. The new scripts are set to go out. Mike has cast a former soap actor to play Marco Corsetti."

Mika closed her eyes, nearly overcome by rage. She took a deep breath, calming her voice. "Christina Landis has publicly retracted her statement and apologized to Abby Farina. This is the last conversation I will have with you. If you attempt to contact any member of the cast and crew of *Corsetti's Will* or Mika Williams Productions, I will seek legal action against you personally." She hung up before he could respond.

Mika walked into the kitchen and poured a glass of wine. After taking a healthy swallow and a few minutes to calm her anger, she called Abby.

"Mika?" Abby sounded frightened.

"Abby, I'm sorry I woke you, but I wanted you to know right away. Christina issued a press release retracting her accusations against you. I've called Binge to let them know we are resuming production. Are you ready to get back to work?" Her words were met with silence. She spoke softly. "Abby?"

"Did she say why she did it?"

"No, only that she was sorry, and you deserved better." Abby didn't say anything. Mika let the silence linger for another few moments before saying, "Are you okay?"

Abby's voice caught. "No. I don't think I am."

After the call, Mika sat in the dark drinking her wine. Her plan had been to call her lawyer to explore legal remedies against her father, Larry Rand, and possibly David. She'd contemplated going as far as getting a restraining order against her father, but since her grievances would be couched in legal terms, it would leave the interpretation of events, and the last word, to him.

But she couldn't expect Abby to resume her role without some public reckoning. She'd had been harmed by Luciana, Christina, Binge, and their fans. Despite her wishes, filming couldn't start on Monday.

Mika finished her wine and stood to go to bed. She had a lot of work to do.

CHAPTER THIRTY-THREE

Abby watched the replay and felt the same drop in her stomach she had the morning it happened. Keisha Armstrong spoke to the camera. "Mika, take me back to that day. What were you thinking when you saw the tweet?"

Mika was seated on a raised stage surrounded by a small audience. "I was stunned. Truly shocked. It was so different from the conversation I had with Christina when she asked to be let out of her contract."

"When you heard it, did you think it was possible Abby Farina had harassed Christina without your knowledge? That Abby wanted Christina off the show?"

"No. I knew it wasn't possible. Christina and Abby were very rarely on set at the same time. Because of the intimate nature of Christina's role, we always filmed her scenes on a closed set after everyone else was done for the week. But that's not the only reason, I was sure." Mika leaned forward to emphasize her words. "Abby Farina brings joy to the set of *Corsetti's Will*. She's kind to the crew, her castmates, and our guests. Abby is, quite literally, the last person I would believe capable of harassment."

"Let's bring her out. Please welcome Abby Farina." At her name, Abby felt the anxiety move from her stomach to her chest. She walked onto the stage and accepted Keisha's hug before settling in the chair next to Mika. She crossed her legs and rubbed her chest, trying to ease the panic. "Abby, what did you think when you saw the tweet?"

She kept her answer short, hoping the quaver in her voice wouldn't be noticeable. "I was shocked. I thought it was a mistake—that Christina's account had been hacked."

"What was your relationship with Christina?"

She swallowed, trying to keep the nerves from rising to her throat. "Friendly. I really didn't know her that well. We saw each other Mondays at the table read, and sometimes Thursdays during lunch when she was coming in and I was heading home."

Keisha looked at the camera again. "Fourteen days after her original tweet, Christina Landis released this statement." The press release appeared on-screen behind the anchor, and Keisha read it aloud. When she was done, she asked, "Abby, what do you think happened?"

The open-ended question was an invitation. The night before, Mika had given Abby a file folder in her New York hotel room. "In there is an explanation of everything that happened to you, why it happened, and who is ultimately responsible. Tomorrow, Keisha will give you the opportunity to reveal the truth. As long as you stick to the facts outlined in there"—she tapped the folder in Abby's hand—"neither Christina nor Luciana can sue you."

"Luciana?"

"Luciana Raithman." Mika walked to the door of the suite and opened it. "The decision is yours."

Up until the moment Keisha asked the question, Abby thought she would reveal everything Mika had shared. But as she started to speak, humiliation flooded her. Luciana Raithman had made her life and her career meaningless. She was someone who was easily sacrificed. Abby realized sharing the story would only make her feel more insignificant. It would let everyone know what Luciana had figured out: Abby wasn't important. She glanced at Mika. "I don't know what happened, but I accept Christina's apology and wish her well."

The studio was silent while Keisha waited for her to add more. When it was clear that was all she was going to say, Keisha gave Abby a small smile and looked into the camera. "There's much more to this story. What happened to Abby Farina and Mika Williams in the fourteen days between the initial false allegation and the eventual retraction is deeply disturbing."

"And we're out," a voice offstage said.

Keisha reached her hand out to Abby. "I'm sorry I didn't get to talk with you before we went on-air. Thanks for having the courage to be here." She squeezed Abby's hand. "Are you sure you want to leave it at that? I can give you another opportunity to share what really happened." Her words caused a wave of emotion, and Abby teared up. "I'm sorry, I didn't mean to upset you," Keisha said.

Abby waved her words away as one of the women from Makeup rushed forward. "This seems to be my new normal. Everything makes me cry." She looked up as the woman sponged makeup under her eyes. "No. That's all I want to say." Out of the corner of her eye, she could see Keisha's nod.

The same disembodied voice counted down and Keisha said, "We're back with Mika Williams and Abby Farina of *Corsetti's Will*." She turned to Abby. "Tell us about that first night."

Abby inhaled deeply. "The network canceled most of our appearances, so I was back home in LA. I had a couple of glasses of wine and decided to check Twitter." She gave a shaky laugh. "The week before, Sara…"

"Sara Silver, your costar," Keisha clarified.

"Yes. Sara and I hosted a karaoke night for LGBTQ+ charities. We had a great time, and a couple of videos from that night ended up on YouTube."

Keisha turned to the screen behind them. "Like this one?" The audience laughed as a clip of Abby and Sara singing "I Got You Babe" played.

"That's one of them," Abby said. "At the time it had gotten thousands of likes. The people who attended that event were friendly and very supportive." She shook her head and cleared her throat. "So that first night, I thought, 'Well, those people like me. They'll defend me.'"

"And did they?" Keisha's voice was gentle.

"No." Abby could barely get the word out. Keisha pushed a tissue box toward her. "Sorry," Abby mumbled as she pulled one out.

"In fact, many of the tweets about you were threatening," Keisha said. "So threatening, in fact, that when Sara Silver saw Abby's Twitter feed, she asked to take over the account. Sara joins us from Los Angeles." Keisha turned to the screen showing a feed of Sara at the studio. "Sara, thanks for joining us. Tell us what you found when you went on Abby's account."

"Hate," Sara said. "There's no other word for what was directed at Abby. I've never seen anything like it. It was horrible."

"You took screenshots before reporting the threats to Twitter." Keisha looked at the camera. "A warning to our viewers, some of these are disturbing." The tweets were projected behind Keisha.

You need to watch your back, bitch. I'm coming for you.

Call your parents and tell them goodbye.

You think it's okay to take someone's job? How bout if someone takes your life?

The next one that appeared on-screen had the first line blurred out. "This one may be the most disturbing," Keisha said. "That's Abby's address we've blurred. The next line is terrifying, *'Looks like it would be easy to burn down. Sleep well.'*"

Sara's face came back on-screen. "Sara, you've said this is deeply personal to you. Tell us why."

Sara's face softened. "Well, first because Abby is an incredible woman who's very special to me and to everyone at *Corsetti's Will*." Keisha reached back and squeezed Abby's hand. Sara continued, "I'm also deeply saddened that members of the gay community and our allies are responsible for spreading hate. As a community, we've been victims of hate and know the depth of the pain it causes. I always believed we took the higher road. I was wrong."

Keisha turned to face the camera. "There's still more, including what happened when protestors showed up outside Abby's home." There was a slight gasp from the audience as they broke for commercial.

Abby felt Mika's touch on her arm. "You doing okay?"

"I think so. How did she know about the protest?"

Mika seemed to be searching for the right words. "There's a video online. A couple of them, actually. You didn't know?"

Abby's chest tightened again. "They're going to show it?"

"Yes."

She looked away from Mika's intense eye contact. When Mika had first proposed they do this interview, Abby had been reticent, but Mika convinced her she needed to tell her story, to reclaim her reputation. But all she was doing was sharing her humiliation with millions of people. Abby closed her eyes. She felt ill.

Keisha brought them back from the commercial. "The day after Christina Landis's tweet, Binge network was flooded with calls to fire Abby. Protestors picketed outside the network's headquarters and a petition was posted on Change.org." Keisha switched positions to look into a different camera. "And then this happened."

Abby shrank in her chair as she watched the women corner her and listened to the bleeps of the censored expletives thrown at her. The noise and the look of terror on her face brought back the emotions of that day, and she started to tremble. When her neighbors shoved through the crowd and pulled her to safety, the audience applauded.

"Abby, how do you feel when you see that footage?"

Abby looked away, then took a deep breath and looked back. "Terrified."

* * *

The interview aired on the network's evening news magazine. Keisha Alexander sat on a stool, one long leg stretched to the ground, the other perched on a rung. "Tonight, you'll see my exclusive interview with Mika Williams and Abby Farina from Binge network's *Corsetti's Will*. Just over three weeks ago, I interviewed Mika, Abby, and actress Sara Silver for what was intended to be an appearance promoting the premiere of their show, *Corsetti's Will*. Less than a minute before we went on, Christina Landis posted her now infamous tweet." The tweet appeared on-screen as the anchor spoke. "In it, Landis, who played the on-screen girlfriend of Silver's Joey Driskell, accused Abby Farina of forcing her off the show so she could take over the role of Joey's love interest." Keisha looked to a second camera. "The story of what happened in the following fourteen days is one of terrifying threats, betrayal, and a shocking power grab."

"How'd she look?" Nathan said when the show went to commercial.

"I couldn't see her—only Keisha."

As soon as Christina's retraction was released, Sara called, but Abby didn't pick up. After the third voice mail, Sara got a text. *I've been in Palm Springs with my parents. Going with Mika to NYC. Talk when I get back.*

When Abby was introduced, the change was noticeable. Her clothes, which were normally an extension of her vibrant personality, were somber—a charcoal pantsuit with a monochromatic blouse. When she reached up to hug Keisha, Sara could see the weight loss. A close-up showed what even an expert makeup team couldn't hide. Her eyes were shadowed and dull. Sara put her fingers over her mouth, fighting back tears. "She looks destroyed."

Nathan looked at his sister. "She's strong. She'll be okay."

When the camera was on Abby's face, it was easy to see she was fighting tears throughout the interview. Her hands stayed in her lap, one gripping her wrist while the other crushed a tissue. Abby usually took up space with her enthusiasm, but now her shoulders were rounded and she was small in the oversized chair. "What's happened to her, Nathan?"

Once the video of the mob played, Sara understood. The women knew Abby was frightened, and they reveled in in it. Some yelled obscenities at her, others laughed at her helplessness, all the while capturing her terror on video. Next to her Nathan sat forward, his mouth tightening in anger. "Those bitches. They're laughing at how scared she is." He stood and walked to the side of the room. "I can't watch."

For Sara, anger at the mob and the studio warred with her own recriminations. "She must have felt so alone." Like Nathan, she wanted to look away but forced herself to watch how she'd abandoned Abby.

At last, two people broke through the crowd and pulled Abby away, shielding her until they got inside the apartment building. The video ended and Keisha introduced Abby's rescuers, joining them from LA via satellite.

"What did you think when you first got out of your car?"

"We didn't know what to think," the woman said. "We heard all this yelling and swearing, but we couldn't see anything but the signs and the crowd."

"I thought it was a fight," the man said.

"When did you realize what was happening?"

"When I walked up, I could see Abby was surrounded, and she looked scared, so I told Becca, 'We gotta help her.'"

"Did you know Abby before this? Did you know who she was or what was going on?"

"I didn't know her name or that she's on TV. I just knew she was my neighbor and what was going on wasn't right."

"Were you scared?"

The woman answered, "Yeah, I was. You were too." The guy nodded. "Some of those women were pretty tough-looking. I was afraid they were going to chase after us."

Keisha looked at Abby. "What were you feeling at this point?"

Abby shifted. "Honestly, I was dazed. I know I felt overwhelming gratitude. They stepped in without considering their own safety." The tears in her eyes spilled over. "I don't know what would have happened if they hadn't helped me."

"Did you call the police?" Keisha asked the couple.

"Abby didn't want us to. She thought it would make it worse, but we were scared to leave the apartment with them out there."

"What did the police do?"

"They said there wasn't much they could do. They told them to move off the property and warned them not to harass anyone."

"Did you ever speak to the police?" Keisha asked Abby.

"No."

"Why not?"

Abby shrugged, and it looked like she wasn't going to answer. Finally, she shook her head. "What could they do?"

* * *

Mika poured a second glass of wine when images of a young Mike Williams with his wife and daughter appeared behind Keisha. "Mika Williams was born into Hollywood royalty. The namesake of legendary producer Mike Williams, she found success in her own right. Her first job was writing for the series *Untimely Death*, where she earned an Emmy for her work. Although the show only lasted two seasons, Mika was hired to head the writing room on *Seattle PD*. From there she went on to create and produce the critically acclaimed *Murder* and *Malice Aforethought*."

Mika tuned out Keisha's voice-over as she watched images of the headlines following her blockbuster deal with Binge. She tuned back in when a recent picture of her father was shown. "As Mika's success grew, the appetite for Mike Williams's brand of entertainment waned. After his last show was canceled in 1991, he closed his company Lonely Hero Productions and seemingly retired."

Off-camera, Keisha had pressed Mika. Why would her father try to sabotage her career? What event in their past had caused such a rift? There were no answers to those questions. The truth was Mike Williams disappeared from her life because he didn't care enough to maintain a relationship with his daughter.

When she was seven, her parents divorced. By eight, she'd met too many of his new friends, all women. He was all but gone from her life by the time she was ten, only to reappear when she started to see success as a television writer. By that time, he hadn't had a show in ten years. Somehow, he convinced *People* magazine to run a story on Mike Williams, former blockbuster producer, and his daughter, the up-and-coming television writer. She'd refused to be part of the article, but he knew the business better than she did. One call to the studio and she was at his home posing for pictures with him. She could still call up the revulsion that had gripped her when he draped an arm around her, smiling for the camera. The article started a pattern: she'd find success, and he'd find a way to cash in on it.

In the days between Christina's retraction and the interview, Mika split time between the *Corsetti* writer's room and her attorney's offices. When she'd explained to her circumspect lawyer what she wanted, Elaine Xiang called in her law partner, and the two spent an hour trying to convince Mika of the recklessness of her plan. It took Mika threatening to find new representation before Elaine finally listened. From that moment, she used her considerable skills and the resources of Lafferty and Xiang to find the corroboration Mika needed to go public. It had taken another couple of days for the network's lawyers to approve the interview, but the documentation Mika's team provided along with pressure from Keisha Alexander convinced the executives.

Mika curled her legs under her and reached for her glass. The interview had already aired in other time zones, and her phone was buzzing with calls and texts. She checked each call, declining them all except one. "Hello, Father."

"You fucking bitch. My lawyers are going to destroy you. When I own your fucking company, I'm going to make that dyke show into a family-values wet dream. Maybe I'll send your man-hating dyke to get converted and she'll end up begging guys to fuck her."

He took a breath, and Mika broke in. "You've always underestimated me. Do you think I would tell my story to twenty-five million people without making sure I had every legal angle covered? But please, call your lawyers and spend what little money you have trying to undo the knots I have you in."

"You think so? One call, and I'll be telling my side of the story. I'll make sure the world knows you're a no-talent loser whose only success came because I gave you my name, and you used it to get to the top. You hate that I had to come in and save your ass, so you made up lies to cover how badly you failed."

"Self-preservation."

"Ha! You admit you lied. I should be taping this fucking call."

"Don't worry. I am. I have every word. But no, it's not my self-preservation I'm talking about. It's David's, and to my utter delight, Larry Rand's. They turned on you. It was harder for Larry, of course, because he was in charge, but he still managed to paint quite the picture of your manipulation. Now, David was especially helpful. He had a lot of documentation. Some of it in your handwriting. In exchange, I've agreed to allow him back into the writing room on my next show. Not only will you not win a lawsuit, if you attempt to spread lies about me in an interview, I'll let my lawyers take care of you. They assure me you will be well and truly fucked."

CHAPTER THIRTY-FOUR

Abby still hadn't called. Sara texted after the interview with Keisha aired telling her how sorry she was for what Abby had been through and how much she wished she'd been there. A few hours later, Abby replied: *Thanks*. The pit in Sara's stomach grew.

She lingered in front of the table of coffee and pastries, making small talk with anyone near. With only five minutes to go before the table read was to begin, there was still no sign of Abby. Sara walked to their table, trying not to read into Abby's absence but feeling like everyone had the same concern she did. Had Abby quit? Is that why she wouldn't talk to Sara? Just as Mika walked to the front of the room, Abby slipped into the chair next to her. Sara tried to catch her eye, but Abby's gaze was fixed on Mika. Sara swallowed back tears.

"Welcome…" That was as far as Mika got before the entire room stood as one and cheered. She took a small step back and placed a hand on her chest. She looked down and Sara could see she was fighting back her own tears. That was all it took for

Sara's emotions to spill over. She reached for her coffee, trying to swallow the tears along with the dregs of her cup.

When everyone was seated again, Mika's face grew serious. "By now you're all aware of the full extent of what took place over the last month. I know you already know this, but I want to make it perfectly clear for everyone. Abby Farina did not harass or intimidate Christina Landis. Abby was a victim." She let the word hang for a moment, and Sara could feel Abby stiffen beside her. "It is incumbent upon all of us to ensure she is not revictimized. While I know she appreciates your well-wishes and support, I'll ask you not to press her for details. The best we can do for her and the show is to return to normalcy." Mika smiled at Abby, then looked around the room. "In other news, views of the pilot have quadrupled, putting us on track to be Binge's number one show."

When the applause died down, she continued, "Originally, Episodes Two, Three, and Four were to be released the day after the television premiere. A former network executive"—she grinned wickedly—"put that schedule on indefinite hold. Now that Mr. Belinski is overseeing *Corsetti's Will*, Episodes Two through Five will be released in two weeks. We have work to do."

* * *

Abby was surrounded by well-wishers after the table read, so Sara left without talking to her. It didn't matter, because by that time Sara was so uncomfortable with the silence between them that she wasn't sure she could have spoken.

Tuesday morning, she walked into Makeup, comforted to see Tanya and Michelle's familiar faces. Sara hugged them both, holding on a little longer than normal. When she sat, Michelle perched in the empty chair next to her. "Where's Abby?" Sara asked.

"She came early. Texted me last night to see if she could come in a half hour before call," Michelle said.

Sara teared up. "Stop it," Tanya scolded as she grabbed a tissue.

"We haven't talked since New York." Sara dabbed under her eyes. "She's avoiding me." Michelle glanced at Tanya, who gave her a slight head shake. Sara looked between them. "Please tell me," she said. "I feel like I've lost my best friend."

Michelle straightened and her eyes flashed. "Best friend? You didn't act like a best friend."

Tanya was applying foundation to Sara's skin, so she had to look sideways at Michelle. Her mouth was set in a hard line. "Is that how she feels?"

"She didn't say that." Tanya gave Michelle a warning look.

"It's okay," Sara said. "I need to hear it."

"Why didn't you do anything? Why didn't you go on TV or do an interview defending her?" Michelle pointed at her. "You let them attack her. She stood by you—"

Tanya's voice rose. "Michelle." The two makeup artists locked gazes in the mirror, one defiant, the other warning.

"They told us we couldn't say anything. Her lawyer said I could make it worse if I made a statement." Her argument sounded weak to Sara's own ears.

"She knows that," Tanya said in a gentle voice.

Michelle crossed her arms over her chest. "You know what? You could have said something. Abby would have. If straight people attacked you for being gay, Abby would have shut it down." Michelle's face and neck were flushed. "You're one of the top gay celebrities. What you say matters, and you didn't say anything. You let them go after her." Michelle stood, gave Sara a long look, and walked out.

Tanya started to speak, but Sara stopped her with a shake of her head. "She's right. I didn't protect her. I didn't even try." She shook her head again, but this time it was to keep the tears at bay.

*　*　*

"Let's take lunch," Celia said. "Back on set at one o'clock."

"Abby, Sara." Mika stepped from behind the cameras. "Your lunches will be delivered to Abby's trailer." She moved closer so her words wouldn't be overheard. "The tension between you is affecting everyone. Get it figured out." Without another word, she walked away.

They stood, watching Mika's retreating back. Sara shoved her hands deep in the pockets of her jeans. "Is that okay?"

Abby shrugged, and they walked together, neither speaking until they reached the trailer. A craft services cart sat outside the door with two covered plates. Abby stepped inside, not bothering to pick up a lunch. She sank into the banquette, suddenly very tired.

Sara followed, carrying two plates. "You have to eat something," she said. "We have a long afternoon." She set a plate in front of Abby.

"You want something to drink?" Abby opened the small refrigerator. "Iced tea?" She held up a bottle, and Sara nodded. She took a water for herself and returned to the table.

While Abby tore at the label on the plastic bottle, Sara picked up her fork and pushed her salad around. Eventually, she placed her fork on the edge of the plate. "I can't eat," she said. "Abby, I'm so sorry, I wasn't there for you." Sara ran her fingers over her lips, and Abby could see it was to hide the tremble. "I thought I was doing the right thing when I left you alone, but…" Sara bent her head, and the tears fell. When she spoke again, the words were obscured by her emotion. "God, Abby, when I saw the video of you being attacked, it killed me. I'm so sorry. I should have spoken out. I just sat at home and let people hurt you. People in my community." Sara choked on those last words.

Abby watched Sara cry, but the image barely registered as she let Sara's words spin in her thoughts. Ever since the first morning when Keisha read Christina's tweet on national television, Abby had existed in a haze of loss and loneliness. The thought that someone could have intervened never occurred to her. Sara raised her head, her blue eyes swimming in tears. "I let them hurt someone I care deeply about. I'm so sorry."

Abby stood, unable to process Sara's guilt or the allusion to their relationship. How did she explain to Sara that New York had happened to a different person? She looked around the trailer, searching for a way to explain the loss she felt. "I can't find who I used to be," she finally whispered. "I used to believe that you got back what you put out into the world, so I thought people would be kind to me. That first night when I pulled up Twitter, I really believed the fans would stand by me. I thought they loved us after karaoke." She stared sightlessly across the trailer. "I found out it doesn't matter what you do or who you are or even what the truth is. If the right person tells people to hate you, they will." Her chest tightened and her eyes burned. She didn't want to cry any more. "After Christina's retraction, I thought I'd feel strong again. Then I thought I'd feel in control once I told my story to Keisha." She hugged her arms tighter to herself. "I should be mad at Luciana Raithman, but I can't seem to feel anything."

Abby couldn't look at Sara. "I don't know what to do with your apology. If you're saying you were the right person to tell them to stop hating me, that you could have done that and didn't…" She crossed her arms and shook her head. At last, she looked at Sara and the dam broke. She started to cry and her deep, wracking sobs filled the trailer. She felt Sara kneel next to her, uncertain hands touching her legs. Abby looked down at her. She could barely get the words out. "Everyone left me. Even you."

CHAPTER THIRTY-FIVE

Mika had taken one look at Abby and rearranged the rest of the afternoon's shoot. Abby protested, but she knew Mika was right. Despite Tanya's skills, there was no way to hide her swollen eyes and blotchy skin. On the drive home, her lunch with Sara played over in her mind. The sharp pain of Sara's admission had faded somewhat, and she was left with the same numbness that had been with her for weeks.

She pulled into the parking lot of her apartment and sat in her idling car for a few minutes, checking her surroundings. No one lingered on the sidewalk in front of the building. A few cars were around her, but they sat empty. She opened the door and listened for the shouts or her name. Nothing but traffic noise. Pushing the door open fully, Abby reached for her purse and stepped out of the car. She turned in a slow circle, and only when she was convinced that there was no one around did she shut the car door and hurry to the entrance of the building.

Safely inside, her heart pounded and her legs shook. How long would it be before she could get out of the car like a normal person? She took the elevator to her apartment and let herself in. Now that the adrenaline was gone, she was overcome with exhaustion. Dropping her purse on the counter, she made her way to her bedroom where she plugged in her phone, stripped out of her clothes, and buried herself under the covers. For once, sleep came quickly.

It was dark when Abby woke. Her eyes burned, and she was stiff from being in the same position for hours. She stumbled to the shower, where she stood under the hottest spray she could tolerate, letting the warmth loosen her muscles. Reaching blindly for the soap, she knocked it off the tray and had to chase it around the bottom of the tub. When she finally managed to grab it, she stood and her back spasmed. "Fuck." She groaned, moving under the spray so the hot water pulsed against her lower back. She vowed to stay in the shower until her muscles loosened or the water grew cold.

She was rinsing the conditioner out of her hair when she heard loud noises, banging and inaudible yelling. She poked her head around the shower curtain but couldn't make sense of the sounds. She turned off the water and listened. A smoke alarm. It wasn't hers, but it was loud enough that she could tell what it was. "God, I hope that doesn't go on all night," she muttered. She threw back the curtain and reached for a towel. The steam was heavy and thick, and she coughed after a deep inhale. Now that the water was off, the smoke alarm sounded much closer. Wrapping one towel around her hair and another around her body, she reached for the doorknob just as the bathroom light flickered and went out. She flicked the switch a couple of times, but nothing happened. With a sigh, Abby opened the bathroom door, but confused by what she saw, she didn't move.

It was night, but normally light from the exterior of the complex came through her sliding glass door. But there was no light now. She gasped, then coughed as the smell hit her. Smoke. Understanding and fear hit at the same moment. Dropping to the floor, she crawled from the bathroom door, down the hall to her bedroom. The depth of the darkness was terrifying. Abby felt for her dresser, yanked open drawers, and threw on whatever clothes she touched.

She needed light. If she could get to the nightstand, her phone was there, charging. Her knee bumped into the bed, and she used it to guide her to the bedside table. The phone lit up when she touched it. She blew out a relieved breath, but the ensuing inhale caused her to start coughing, and she dropped back to the floor.

Abby was almost out of the room when she remembered shoes. She flipped around and army-crawled to the closet, finding it when she slammed headfirst into the closed door. "Ouch, fuck," she cursed as she reached for the handle. Her hand scrabbled over the surface of several shoes until she felt a pair of running shoes. She jammed them on bare feet, then turned to crawl out of the closet. The turn caused her back to spasm again, and she dropped to her stomach.

For the first time, the possibility that maybe she couldn't escape the fire hit her, and for a second, she considered her own death. Maybe the best thing would be to breathe deeply and let the smoke take her before the fire could. She closed her eyes and let her body sink down into the carpet.

Something about surrendering to her fate, to this fate, infuriated her. What was she doing? Burying her face in beige, apartment-grade carpet and giving up? The indignity of that death pushed her to her knees. She looked at the phone and groaned at her own stupidity. She dialed 911 and started crawling.

If possible, the air was heavier, the smell intensifying as she moved through the living room to the front door. She reached it in seconds and put her hand against it, needing the leverage to stand. The heat was intense, and she pulled her scorched hand away.

"9-1-1, what's your emergency?"

Abby wanted to cry in relief when she heard the woman's calm voice. She tried to match it. "I'm in Studio Towers apartments, and there's a fire. It's not in my apartment, but the smoke is bad. I just touched the door and it was too hot to open."

"Do not open that door. I'm letting the fire department know you're in there. What's your name?"

"Abby Farina."

"What apartment number?"

"Three-eleven."

"Okay, I'm giving them the information while we talk. Do you have a balcony?"

"Yes."

"Good. Stay low to the floor and crawl to your balcony. The fire department is on scene, and they're coming to get you."

"Okay." Abby turned from the door, trying to get her bearings in the thick darkness. Her eyes and nose burned. She kept her breathing shallow, but her body craved air and she couldn't help taking a deep breath. She stopped moving, overcome as her chest heaved and her lungs forced out whatever poisons they'd taken in. Gasping, she took in more smoke and the coughing intensified. She was confused. What direction was she supposed to go?

"Abby, can you hear me?"

She'd forgotten the 911 operator. "Yes."

"They're almost there. Have you made it to the balcony?"

"No, I'm not sure where I am."

"Are you still by the door?"

Abby reached back and her fingers grazed the metal. "Yes."

"Do you know which way the balcony is?"

"Yeah."

"Okay, I want you to crawl to the balcony. Can you do that?"

"Don't hang up, okay?"

"I won't, Abby. Crawl to the balcony."

The slider was across the room and to the right of the door. If she moved in a straight line from the door, the back of the couch would be to her right. Abby touched both feet against the door to line herself up and started crawling. She let out a tiny relieved breath when she felt fabric. With her shoulder brushing the couch, she increased her speed.

At the edge of the couch, she knew she only had a few feet to the wall, so she slowed, careful not to hit her head again. Once she touched the hard surface, she put her left shoulder against the wall and crawled. But now, she was inhaling more smoke as exertion and panic stole her breath. Another coughing spasm, and she was forced to stop as it overwhelmed her. Her chest burned and her body wouldn't obey her command to move. Distantly, she heard the 911 operator calling to her, but she couldn't speak. Against her will, she sank into the carpet.

CHAPTER THIRTY-SIX

"That's as much as I know," Mika told the writers. "I don't know how long Abby will be hospitalized." Mika looked at their stunned faces. Several were openly crying. "As I see it, we have three possibilities. Abby returns quickly and our current arc stays intact." She paused, letting them get ahead of where she was going. "Or, Abby is unable to return this season, and we need to rewrite the episodes but can maintain the current story."

Mika looked down. Everyone knew what she was going to say next. She sighed heavily, then looked up, letting them see the weight of what she was about to say. "We also need to have a plan in case she is unable to return. It's the outcome no one wants to imagine, but we must. A show can lose a star, but it can't survive bad writing. It's up to us to make sure we do our best to save *Corsetti*. Not for me or for those of us in this room, but for the people who work with us and are counting on us to protect their livelihood."

At a knock, she called, "Yes?"

Renee stepped into the room and whispered, "There's a Chief Whitby of the Studio City Fire Department on the phone for you. He says he needs to speak to you right away."

Mika looked at her new head writer. "Get them started. I'll be back as soon as I can."

In her office, she picked up her phone. "This is Mika Williams."

"Ms. Williams, I'm Chief Roger Whitby of the Studio City Fire Marshal's office. We're investigating the fire at Abby Farina's apartment complex. I've watched the interview you and Ms. Farina did with Keisha Alexander. I have some questions regarding the incident with Ms. Christina Landis."

"Of course."

"Which of Ms. Landis's statements do you believe to be truthful?"

It was not the question Mika expected. "The press release was the only truthful statement." She emphasized the word "only."

"Why do you believe that?"

"It's not a belief. It is a fact. I had my lawyers investigate the incident. I was prepared for the full story to be told on national television, so I had to ensure that my information was accurate."

"You believe the full story, as you call it, is that Ms. Landis was confused? She perceived harassment where there was none?" The skepticism in his voice was obvious, and in that moment, Mika realized the mistake she'd made not revealing Luciana Raithman's manipulation when she had the opportunity.

"No. What I know is Abby was the victim of a Hollywood producer seeking publicity so she could fund her new film. I have evidence of that, and I offered that evidence to Ms. Farina to present during the interview with Keisha Alexander. She elected to take the higher ground."

"Could you be more specific?"

"Chief Whitby, I can email or fax the documents my lawyers prepared for Ms. Alexander's network. It's very thorough, and I believe will answer your questions better than I can."

"That would be helpful, thank you. I'll send a member of

our investigative unit to your office." He paused, and she heard paper shuffling. "What can you tell me about the threats against Ms. Farina. Did you take them seriously?"

Mika thought for a moment, then spoke carefully. "I'm not sure how to answer your question. I took the fact that she was getting threatened very seriously, but I did not take any action in response to individual threats."

"Did you assign security to Ms. Farina?"

"No, and in hindsight, I should have. I'm sure you saw the footage of the mob outside her apartment."

"Yes."

"At the time, I was dealing with my own threats to the show. I was also instructed by the Binge legal department not to have contact with Abby." She sighed. "I should have foreseen that she would need more support."

"I've also watched video of…" He paused, and Mika heard papers shuffling. "Corsetti Karaoke?" Mika waited for his question. "Would you say Ms. Farina often seeks the spotlight?"

"No more than any other actor. If you're suggesting that Abby started the fire to get attention, you're wrong. She's been struggling with the exposure from this incident. That's one of the reasons she didn't share the full story on national television. She wanted it all to go away."

"Has she been depressed?"

Mika silently cursed herself. "She's getting better, but she feels vulnerable. That's different than being depressed."

"I need to speak with Sara Silver. Could you give me her contact information?" Mika took the number off her phone and recited it to him. "Thank you for your time. Someone will be at your offices shortly. I may need to contact you with further questions."

"That's fine. I'll let Sara know you'll be calling." They hung up and Mika sent a quick text to Sara. Then she called Dani. "We need to meet," she said. "My office. Ninety minutes."

* * *

Dani took notes as Mika told her about the call. When she

got to the questions about the Twitter threats, Dani's brow furrowed. "Did he ask for any specifics? Twitter handles? Names, pages?"

"No, but he was going to call Sara. I'm sure he wants the screenshots she has. What she shared with Keisha was just a fraction of the threats she reported. I imagine he's already found the original video of the mob outside Abby's apartment and is working on identifying the participants."

"Most of them have been already been identified," Dani said. "As soon as Keisha's interview aired, people started to name the mob. In my opinion, fans have been taking out their own guilt on those women. So far, anything too ugly has been shot down by other users, but the fire may escalate things."

"What do you recommend we do as a studio?"

Usually, Mika enjoyed watching Dani process as every thought played across her face. Today wasn't one of those days, and she worked to tamp down her impatience. At last, Dani looked at her and blew out a long breath. "Do you mind if I think out loud?" At Mika's nod, she continued, "It will come out that some of our fans are being investigated. Our fandom will probably split their loyalties. Either they'll support the fans who made the threats by claiming freedom of speech, or they'll turn on each other, similar to what has happened with the mob. Neither is an outcome that is good for our fans or the show." Mika watched Dani's crossed leg bounce as she talked. She waited, knowing that the younger woman was coming to a solution.

"We could also make the choice for them." Dani looked at Mika, who crooked an eyebrow. "We make a statement that we believe in freedom of speech, but that doesn't mean freedom from consequences. We follow that with our stance against any hate speech, maybe using some of what Sara said in the interview with Keisha. We can partner with an anti-bullying organization and ask people who want to support Abby's recovery to donate in her name. We'll also give them ways to contact their local organizations to volunteer their time."

Mika exhaled. "That feels good. It gives everyone a way to

use their energy. How quickly can you get something together?"

"I'll get right on it."

Mika stood and walked to the window, staring across the lot while she spoke. "What if one of them did start the fire?"

* * *

Mika watched video of the chief's press conference. The news coverage started with footage of thick black smoke pouring out of broken windows on the side of the building. Then tips of orange fire appeared through the windows as the flame chased oxygen. In a sudden burst, the roof caught fire. What had been a relatively calm scene of water pouring on smoke suddenly changed, and fire personnel ran toward the building. A thick arc of water moved from the side of the building to a third-floor balcony. The video zoomed in tight as a ladder was moved into place and a pair of firefighters climbed. As they got closer, the water moved away from that balcony to one nearby. The first figure used his axe to break through the glass door. Smoke billowed out, obscuring the rescuers from view.

A figure emerged from the smoke carrying a limp woman over his shoulder. She was handed to yet another firefighter who descended the ladder, her unconscious body held tightly against him. At the bottom, paramedics surrounded them. A gurney rolled into the frame, then was blocked by the circle of first responders. When the circle opened, the camera followed a group hurrying to the open doors of the ambulance. There was only the briefest view of Abby, her face hidden behind an oxygen mask before the doors closed.

"That's raw footage of actress Abby Farina's rescue from a burning apartment in Studio City. We've been awaiting the start of a press conference by the Studio City Fire Department. As of the last update, Farina is listed in serious condition. Let's go live to the press conference."

"I'm Chief Roger Whitby, Fire Marshal for the Studio City Fire Department. I'll read a statement and then take a few questions." He looked up as if to make sure they were all listening. "Last night Studio City Fire responded to a call an apartment fire at 2541 Mission Avenue East. When firefighters arrived, the structure was fully involved with active fire in one apartment and throughout the corridors. As firefighters were checking apartments, we received a 911 call from the occupant of apartment three-eleven. Firefighters entered the apartment through the balcony and found the victim unconscious. She was transported to Memorial Burn Unit. No other residents or fire personnel were injured." He looked up. "Evidence suggests the fire was deliberately set. We are asking anyone with information or video of the fire to contact the Studio City Fire Department. I'll take a few questions."

"Was Abby Farina the target?"

"At this time, we have no motive for the fire."

"Did the fire start in Ms. Farina's apartment?"

"No. The fire started in an empty apartment."

"Do you suspect Ms. Farina of starting the fire?"

"At this point, we have no suspects."

"How badly burned is she?"

"The hospital will release all information on Ms. Farina's condition."

"But your people saw her. Is she disfigured?"

Chief Whitby didn't bother to hide his disgust at the question. "That's all for now. Thank you."

CHAPTER THIRTY-SEVEN

"Abby, honey, wake up." Abby blinked her eyes open and turned to look at her mom. "The respiratory therapist is here with your treatment." Her mother bent closer and whispered, "And the fire marshal wants to talk with you if you feel up to it."

Abby widened her eyes but didn't speak. Talking led to coughing, and her throat was raw. She watched the therapist load the medication and prepare the soft mist inhaler. "Hi, Abby, are you ready?" She nodded. "Inhale and breathe out slowly." The woman's hand was on Abby's stomach. "More. That's it. A little more." She moved the inhaler to Abby's mouth, and without instruction Abby wrapped her lips around it, creating a seal. The therapist pressed a button. "Inhale. Good. I know it's hard, but try not to cough yet. And, ten, nine, eight, seven, six, five, four, three, two, one. Exhale." Abby let out her breath and immediately started coughing. The therapist reached for a kidney-shaped basin and a tissue. "That's good. Get all of that junk out of your lungs." Abby coughed and spit blackened mucus into the basin. "Still got quite a bit in there," the therapist said as she handed Abby the tissue. Abby nodded weakly. "As much as you can, keep coughing. I know you're tired, but you need to clear your lungs."

Carol Farina stood on the opposite side of the bed. "The fire marshal wants to talk to her. Do you think that's okay?"

"That depends on Abby. Do you feel up to it?" Abby shrugged. "It's up to you, but if you decide to talk to him, not too long, okay?" She nodded, and the therapist moved to the computer to document her treatment.

"I'll talk to him," Abby whispered. Whispering was less stress on her throat and felt less likely to lead to a coughing fit.

Her mother gave her a long look. "Okay, but I'm staying." Abby nodded and closed her eyes.

She'd been vaguely aware of the fireman stumbling over her as he entered the apartment. She didn't remember being carried out or the descent down the ladder. The blast of cool oxygen from the mask over her face brought her to consciousness. Then she was lifted and moving. After that, her memory was of isolated events. The arrival at the hospital. Her clothes being cut away. Someone asking her name. A thin tube inserted down her throat. Her mother and father crying.

According to her mom, she'd been in intensive care for the first twelve hours while doctors monitored her breathing. Once they determined her lungs weren't seriously damaged, she was transferred to a regular room. The doctors emphasized that the effects of the smoke could still present or worsen over the coming days, so she was being closely monitored by a respiratory team. Abby listened to everything she was told but retained less than half of it.

At the sound of a knock, Abby opened her eyes and watched the man enter the room. "Ms. Farina, I'm Chief Roger Whitby, fire marshal for the Studio City Fire Department." He cast a questioning look at her mother, who extended her hand.

"I'm Abby's mom, Carol Farina." He took her hand and she offered him a chair near the bed. Without asking, Carol took the chair on the opposite side.

"How are you feeling today, Ms. Farina?"

"Better, thanks to your department."

Carol interjected, "Do you have the names of the people who rescued my daughter? We'd like to thank them."

Whitby opened his notebook and scribbled inside. "I'll get them for you." He looked at Abby. "Do you feel up to answering a few questions?" At Abby's nod, he leaned closer to her bed. "The firefighter who entered your apartment reported that the smoke detector was not functioning. Did you remove the batteries from your smoke detectors?"

Mrs. Farina made a sound of protest. Abby looked at the man, confused by the question. "Did I take the batteries out of the smoke detectors in my apartment?" She frowned. "No. Is that why they weren't going off?"

"Yes. Did you hear the alarms in other apartments?"

"Yeah. When I was in the shower, I thought I heard something, but I wasn't sure until I turned the water off." He wrote as she talked.

"You were in the shower when the fire started?" he asked, still looking down.

"I don't know," she whispered. "I don't know when the fire started, but if I had to guess, it was while I was showering. There wasn't any smoke when I woke up, but I could smell it when I got out of the shower. Was the fire ever in my apartment?"

"No. You were asleep before you took a shower?"

"Yes."

"Is that usual for you?"

"No. I came home from work early, and was tired."

"What time did you arrive home?"

Abby thought back. Was it yesterday? The day before? "Um, I think between two and three."

"Can you be more specific?"

She closed her eyes, trying to remember. "Closer to three."

"Why are you asking about Abby's day?" Mrs. Farina asked.

"We're trying to ascertain the activities of all the residents that day." He looked back at Abby. "Your apartment was a total loss. Do you have insurance?"

"Yes. I have renter's insurance."

"What would you estimate the value of the contents of your apartment?" he asked.

Abby looked up, considering her answer. "I don't know. I had a TV, laptop, tablet, furniture, and my clothes. That's it. I guess not a lot."

"Would you say the contents were worth less than a hundred thousand dollars?"

Carol spoke before Abby could answer. "Does her answer to this question impact her insurance claim? If she says it's under a hundred thousand, and later, when she's itemizing her belongings, realizes it's more, will that be a problem?"

"It depends on how much more."

Abby looked between them. "I really don't know the value of what I had, but nothing was very expensive. I can't imagine it would be more than that."

He nodded and paged through his folder. "You're an actress, correct?"

"Yes."

"Are you currently employed?"

"Yes, I'm employed by Mika Williams Productions."

"What was the most valuable item in your apartment?" he asked, looking up from his notes.

"A signed copy of *Tuck Everlasting*." At her words, her mom inhaled sharply.

"Is that a book?" he asked

"Yes."

"Estimated value?"

"Probably five dollars. Maybe the signature makes it worth more, but it's not in good condition."

Whitby frowned at her. "The most valuable item in your apartment was worth five dollars? Nothing else you claim will be worth more than that?"

"It means the most to me. It was a gift from my mom." She reached for Carol's hand. "You asked me what was the most valuable. The most expensive item in my apartment was either the TV or laptop."

For the first time, Whitby smiled at her. "I'll do a better job with my questions." He pulled out a sheaf of papers. "Is there anyone who would wish to harm you?"

Carol made a disgusted sound. "Abby has been harassed and threatened repeatedly in the last month."

Whitby acknowledge her words with a nod, then repeated his question to Abby. "Is there anyone in particular who would like to see you harmed?"

"No," she answered. "And the threats I received were online, not in person."

"Except for that mob," Mrs. Farina said.

"What about Christina Landis?"

"Christina wasn't really angry with me. It was a publicity stunt. Another woman put her up to it."

"That would be Luciana Raithman?"

Abby blinked. "Yes. How do you know that?"

He continued as if she hadn't spoken. "And you were threatened as a result of this publicity stunt?"

"Yes."

He shuffled through a file, found what he was looking for, and lifted the paper as he read: "'Looks like it would be easy to burn down. Sleep well.' As you know, your address was on that post."

Abby felt pressure in her chest and the suffocating feeling of smoke in her lungs. She squeezed her eyes shut and took a deep breath. That set off a spasm, and she started to cough. Her mother reached for a tissue and helped Abby sit up. At last the coughing eased, and Abby turned embarrassed eyes to her mother. "It's okay." Carol rubbed her back. "Spit it out." Abby took the bowl her mother handed her and once again spat blackened mucus into it. She wiped her mouth and lay back, spent by the effort. Carol looked at the chief. "I think that's enough for today."

"Do you really believe one of those people started the fire?" Abby whispered.

"This is just one of the areas of investigation. Online threats, while upsetting, don't usually result in actual violence." He held

CHAPTER THIRTY-EIGHT

Sara reluctantly agreed to stay away from the hospital. The press of media was more than hospital security was able to handle, and they'd politely suggested that their resources were better spent healing Abby than dealing with the extra attention high-profile visitors would garner.

Mika was the contact between the Farina family and the show. She was good at keeping them up-to-date on Abby's condition, but Sara was done being sidelined. After learning that Abby had been moved from ICU, she called.

"Mika, can you give me the number for Mrs. Farina?"

"I promised her we wouldn't overwhelm the family with calls and visits," Mika told her.

"I understand, but Abby and I…" Sara paused, not sure how to finish the sentence.

"Are close," Mika said. "I know. I'll text and see if she minds that I share her number with you."

Fifteen minutes later, Sara's phone rang. "Hello."

"Is this Sara?"

his hand up when Carol looked like she was going to interrupt. "There are always exceptions, which is why we're investigating everything." He stood and offered his hand to Abby and her mother. "I'll get the names of the firefighters for you."

"Yes."

"Hello, Sara. I'm Abby's mother, Carol. How are you, dear?"

Sara stood and walked to the window in the kitchen where she could look out at the pool. "Mrs. Farina, thank you for calling me. How's Abby?"

"Would you like to talk with her?"

Sara caught her breath. "Yes." Then a thought crossed her mind. Was this Mrs. Farina's doing? Was Abby in the background waving her arms? "Does she want to talk to me?"

"Sara?" Abby's whispering voice was hard to hear. She pressed the phone hard against her ear and tried not to cry.

"Abby. It's so good to hear your voice."

"It's good to hear yours too."

"Are you okay?" Sara knew the question was silly and inadequate.

"I am," Abby answered. "How are you?"

Sara forced out a laugh. "I'm much better now." She couldn't choke back the emotion. "I've been so scared."

"I was too, but I'm okay, now." Abby's voice sounded tight. "Can you come and see me? We need to talk." Abby started to cough, and Sara listened helplessly while she struggled to take in a breath.

After nearly a minute, Carol Farina spoke. "Sara, she had a little coughing attack. The doctors say it's perfectly normal and necessary. She has a lot of gunk in her lungs that she has to cough out." Sara could still hear coughing in the background, but the intensity had subsided.

"Is it okay if I visit her? I promise I won't stay long."

Carol laughed. "If you can get the hospital to let you in, I know she'd love to see you. Maybe you could come by this afternoon?"

"I will. I'll let you know when I'm coming."

* * *

It took a call to the hospital security chief and the promise of an autograph and a selfie, but she got permission to visit.

Despite their precautions, someone in the press recognized her and they shouted questions after her.

"Did Abby start the fire?"

"Will she be able to work again? How bad are the burns?"

"Will the show get canceled?"

Once safely in the elevator, she touched the arm of the security chief. "I'm sorry I added to the chaos. Are they always that bad?"

"That's nothing. It's when they try to sneak in that we have problems. We've had to warn hospital personnel to keep track of their security badges at all times. They're not above stealing to get in."

She took off her hat and glasses outside Abby's door, so he could take his selfie. "Don't worry," he said. "I won't post anything on social media. I hate that stuff."

"I'm starting to," she said, then knocked lightly on the door. She was about to knock again, when a middle-aged woman in leggings and a long sweater opened the door, stepped out, and closed it behind her. The slight frown between her eyes transformed into a welcoming smile. "Sara. It's so nice of you to come." She reached up and pulled Sara into a fierce hug. "She had her treatment a half hour ago and you know it just wipes her out. She's sleeping, but come in."

Sara was surprised how much the sight of Abby in a hospital gown, hooked to an IV, her face covered by an oxygen mask, reassured her. She released the breath she'd been holding. Carol patted her arm in understanding. "I felt better when I first saw her too. She's going to be just fine." Sara nodded, too overcome to speak. She rubbed a hand over her mouth to hide her quivering chin. "If you don't mind, I'd like to go to the hotel and get cleaned up. Would you stay with her until her father or I get back?" Carol didn't wait for an answer, just pushed Sara to the other side of the bed. "That's the better chair." Then she gathered her purse and, with a squeeze of Sara's hand, slipped out the door.

Sara covered her mouth and let the tears fall. She wanted to take Abby's hand but was afraid to wake her, so she comforted herself by checking over every inch of Abby that was visible. A red, raw patch on one of Abby's arms drew her attention, and she stood to get a closer look. "Rug burn," a voice croaked. Because Abby's bed was raised, the voice was in Sara's ear. She jumped, and Abby gave a husky laugh. "Did I scare you?"

Sara took her hand and wiped at her cheeks, trying to cover her tears. "I'm so happy to see you."

Abby squeezed. "I'm happy to see you too." She lifted the arm Sara had been inspecting and turned it so she could see the extent of the injury. "I have rug burns on my elbows and knees." Abby put her arm down and looked up and saw the tears. "Hey, I'm okay."

Sara stopped pretending. "I was so scared," she whispered.

"Me too," Abby admitted. She pulled off the oxygen mask and let it fall into her lap. "When I touched the door and realized I couldn't get out of the apartment, I was terrified." It was Abby's turn to cry.

"Oh, Abby." Sara sat on the edge of the bed.

"I wanted the smoke to get me before the fire did. I was afraid of being burned…" Abby leaned forward and wrapped her arms around Sara.

Abby pulled back first. She wiped her eyes, and Sara reached for a couple of tissues. They wiped their eyes and gave each other watery smiles. Abby took Sara's hand. "Where's Mom?"

"She went back to the hotel to shower. Is that okay? Do you need anything?"

"Sometimes I pretend I'm asleep just so she'll stop talking. Thanks for rescuing me."

Sara laughed, so happy to hear the playfulness in Abby's voice. "I would have been here sooner, but the hospital didn't want us to add to the chaos outside."

"Yeah, Mom said there are a lot of reporters. Is it bad?"

Sara shrugged. "After the first morning, I haven't watched any of the coverage." She rubbed her thumb over Abby's hand. "Have they…" Sara hesitated.

"The fire marshal questioned me." She held Sara's gaze. "It was arson."

"Do they know who did it?"

"I don't think so. At first Mom and I thought he was accusing me." She shook her head. "Did he call you?"

"Yeah, he wanted the screenshots I took off Twitter."

"Even though I don't think it's more than a coincidence, I'm glad he's going to question them."

"Have you thought about where you're going to live?"

"Mom and I talked about it. She wants me to find an apartment with security." Abby gave a little laugh, then started to cough. Sara watched her carefully, but Abby waved away her worried expression. When she could catch her breath, she said, "I'll stay in a hotel for a while."

"Nathan and I want you to live with us." At Abby's blank look, she rushed on. "You know how many bedrooms the house has. You'd have plenty of privacy, and there's the gate, so you wouldn't need security."

"And what about us?"

Sara's eyes widened, stunned by the question. "Us?" Abby didn't look away. Sara swallowed. "Is there an us?"

"I want there to be an us."

"Are you talking us as friends, or…" Sara paused, trying to find the right words. "Or New York us."

Abby's smile was bright. "New York us." Then her expression sobered. "I know you blame yourself for not standing up for me publicly. But if you had, people would always question Christina's retraction. They would wonder if she was pressured by you. I would always live under the shadow of her accusation." She lifted her hand and interlocked their fingers. "I pushed you away. I pushed everyone and everything away. The threats and the hate scared me, but being scared nearly cost me my happiness. I don't want to lose you."

"You can't lose me." Sara kissed her softly. "Will you move in with us?"

Abby kissed her back.

CHAPTER THIRTY-NINE

The first few days out of the hospital, Abby's mom stayed in the room next to Abby's at Sara's house. It was a relief to have the older woman there while Abby continued her respiratory treatments, but after a few days, Mrs. Farina kissed Abby, hugged Nathan and Sara, and returned to Palm Springs.

Since they'd agreed that it was too soon to tell anyone other than Nathan that they were dating, Abby was glad to see her go. She wanted to emotionally and physically restart their relationship, but every time she tried to get close to Sara, she was rebuffed. Abby supposed it was that Sara was afraid to hurt Abby, and admittedly, Abby was still weak. It was all understandable, but she was getting impatient.

The sound of an alert on her phone woke her from a nap. She rolled over and read the banner on her screen. *Arrest made in arson fire that injured actress Abby Farina.* Seeing that she had a voice mail, she played the message. "Ms. Farina, this is Chief Whitby. A suspect was arrested this afternoon for the arson fire that destroyed your apartment. I'm sorry I can't give you more details over the phone, but there will be a press conference later today." He paused, then added somewhat awkwardly, "Thank you for your assistance."

Muffled voices outside her door told her Sara and Nathan had also heard about the arrest. "Come in," she called before they could knock.

The door opened slowly, and Sara poked her head in. "You awake?"

"Yes. Tell Nathan he can come in too." The door opened all the way and the siblings walked to the side of her bed. Abby scooted over so Sara could sit. "So, you heard?"

"Yes." Sara reached for her hand. "I thought he was going to call you first."

"He did." She gave Sara a lopsided grin. "I was asleep."

"Do you want to come downstairs and watch the press conference?"

Abby looked down at their joined hands. "What if it's a fan?" She looked into Sara's eyes. "It won't be over. There'll be a trial, and I'll have to testify. So will you."

Nathan took a giant step backward. "I'll go turn on the TV. How 'bout I open a bottle of wine too?" He was out the door before either could answer.

Sara leaned over and took Abby's face in her hands. "Whatever happens, I'll be with you." She gave her a soft kiss and leaned back. "Do you want to go down and watch?"

Abby threw back the covers. "Lead the way."

They'd just settled onto the sectional when the anchor announced they were going live to the press conference.

"I'm Chief Roger Whitby of the Studio City Fire Department. This afternoon we arrested John Massey and charged him with first-degree arson in the fire at the Studio Towers apartments." Abby gasped when she heard the name. Whitby continued talking, but she wasn't listening.

When a mugshot appeared on the screen, Sara turned to her. "Oh my God. Is that your neighbor? The guy who was on Keisha's show?" Abby could only nod.

"At this time, we aren't releasing any more information. Thank you." Even though the chief walked away, the reporters shouted questions to him.

"Do you have a motive?"

"Was Abby Farina the target?"

One reporter made the connection. "Was he looking for fame?"

Whitby kept walking.

* * *

Keisha Alexander's interview aired the next week. Once again, the show opened with her seated on a stool. She looked tired, but her voice was strong when she spoke. "Tonight, I'll speak exclusively with actress Abby Farina of *Corsetti's Will* and with John Massey, the man who has admitted to setting the fire that destroyed the Studio Towers apartments and seriously injured the actress."

Keisha turned on the stool to face a second camera. "In the days since Massey's arrest, the sometimes intertwined and sometimes conflicting roles of social media and broadcast media have been debated. Tonight, I'll reflect on those conflicts, and the responsibilities that come with them. But we begin with our first contact with John Massey."

Over a still photograph of Massey from the earlier show, audio from a phone conversation played.

Producer: We'd like you to appear on the show and tell our viewers what you witnessed that day.

Massey: On the show? Really?

Producer: Yes. We'll send a crew to your home to film you and your girlfriend. Keisha Alexander will be in-studio and interview you.

Massey: So, I'm not going to New York?

Producer: No, you can stay right there. Is your girlfriend available?

Massey: Um…I don't know. Can I let you know?

Producer: We'd really like to have both of you.

Massey: And we'll be on national television? On the morning show?

Producer: Yes, it's national, but you'll be on our primetime show. It will air at nine on the West Coast.

Massey: Wow. Okay. I'm sure I can get her to be here.

The camera returned to Keisha. "This week, I spoke to John Massey in the Studio City jail where he is awaiting sentencing." They cut to video of Massey sitting in a folding chair across the room from Alexander. His hair was shorter, his now clean-shaven face a departure from the earlier interview. "Why did you set the fire?" Keisha asked.

"Becca broke up with me a week after we helped Abby, so when the show called, I thought it'd be a good chance to get her back. I told her about the interview, but I said that you"—he inclined his head at Keisha—"thought we were still a couple." He looked embarrassed. "I told her we needed to pretend we were still together if we wanted to be on your show."

The image changed to the earlier interview.

"What did you think when you first got out of your car?" Keisha asked.

"We didn't know what to think," the woman said. "We heard all this yelling and swearing, but we couldn't see anything but the signs and the crowd."

"I thought it was a fight," the man said.

"When did you realize what was happening?"

"When I walked up, I could see Abby was surrounded and she looked scared, so I told Becca, 'We've gotta help her.'"

"Did you know Abby before this? Did you know who she was or what was going on?

"I didn't know her name or that she's on TV. I just knew she was my neighbor and what was going on wasn't right."

"Were you scared?"

The woman answered, "Yeah, I was. You were too." The guy nodded. "Some of those women were pretty tough looking. I was afraid they were going to chase after us."

Back in the jail, Keisha asked, "What happened after the interview aired?"

"Our phones blew up. People thought it was so cool what happened, how we helped Abby. One of my friends threw a party for me, and I convinced Becca to go." He smiled at the memory. "It was a great night, and everyone was really excited. I thought we were getting back together, but Becca wasn't interested." He straightened to look Keisha in the eye. "I don't want you to think she played me for the fame. She didn't. It was all me."

"What happened next?"

"I went a little crazy. I thought if I saved Abby again, Becca would want me back." He looked away. "She never said anything like that. It was all me."

"You told my producer that you wanted to make sure Becca isn't blamed for the fire. Is that just another way for you to get back with her?"

He laughed without humor. "I'm going to prison for nearly killing an innocent person. I won't ever have someone in my life again. I want to make sure everyone knows Becca had nothing to do with the fire. When she helped Abby, it was because she knew it was the right thing to do. She had no idea I would do something like this." He looked down at his clasped hands. "I didn't know I would do something like this."

"What did you do?"

He sighed. "I had a key to one of the empty apartments. I used to take care of a guy's cat when he went out of town. When he moved, he forgot to ask for the key back."

"That's where you started the fire?"

"Yeah. I didn't know how to make it look like an accident, so I just sprayed lighter fluid around and tossed a match. I watched it burn for a while to make sure it would catch. Then I started banging on doors for people to get out."

"What about the hallway? The arson report said there was accelerant in front of Ms. Farina's door."

"When everyone was out, I said I was going back to check one more time. People told me not to go, but I broke away. I needed it to look like the mob came back for Abby, so I grabbed the rest of the lighter fluid. I banged and yelled on the doors one more time, then emptied it in the hall and threw the can in front of Abby's door."

The image changed to video of the fire. "But Abby Farina wasn't out of the apartment. She was in the shower when the fire started." Over an image of smoke pouring out of Abby's apartment, the audio transcript of the 911 call played.

"I'm in Studio Towers apartments, and there's a fire. It's not in my apartment, but the smoke is bad. I just touched the door and it was too hot to open."

"Do not open that door. I'm letting the fire department know you're in there. What's your name?"

"Abby Farina."

"What apartment number?"

"Three-eleven."

"Okay, I'm giving them the information while we talk. Do you have a balcony?"

"Yes."

"Good. Stay low to the floor and crawl to your balcony. The fire department is on scene, and they're coming to get you."

"Okay." There's silence, then coughing. A gasp of air followed by even more coughs.

"Abby, can you hear me?"

"Yes."

"They're almost there. Have you made it to the balcony?"

"No, I'm not sure where I am."

"Are you still by the door?"

"Yes."

"Do you know which way the balcony is?"

"Yeah."

"Okay, I want you to crawl to the balcony. Can you do that?"

"Don't hang up, okay?"

"I won't, Abby. Crawl to the balcony."

A long period of silence is punctuated by Abby's coughing. Then the coughing stops.

"Abby? Can you hear me?" A pause. "Abby?" The dispatcher's voice is professional, but urgent. "Fire rescue, be advised. Occupant is unconscious."

Keisha frowned at Massey. "Did you disable the smoke detectors in Ms. Farina's apartment?"

He leaned forward. "No. I was never in her apartment."

Keisha's voice narrated over a still image of a criminal complaint. "Two months before Abby Farina moved into the Studio Towers apartment complex, an eviction notice was filed against two men. One month later, they were both charged with vandalism and theft for damaging appliances, destroying plumbing, and stealing the microwave. The apartment listed? Number three-eleven—Abby Farina's future apartment. The only apartment where the smoke detectors malfunctioned the night of the fire."

Back in the jail, Keisha asked, "Why a fire, John?"

"Because of the tweet you showed on the show. The one where they threatened to burn the apartment down and gave the address. I thought that person would get blamed."

The second half of the show took place by Sara's pool. Keisha and Abby sat at the table under a large umbrella. "How do you feel?"

"Much better. My lungs are still healing, but I was fortunate that the Studio City Fire Department found me and got me out in time." Another voice-over from Keisha accompanied video of Abby being carried out of the apartment. "Abby asked that we share this video and acknowledge Engine Company 7 and firefighters Austin Waters and DeShawn Jacobs along with paramedics Kelly Sanders and Albert Munoz." When the video ended, Keisha asked, "What do you remember about that night?"

"I was in the shower and thought I heard yelling and banging in the hall. When I turned the water off, I could hear the smoke detector in the apartment next to mine, but I wasn't that concerned. I remember getting out of the shower and thinking the steam was thick. It took me until the lights went out before I realized something was going on, and even then, I just thought it was a power outage."

"When did you realize it was a fire?"

"Really not until I smelled the smoke." She gave a little laugh. "Which is ridiculous, because the smoke was so dense it blocked the light from the windows."

"Do you remember what your first thoughts were?"

"My first thought was to get dressed. Then to grab my phone, but I was only thinking of it for the light. It was a while before I thought to call 911."

They talked more about the fire before Keisha brought up the earlier interview. "There are those who say that John Massey would have never started the fire if I hadn't publicized the Twitter threat. Where do you place blame?"

Abby took her time answering. "Well, there's certainly plenty of blame being passed around, but there is only one person to blame for the fire, and that's John Massey." She took a deep breath. "He's the only one I blame, but there are others I'm angry with. I'm mad at the people who attack others on Twitter. I'm angry at the sanctimonious people who blamed you, but don't condemn social media. I'm even mad at Binge network and my show for using social media to market our product. But mostly, I'm mad at myself for not saying no. Not to Binge, not even to the haters, but to myself. I gave them power. I read their tweets and took them to heart. I let their words hurt me. I can't control what they say, and I can't control the fact that I have to have a social media presence to do a job I love. But I can control how I respond.

"I'll continue to post anything I think will be of interest to fans of *Corsetti's Will*. The first post I'll share is an article on how to block comments on social media platforms. I've already done it on all of mine." She smiled at Keisha. "I'll show you how."

Keisha threw her head back and laughed. "I'll take you up on that." Then she cocked her head. "You've changed since our last interview. Your confidence is back. I honestly expected you to be even more timid."

"I got angry. I've never been scared like I was when those women surrounded me. Even crawling to get out of the fire, I wasn't as frightened as I had been that day. Afterward, I realized that I was allowing them to take away the things I value: my confidence, my trust. No one can live like that. In the hospital, I decided I wanted my old self back."

"You stopped feeling like a victim?"

Abby paused before answering, "I guess it's more that I like who I am, and I refuse to let someone else take it from me."

CHAPTER FORTY

Sara finished the script and threw it across the room in disgust. "What the fuck?" she yelled. She heard footsteps in the hall, and Abby's face appeared around the doorjamb.

"You finished? Finally." She walked over to Sara's bed and plopped down.

"What the fuck is she thinking? She won't really make him the bad guy, will she?"

"Keyser Söze," Abby said.

"No, no, no. Not with Corsetti. I like him too much. He can't be the bad guy. Plus, you can only have one movie like *The Usual Suspects*. Everything else gets compared to it."

"*Us*?"

"Okay, but Lupita Nyong'o is the star of that movie. No one would ever suspect her of being evil."

"There are plenty of movies with a main character who isn't playing true. It would be a great plot twist if Corsetti faked his death."

Sara reached for her script and whined, "I don't want Leo to be a bad guy."

Abby scooted up the bed and took the script out of Sara's hands, laying it on the bedside table. "There's still one more episode. It doesn't make sense for Mika to have the climax happen in the penultimate episode."

"Penultimate, huh?" Sara grinned crookedly at her.

"I thought that would impress you." She leaned down so her lips were inches from Sara's. "I know a couple of other things that impress you. At least they did in New York."

Sara let her eyes close as Abby leaned in for a kiss. It started soft, but Abby deepened it, and Sara couldn't help responding. Abby moved a hand to Sara's hip, running her thumb over the patch of exposed skin. That was all it took for Sara to pull away.

"I don't think we're ready," she whispered.

Abby looked at her for a long moment, her expression guarded. "Good night, then." She gave her another soft kiss and left the room.

Sara watched her go. Abby had said she wanted to go back to who they were in New York, but Sara was afraid. They'd only had that one day and night together, and so much had happened since. What if it was too much to come back from? Sara wasn't sure her heart could take losing Abby again.

* * *

Alan Fletcher walked in, and someone called out, "I see dead people."

Abby snorted. "I wish I'd thought of that."

"I feel sorry for him. Look, everyone's avoiding him. Do they know something we don't?" Sara tilted her head toward the food tables where cast and crew usually congregated before the table read. Fletcher was the only one filling a plate.

"Good morning, everyone," Mika said, and waited wh. all settled into their places. "By the buzz in the room, I c: most of you have read the script. This is a good time to rer you of the confidentiality clauses in your contracts. No one, not even your significant others can know the storyline." No one moved or spoke. They all knew breaking the confidentiality clause led to immediate dismissal and a guaranteed end to their careers. "Let's get started." She nodded to the first AD to begin.

Interior. The Corsetti home. The sound of pounding on the door.

Detective 1: *Police. Open up! We have a warrant.*

More pounding. Bria, in pajamas, walks to the door, looks through the peephole, then opens it. Detective 1 pushes through the door, followed by three other men. He hands Bria a folded piece of paper.

Detective 1: *That's a warrant to search the premises.*

B. Corsetti: *For what?*

Three men disappear into the house. One stays with Bria.

Detective Sullivan: *I don't think we've met before. I was a rookie when your dad retired. Detective Shawn Sullivan.*

B. Corsetti: *What's going on? Why are you searching my house?*

Sullivan looks around to make sure no one is listening, then takes Bria's arm and leads her to the couch where they both sit.

Detective Sullivan: *The department's been getting a lot of pressure from the media to arrest someone in Noelle Prado's murder. City Hall's been threatening to bring in the state police if something doesn't break. Last night they found your dad's informant.*

B. Corsetti: *The guy he was going to meet when he was killed?*

Detective Sullivan: *You knew about that?*

B. Corsetti: *Joey was able to decipher the code he used in his calendar.*

Detective Sullivan: *Look, there's no easy way to say this. He implicated your dad in a murder-for-hire ring. He said Leo ran it.*

B. Corsetti: *That's bullshit. Who's this informant?*

Detective Sullivan: *A detective in the department. When your dad retired, he needed someone on the inside. He was blackmailing this guy to keep track of the investigations.*

B. Corsetti: *I don't believe it. I want to talk to him.*

Detective Sullivan: He's dead. They found him this morning. He ate his gun. He left a note implicating Leo and confessing to killing him.

B. Corsetti: Come on, detective. That's an obvious setup.

*A shout. **Detective 1 enters the room carrying a wrapped package.***

Detective 1: Right where he said it would be.

B. Corsetti (to Sullivan): Was that your job? Keep me distracted while he planted evidence?

Detective Sullivan: Your father was my hero. This hurts more than you know.

* * *

Abby finished her scenes early the next day. When she got home, Nathan's head was buried in the refrigerator. He looked up at the sound of her purse dropping on the counter.

"I think I'll change and sit by the pool for a while. Wanna come?" she asked.

"Nah, there's a game I want to see." His eyes brightened "We should get a TV out by the pool. Then we could float around and watch sports."

"Yeah, 'cause listening to you scream at the refs is super relaxing. No thanks."

By the time she returned to the kitchen two hours later, she had more than a little buzz going. She found a piece of notepaper and wrote, *Wake me up when you get home. Please.* She added a heart, then worried it was too much. Could she cross it out without being noticeable? What was worse: a premature love declaration or a scribbled-out love declaration? She was about to throw the note away and start over when Nathan came in carrying a bag of chips.

"Want some?" he asked through a mouthful of Ruffles.

She hastily slid the note by her purse. "No, I'm good. Is the game still on?"

"There is always a game on," he answered. "Wanna watch it with me?"

"Not tonight."

"That's what she said." He shook his head sadly.

She groaned. "God, that is so old. Or have people in Minnesota just discovered *The Office*?"

"It's a classic line that will never age, especially when a beautiful woman tells me, 'Not tonight.'"

She patted his cheek. "Poor baby. I'm heading up."

He shoved more chips in his mouth and moved toward her with outstretched arms. "Want a kiss good night?"

Laughing, she pushed him away. "Another time, maybe," she said over her shoulder.

"Your loss," he shouted. She was sure he spewed crumbs as he did.

* * *

Sara followed the sound of the television to find Nathan snoring on the couch. Hands on hips, she contemplated her brother. He was a good person, and when his mouth was hanging open like it was now, he was kind of cute. She shook his foot. He groaned, made a grunting noise, and opened his eyes. "What are you doing home?"

"It's nearly midnight. Are you planning to sleep down here?"

"Huh," he said, sitting up and rubbing a hand over his face. "Wonder who won the game."

She smiled indulgently at him. "Why do you bother watching? You never see the end."

"I'm fine when the game's on, but the commercials kill me."

"Well, I'm going to bed. See you in the morning."

"Wait. Did you see her note?"

Sara frowned. "What note?"

He led her into the kitchen and handed her a slip of paper. "Here. She tried to hide this under her purse, but lucky for you I'm an excellent detective. Go wake your girl, but keep it down. I need to get my rest."

Sara read the note, then looked up at her brother. "Nathan, do you think this is a bad idea? You know, because of the show? What if it doesn't work out?"

He put his hands on her shoulders. "For once you need to think of yourself, not the band, not the show. Think about what you want. Abby makes you happy." He pulled her into a hug. "You're allowed to be happy."

* * *

Sara tapped on the door before opening it. "Abby?" she whispered. When she got no response, she walked toward the bed. "Abby," she said in a normal voice.

"Sara." The covers rustled, and Sara could just make out Abby sitting up.

"Hi." She sat on the edge of the bed. Abby's sleepy eyes and mussed hair were adorable. She tucked a couple of strands back in place. "Sleeping with a pillow over your head?"

Abby ran a hand through her hair. "I'm sure it looks that way. You got my note?"

"I almost missed it. For future reference, if you want to leave me a note, hiding it under your purse is not a great place. Also, don't bother trying to hide anything from Nathan. If he thinks you have a secret, he'll go to great lengths to discover it."

"Ohhh...I forgot I put it under my purse. He came in just as I finished writing, and I didn't want him to read it."

Sara laughed. "He read it." She paused. "You doing okay?"

"Yes. No. I can't believe we live in the same house and work at the same job but hardly see each other." Abby rubbed Sara's thigh as she spoke.

"I know." Sara moved closer to her. "I've missed you." She leaned in and gave Abby a light kiss.

"Take off your clothes," Abby whispered.

"Are you sure?"

"Stop asking me that. Trust that I'm sure. I wouldn't be lying naked in my bed waiting for you to come home if I weren't sure. Get undressed."

Sara paused only a moment before pulling off the T-shirt and pajama bottoms she'd put on before coming to see Abby. When she pulled back the covers to slide next to her, Abby stopped her. "No. I want to feel you on top of me."

"What about your lungs? Will you be able to breathe?"

"I'm fine." Abby shifted and Sara slid a thigh between Abby's legs and moaned. Abby was already wet.

"I've been thinking about you," Abby said. She pulled Sara down for a kiss, lifting her head to meet her.

All hesitancy was gone. The kiss was deep and passionate, making Sara wonder why she'd been holding back. She moved up to change the angle of the kiss and felt her own wetness on Abby's thigh. She opened her legs farther and pushed into Abby. "I want you in my mouth," she murmured. Abby's moan was all the answer she needed.

Sara broke the kiss and moved down Abby's body. She lightly scratched over a nipple, watching it harden, then took it into her mouth and sucked. Abby moaned and ran her hand through Sara's hair. Sara looked up, locking eyes with Abby before gently taking the nipple between her teeth. Abby's eyes closed, and Sara moved to the other breast. Her mouth worked the hardened tip as she hooked her hands under Abby's knees and lifted. The position opened Abby to her, and her wetness coated Sara's stomach. It was a position that never failed to excite her.

"Sara," Abby whispered. With one more tender bite, Sara moved down her body. She spread Abby open and ran her tongue the length of her. The touch was light enough that Abby knew she was there, but not enough to satisfy her. Abby groaned, and Sara looked up to see her arch her neck and lift her hips. She ran her tongue over Abby again and moved down to her entrance, making lazy circles with her tongue, then moving back to suck her clit. "Sara, please," Abby said. "I need you inside me."

Sara lifted a little and entered Abby with two fingers. Abby's groan of pleasure was almost her undoing. She watched her fingers move in and out of Abby, so taken with the beauty of the woman under her. When Abby was close, she bent once again and swirled her tongue around her clit. Abby's movements became erratic, and her moans louder. Then everything stopped as her orgasm hit. She cried out, hands scrabbling for Sara's head as she pushed herself into Sara's mouth.

They lay like that for a few moments while Abby took gasping breaths. Finally, she said, "Jesus, Sara. It's never been like that."

Sara lifted her head from Abby's stomach and carefully withdrew her fingers. "You're beautiful."

Abby smiled. "Come here." Sara eased back up Abby's body, enjoying the tiny aftershocks as her leg contacted Abby's sensitive clit.

"I want to do that to you," Abby said. "I want you to feel like I do."

"I don't know if I can feel any better than I do right now," Sara whispered before kissing under Abby's ear.

Abby took Sara's face in her hands. "Let's find out."

* * *

Abby woke earlier than normal. Sara's arm was draped across her middle, and one leg had her pinned to the bed. She loved the show of possession, but she had to go to the bathroom. With a quick kiss, she eased out from under Sara. After using the bathroom, she washed her face, brushed her teeth, then carefully opened the door. The bed was empty. Disappointed, she pulled on a T-shirt and shorts, then went back into the bathroom to brush out her hair. A couple of thumps on her bedroom door signaled Sara's return. Abby opened it to find Sara with a cup of coffee in each hand. "I was starting to feel like a one-night stand," Abby said.

"I think I just did a walk of shame in my own house. Luckily, Nathan isn't up yet."

"Is it a walk of shame if your makeup isn't smeared?"

"Excellent point." They were back in bed and Sara leaned over to kiss her. "Good morning." She took Abby's free hand. "You okay?" Sara's voice was gentle, but Abby could hear the concern.

Abby gave her a light kiss, then turned to put her mug on the nightstand. She rolled on top of Sara, balancing her weight on a knee and an elbow. With the other hand, she moved Sara's hair off her face before returning to trace her nose, then lips. "I'm happy." It was the simplest, most honest answer she could give. Everything about last night felt right. There was nothing to question, nothing to doubt. "What about you? How are you this morning?"

"I have never felt closer to anyone than I feel with you right now." The vulnerability in Sara's words took Abby's breath away. She let more of her weight rest on Sara as she kissed her.

"I feel the same. Thank you." The kiss turned passionate, and Abby felt the heat building. She reached for Sara's breast, but Sara pulled her mouth away. "I didn't set an alarm last night. What time is call?"

Abby groaned and kissed Sara's neck. "It's early, isn't it? Six? What time is it now?"

Sara threw an arm toward the nightstand, slapping its surface until she found her phone. "Five twenty-two." She dropped her head back on the pillow. "What time do you want to get up?"

"I don't." Abby rolled off Sara. "Is that the call time for sure, or do I need to check?"

"It's the call time." Sara moved so this time she was on top of Abby. "We have fifteen minutes if we want breakfast, thirty if we grab something stale from the canteen."

Abby ran her fingers over Sara's nipple. "It's not even a question."

CHAPTER FORTY-ONE

Mika sat alone in the screening room. The final edits of the season finale were done, and despite all of the obstacles, she'd accomplished her dream. *Corsetti's Will* was a mainstream series with a lesbian lead character. Joey's relationship wasn't what she had envisioned, but it would get there. If Binge would let it.

Despite strong numbers, the network had yet to order a second season. Mika assured the cast and crew it was just a formality, but she hadn't convinced herself. So much had happened in the months since filming began, she worried Belinski didn't think the ratings were worth the turmoil.

"Leo wasn't dirty. They'll never convince me of that." Joey walks over to Corsetti's desk—the one Bria uses now. She opens drawers, searching through the contents. She finds the note Noelle put on his container of cookies. She puts her hand over her mouth and cries.

She puts the note on the desk and runs her fingers over the writing. As she does, she remembers that day.

"That's not a ring box. I thought you were going to propose."

"Why do I have to be the one to propose?"

Corsetti picks up a framed photograph. "Because you don't want to waste one moment. You don't know how long you'll have her." He dusts off the picture, then turns it over and makes sure the back is secure. "You know, if you are ever in doubt, the key to everything is right here." He touches his heart. "And here." He touches the photograph.

Joey snaps out of the memory and picks up the photo. "It can't be this easy." She turns it over and removes the back. She lifts up a key and a slip of paper. "Right here the whole time."

* * *

Joey sits on the floor of the storage unit, surrounded by file boxes. She's holding a piece of paper which she begins to read aloud. After the first words, Leo Corsetti's voice takes over.

"Joey,

"If you're reading this, I'm gone and you have to go it alone. I'm sorry about that, kid.

"So, you figured out my message. I hoped you'd remember what I told you.

"By now, you know I put you in control of the business. I knew if they got to me, you wouldn't let go until you had the answers. I just had to make sure Bria gave you enough time to find them. Well, here they are.

"Whatever you do, don't trust anyone in the department. Take this to the Feds or the state police. I'm going to meet with someone I trust, but if I'm gone it means everyone is dirty.

"I understand if it's too much. If it is, sell the business. Tell Bria to go back to her life. Take Noelle and get far away from here. You can say it's guilt over my death. They'll believe it because they think you're weak. But they don't know you like I do. The day I saw you at Drummond's funeral, I knew they were going to set you up for his murder. You had so much guilt you would have gone down without a fight. I couldn't let them do that to you. When those assholes spouted off at the diner, I saw a way to get you out.

"That story about me having a bad heart is all bullshit. My heart's fine. I'd played dumb as long as I could, but I was running out of time. Sooner or later, someone was going to approach or take me out.

I couldn't decide which was worse. I faked a heart attack and retired from the force.

"You were the best partner I could have asked for. You're decent and honest. Never change. And damn it, marry that girl. She's way out of your league, so you better seal the deal before she realizes it.

"Take care of Bria for me. She and Noelle are just alike. Too good for us and too good for our world.

"Love you, kid.

"Corsetti"

Joey starts to cry. "Damn it, Leo. Why didn't you tell me? Maybe I could have saved you and Noelle." She turns a few pages and scans the document. "It was all of them. They're nothing more than hired guns." She looks up from the paper and wipes tears from her face.

"Yes," a disembodied voice says. Two men in suits step into the light. "Thank you for finding this for us." The speaker looks at the man with him. "You were right. They weren't in the apartment."

"It was you?" Joey stands and points. "You killed Noelle?"

"Yeah, sorry about that. I really thought you had Corsetti's files." He lifts his gun. "You'll be with her soon."

Joey runs at him, but he sidesteps her easily and kicks her legs out from under her. She falls hard.

His partner looks at her prone body. "Should we do it here and lock her in?"

"No, she can't disappear. The chief's already threatening to call in the Feds. It needs to look like a suicide."

The room is flooded with noise. Several voices yell at once.

"FBI! Drop your weapons!" The two men lower their guns to the ground. They are immediately handcuffed.

"You okay, Driskell?" Detective Sullivan squats next to her.

"Yeah, you get that? They killed Noelle."

"We got every word." He helps her up. Bria rushes into the room and throws her arms around Joey.

"You scared the shit out of me." She pulls away and frowns at Joey. "Why'd you have to go at him? That wasn't the plan."

"When he was so casual about killing Noelle, I couldn't take it."

Bria pulls her back in. "Don't ever do something stupid like that again. I don't know what I'd do without you."

This time, Joey pulls back. "Well, you'll have to do without me when you go back to your old life."

"I'm not going back."

"But all the cases are closed. You can sell the building and the agency. You fulfilled the terms of the will."

"We still have an open case."

Joey frowns. "No, we don't."

"I took one yesterday. I don't want to sell the business. This is what I want to do. If I have to, I'll keep taking cases until you agree. You need this, and so do I."

Joey gives her a long look. "You think you know what I need?"

Bria takes her hand. "I'm sure of it."

CHAPTER FORTY-TWO

"Please welcome back the queen of *Corsetti's Will*, showrunner Mika Williams." Mika strode onstage, smiling broadly. She took the microphone offered to her and sat in the chair next to the moderator.

"I was going to introduce the next two actresses separately, but why bother?" The audience laughed. "You know them as 'Broey' on *Corsetti's Will*. In real life they're Sara Silver and Abby Farina!" The crowd that stood at Mika's introduction went wild when Abby and Sara came onstage hand in hand. They smiled and gave identical waves before climbing into their own chairs.

"Mika, you have an announcement?" the moderator said.

Did she imagine it, or did the entire room inhale a collective breath? "Last year, I asked you to tell your friends about *Corsetti's Will* and convince them to give us a try. You did, which allowed us to film a second season. Thank you for that." She waited while the audience applauded. "I'm thrilled to announce our show"—she gestured to include the audience—"continues to grow in popularity. So much so, that Binge has ordered eight more episodes. Thanks to you, Season Three is coming!" she shouted over the cheers.

"We'll talk more about the show, but I know everyone here wants me to ask…" The moderator looked at Sara and Abby. "How does it feel to be engaged?"

"Amazing," Sara answered. "Incredible. I'm so blessed." She reached for Abby's hand. The collective "ahs" from the audience caused everyone to laugh.

"Have you set a date?" she asked Abby.

"Sometime in the summer. Sara will be playing a few shows with Range Street, so we'll pick a date that works with her schedule."

"Will we get to see a wedding video?"

Abby's legs were crossed, and she looked to be relaxed, but Sara looked tense. She opened her mouth to answer but Abby spoke first. "Well, as you know, we are very private, but we do want to share a small part of our lives with you. A small part." She emphasized with a smile. "A few wedding photos will appear in *People* magazine in exchange for a donation to the Trevor Project." The audience cheered.

"Speaking of the Trevor Project," Sara said. "We have a surprise for our you. We are hosting another edition of Corsetti Karaoke. Raffle tickets are available online and all sales will benefit local LGBTQ+ charities."

"Tell them what you'll be singing," Mika said.

Sara looked at Abby, her eyes full of love. "We'll be doing another duet. This year it's 'Islands in the Stream' by Kenny and Dolly." The audience was divided by cheers and an equal number of groans. Sara laughed at their response. "I'm not sure who will sing which part." She looked at Abby. "Forget it. We all know she'll make me laugh and end up singing both parts." The crowd cheered.

Mika watched warily. She wanted to join the celebratory atmosphere. After all, *Corsetti's Will* continued to be the most-watched program on Binge. But she couldn't let herself relax. The same people who booed her when she announced a character would die on a television show, who threatened Abby because she was straight, were cheering them.

But for how long?

What if next season she decided to take another risk? Would they be supportive, or would they turn against her?

She looked out at the women she'd so desperately wanted to see represented on television and wondered if she knew them at all.

Then she started looking not at the crowd, but at the women, and she saw it. The woman in the third row, her face glowing with happiness. The group seated together in the middle all wearing "Corsetti Queens" T-shirts. All throughout the audience were people who understood her vision. Her mood lifted, and she started to smile.

Then she caught sight of Dani Copeland seated off to the side in the back row wearing a white T-shirt with large black letters. A joyous laugh bubbled out of her as she read the words.

We Chose Love.

Bella Books, Inc.

Women. Books. Even Better Together.

P.O. Box 10543
Tallahassee, FL 32302

Phone: 800-729-4992
www.bellabooks.com